Trial of the Trinity

Including Timeline of the 4TH Beast that Terrified Daniel

By

Russell Wooten

Table of Contents

Part 3 Turning It Over

Part 4 Zechariah 13

Introduction

"In all the vehement universal and lasting controversy about the trinity in Jerome's time and both before and long after it, this text of the 'three in heaven' was never once thought of. It is now in everybody's mouth…" (Issac Newton), who wrote more about the Bible than science and mathematics.

Controversy over the trinity began before the fourth century when it was made official by the church in Rome. Either Jesus is God, or an equal "person" to God; or he's not. Either the trinity is true and holy; or it's idolatry.

Plaintiff is representing the Trinity. His Lord and savior Jesus Christ. The Great Commission found in Matthew, Mark, Luke, John, and Acts. Go therefore and make disciples of all nations baptizing in the name of the Father, and of the son, and the Holy Spirit. That forgiveness of sins and life everlasting is through believing in Jesus' death and resurrection. He was taught that baptism is cause for great celebration. That angels in heaven rejoice whenever anyone accepts Jesus as their Lord and savior. He claims the Christian New Testament fulfills the Old Testament AKA Jewish Bible; that we're in the New Covenant and covenants in the Torah are obsolete.

Defense' position is that whenever a Jewish person is baptized Christian, they're breaking the covenant, which is arguably worse than death. He contends that the Jewish Bible opposes the New Testament. Citing Moses, Jeremiah, Habakkuk, etc., paired with current events, claiming we're not yet in the New Covenant. He's defending the oneness of the God of Abraham, Issac, and Jacob. The God who said you saw no image and don't you dare make one. My promises are forever. If you can see

the moon and stars, I'm still keeping My covenants even if
you aren't. The God who shares glory with no other. He's
representing God the Father alone; not the second person
of any trinity. That's the difference. His loyalty is to the
Speaker recorded by Isaiah 42:8-43:11, alone. To the
Name we're told is to be used forever, by all generations in
Exodus 3:15, alone, praising no other.

It's fundamentally impossible that he and plaintiff are both
correct. What are the consequences of being wrong? What
does the first "person" of the Trinity say?

Imagine the courtroom setting "Assemble yourselves and
come; draw near together, you survivors of the nations!
They have no knowledge who carry about their wooden
idols, and keep on praying to a god that cannot save.
Declare and present your case; let them take counsel
together!..." (Isaiah 45:20-23).

The prequel is both sides of every major point argued
extensively. This book is Defense' closing argument,
heavily objected to. There's no straw-man. Both make
every effort to win. Most points from earlier in the trial
raised again, argued with the same passion, but more
concisely.

This isn't just a legal battle. It's the story of what happened
to most of our ancestors, tough choices they faced. How
and why Christianity and Islam expanded into the world's 2
largest religions, while Judaism became the smallest. It's
the story of Deuteronomy 4:27-29. Why millions left their
homelands for the New World. It was prophesied by Moses
and Daniel with terrifying accuracy, and what's to be
realized by the entire world according to Zechariah 13 is
even more shocking!

This is not an instruction manual on standard courtroom procedure. If objections played out like in courtrooms today, and there were no interruptions; it would be hundreds more pages. Instead, it condenses centuries of debate into a gripping narrative.

In 1239-40 CE Paris, which we'll get to, in context, on the timeline, King Louis IX ordered Jewish texts put on trial. After defense counsel lost, handwritten copies of commentary on the Torah were burned by the cartload across from Notre Dame Cathedral. This time both lawyers are allowed equal speech, making their cases without fear of execution. You are the jury.

Part 1

Firstborn, Servant and Witness

Chapter 1

Katarzyna Weiglowa's Last Words

Judge: You may proceed with your closing argument.

Defense Counsel: Before I commence, several points from Plaintiff's closing need to be addressed. We'll start with Psalm 2:12 which is mistranslated in 24 of the top 30 versions listed on Biblehub.com. Here's the context altering mistranslation we find in the King James Version:

"Kiss the Son, lest he be angry, and ye perish from the way, when his wrath is kindled but a little. Blessed are all they that put their trust in him." (Psalm 2:12, KJV) Might as well say kiss Jesus. How do Jews not comprehend that? How do they reject prophecy, in their own Bible, so obviously foretelling of Jesus?

The accurate translation of Psalm 2:12 from Hebrew to English is:

"Arm yourselves with purity lest He become angry and you perish in the way, for in a moment His wrath will be kindled; the praises of all who take refuge in Him." (Psalm 2:12, Chabad.org, The Complete Jewish Bible)

"He" and "Him" is God. However, God is not a he or him because God is not a man (Numbers 23:19). But not even David could find a better pronoun. God's Name forever is "The LORD the God of your fathers, the God of Abraham, the God of Isaac, and the God of Jacob" (Exodus 3:15). Lord of Hosts is His title.

The Hebrew word for 'purity' is accurately translated in Psalm 18:20, 18:24, 19:9, 24:4, 73:1 and everywhere else in the King James and ESV except Psalm 2:12 where "purity" is mistranslated into "Kiss the Son." The Book of Psalms is quoted over 100 times in the New Testament. Yet "Kiss the Son" isn't quoted because the fraudulent mistranslation, even capitalizing the word son, wasn't concocted until after the New Testament was written.

Plaintiff Counsel: Objection. Speculation. Judge: Sustained. You can't prove why Psalm 2:12 isn't quoted in the NT.

Defense Counsel: The Hebrew word for 'son' is 'ben.' My son is 'b'ni.' Children is 'b'ney,' as in b'ney Israel (children of Israel). The word ben in those forms appears about 1,700 times in the Jewish Bible. One place it does not appear is in Psalm 2:12. It's used in the same chapter though. Just a few sentences earlier, in verse 7, ben is accurately translated to son in English Bibles. The LORD God is calling David His son.

"I will declare the decree: the LORD hath said unto me, Thou art my Son; this day have I begotten thee." (Psalm 2:7, KJV)

"I will tell of the decree; The Lord said to me, "You are My son; this day have I begotten you." (Psalm 2:7, Chabad.org)

I will tell of the decree: Said David, "This is an established decree, and [one] that I have received to tell this and to make known."
The Lord said to me through Nathan, Gad, and Samuel.

You are My son *The head over Israel, who are called "My firstborn son." And they will endure through you, as is stated concerning Abner (II Sam. 3:18): "for God said, etc., 'By the hand of My bondsman David shall I deliver… Israel.'" And for their sake, you are before Me as a son because they are all dependent upon you."*
this day have I *for I have enthroned you over them.*
begotten you *to be called My son and to be beloved to Me as a son for their sake, as it is stated (II Sam. 7:14) concerning Solomon: "I will be to him a father, and he shall be to Me a son." We find further concerning David (Ps. 89:27) "He shall call Me, 'You are my Father, my God, and the Rock of my salvation.'" (Rashi's commentary, Psalm 2:7, The Complete Jewish Bible)*

Psalm 2:7 is even more evidence that the most famous verse in the New Testament, John 3:16 is a lie. An easily verifiable lie...

Plaintiff: OBJECTION! How dare you! Jesus paid the ultimate price, whipped, beaten, nailed to a cross for our sins. "For God so loved the world, that he gave his only begotten Son, that whosoever believeth in him should not perish, but have everlasting life." (John 3:16, KJV) That's the word of God! The foundation of our faith. Show some respect, please.

Judge: Both parties agree that Psalms 2:7 is the word of God. Explain how Jesus can be God's only begotten son when God said to David "You are My son; today I have begotten you."

Plaintiff: Psalm 2:7 is prophecy foretelling of Jesus. "One Lord Jesus Christ, the Only Begotten Son of God, born of the Father before all ages. God from God... true God from true God, begotten, not made," (Nicene Creed)

Judge: My question is about the word "only" in John 3:16. How can Jesus be God's only begotten son, when God called the same King David who slayed Goliath as a youngster and was not born of a virgin, His begotten son?

Plaintiff: God gave the promise of Jesus through the line of David. Rashi's commentary is correct up to a point. Psalm 2:7 is indeed about the bloodline of the future Messiah. "For God never said to any angel what he said to Jesus: "You are my Son. Today I have become your Father." God also said, "I will be his Father, and he will be my Son." (Hebrews 1:5, NLT)

The disconnect here is explained by Saint Paul: All Jews, that includes Rashi, have such hardened minds and hearts that they can't even grasp the depths of their own Old Testament because they haven't accepted Jesus who's their only remedy (2 Corinthians 3:14-15). The context of John 3:16 is that God loved us so much He sent His only begotten Son Jesus to pay the price for our sins. Supporting evidence is John 1:29, 3:16, 14:6, Romans 5:8, 1 John 2:1.

Defense: That's the opposite of what the "First Person" of Rome's trinity says in Ezekiel 18. Where it's repeated over and over that nobody dies or pays any price for anyone else's sins. The LORD God the Father alone is our savior (Isaiah 43:11)! God shares glory with no other (Isaiah 42:8). God is not a man, and that's why God's mind doesn't change (Numbers 23:19).

"…no atonement can be made for the land for the blood that is shed in it, except by the blood of the one who shed it." (Numbers 35:33, ESV)

"Fathers shall not be put to death because of their children,
nor shall children be put to death because of their fathers.
Each one shall be put to death for his own sin."
(Deuteronomy 24:16, ESV)

"Therefore I will judge you, O house of Israel, every one
according to his ways, declares the Lord GOD. Repent and
turn from all your transgressions, lest iniquity be your ruin."
(Ezekiel 18:30, ESV)

"I, I am the Lord, and besides me there is no savior."
(Isaiah 43:11, ESV)

"But I am the LORD your God from the land of Egypt; you
know no God but me, and besides me there is no savior."
(Hosea 13:4, ESV)

"Yet you say, 'The way of the Lord is not just.' O house of
Israel, I will judge each of you according to his ways."
(Ezekiel 33:20, ESV)

Recall Deuteronomy 4:2 where we're explicitly instructed
never to add, remove, contradict, or change a word of the
Torah, ever. "Then you shall say to Pharaoh, 'Thus says
the LORD, Israel is my firstborn son." (Exodus 4:22, ESV)

The designation of Israel as firstborn, witness, and servant
go together (Isaiah 41:10). That's Israel's chosen
responsibility to preserve, protect and share the Torah with
the world. We're created in the image of God. Often,
firstborns are given additional responsibilities. It's pretty
much that simple; doesn't mean younger siblings are loved
any less. The firstborn's responsibility to serve as
witnesses to the Oneness of God is the opposite...

Plaintiff: Objection! Jesus is the firstborn! Romans 8:29, Colossians 1:15 and 18, Hebrews 1:6...

Judge: Clarify your position. Is Jesus God's firstborn son, only son, only begotten son, or all the above? Clarify also, how Jesus can be God and the son of God simultaneously.

Plaintiff: "...Father unborn, Son born of the Father, Holy Spirit proceeding from Father and Son; that the Father is not Son or Holy Spirit, that Son is not Father or Holy Spirit; that Holy Spirit is not Father or Son; but Father alone is Father, Son alone is Son, Holy Spirit alone is Holy Spirit.." (Cantate Domino, Papal Bull of Pope Eugene IV, AD 1445)

Defense: "Holy Spirit is not Father" What? Think...

Plaintiff: Your honor, Pope Eugene IV was summarizing the Holy Bible, which confirms the Holy Trinity. Father, Son, and Holy Spirit are identical in essence but distinct in person (John 14:26). Jesus is the Creator (John 1:14). Jesus is firstborn of creation (Colossians 1:15-21). Jesus is God (Hebrews 1:3). Jesus is designated as God's Son because he was conceived by the Holy Spirit instead of by a human father (Matthew 1:18).

Defense: How many times must we prove the child Immanuel was Isaiah's son? Explicitly conceived by a human father, NOT born of a virgin Isaiah 8:3! Again, Isaiah's son was to be called 2 different names: Immanuel by his mother who was a young woman and a prophetess (Isaiah 7:14). And, Maher-shalal-hash-baz by his father (Isaiah 8:3). The reason Isaiah's son was to be called 2 names was to signify the abandonment of 2 kings, bringing forth a time of peace (Isaiah 7:16 and 8:4). The prophecy was fulfilled, both kings were abandoned and both invasions failed over 700 years before Jesus of Nazareth was born.

It is impossible that both the anonymous author of Matthew and the Prophet Isaiah are telling the truth. As a matter of fact, somebody's lying. Remember, when Matthew is conclusively proven to be a liar, that has no bearing on the credibility of The LORD God or Isaiah whatsoever. The New Testament is entirely dependent on the Jewish Bible AKA Old Testament. Conversely, the Jewish Bible stands on its own, making no claim whatsoever to be the fulfillment of any other religion's texts.

The Hebrew word for "alma" is "young woman," and "betulah" is "virgin." Those words are accurately translated 108 of 109 times in Old Testaments; everywhere except Isaiah 7:14 where alma is mistranslated to virgin in 27 of the top 32 listed versions on Biblehub.com. Israel's designation of firstborn son (Exodus 4:22), witness and servant (Isaiah 41:10) is the very reason...

Plaintiff: Pardon. Your honor, we concede that God the Father called Israel His firstborn. However, Exodus 4:22 obviously isn't literal.

Defense: The second half of the sentence is as literal as it gets: "and I say to you, "Let my son go that he may serve me." If you refuse to let him go, behold, I will kill your firstborn son."" (Exodus 4:23, ESV). That happened, literally. Serve Me means serve the "first person" of your trinity, ALONE.

Plaintiff: The Old Testament, which is only a shadow of things to come, was pointing to Jesus. "For those whom he foreknew he also predestined to be conformed to the image of his Son, in order that he might be the firstborn among many brothers." (Romans 8:29, ESV) Jesus is firstbo...

Defense: "Bring out the people who are blind, yet have eyes, who are deaf, yet have ears! All the nations gather together, and the peoples assemble. Who among them can declare this, and show us the former things? Let them bring their witnesses to prove them right, and let them hear and say, It is true." (Isaiah 43:8-9, ESV)

Plaintiff: Stop clinging to your Old Testament, and hear what God says in the New and living Testament of the Holy Bible. Jesus is to be worshipped as God's firstborn, by you, by everyone, even by the angels:

"For to which of the angels did God ever say, "You are my Son, today I have begotten you"? Or again, "I will be to him a father, and he shall be to me a son"? And again, when he brings the firstborn into the world, he says,

"Let all God's angels worship him." (Hebrews 1:5-6, ESV)

Defense: Jury, who are you going to believe: The anonymously authored letter to the Hebrews, added to the Bible under Pope Damasus I; or The LORD God as recorded by Moses, David, Hosea, and Jeremiah?

The LORD God says, "Then you shall say to Pharaoh, 'Thus says the LORD, Israel is my firstborn son" (Exodus 4:22, ESV))

David said, "I will tell of the decree; The Lord said to me, "You are My son; this day have I begotten you." (Psalm 2:7, Chabad.org)

The LORD God says, "With weeping they shall come, and with pleas for mercy I will lead them back, I will make them walk by brooks of water, in a straight path in which they shall not stumble, for I am a father to Israel, and Ephraim is my firstborn." (Jeremiah 31:19, ESV) *Ephraim is the firstborn tribe of Israel.*

The LORD God says, "When Israel was a child, I loved him, and out of Egypt I called my son." (Hosea 11:1, ESV)

Additionally, we can go back to Genesis 6:2 to know that nobody is the only son of God. And Deuteronomy 14:1 to know that we're all children of God.

Plaintiff: The beautiful message of John 3:16 is followed by a very serious promise. All that's required of us is to believe in Jesus Christ the only Son of God. Consequences of rejecting him after he willingly paid the price for our sins are severe: "Whoever believes in him is not condemned, but whoever does not believe is condemned already, because he has not believed in the name of the only Son of God." (John 3:18, ESV)

Judge: Genesis 6:2, Exodus 3:15, 4:22, Deuteronomy 4:2-6:4, 14:1, Isaiah chapters 40-46, Ezekiel 18 and 33, Jeremiah 31:19, 31:35-36, Hosea 11:1, Zechariah 14:9, Psalms 2:7 and 89:27 are why your objection's overruled.

Defense: I'm not sure the jury understands the seriousness of what we're arguing. Katarzyna Weiglowa understood. She was baptized and raised Roman Catholic; later converting to Judaism. 1530 CE, Diocese of Kraków Poland: The 70-year-old widow was sentenced to prison until she recanted her "mistakes of the Jewish faith," her "heresy" of rejecting Rome's "Holy Trinity" and refusing to say Jesus is the only son of God.

On April 19, 1539, Bishop Piotr Gamrat used anonymously recorded words of Jesus to sentence the 80-year-old widow to death. She was burned alive over the same argument that Plaintiff and I just had. Eyewitnesses recounted, while being walked to the stake and given one last chance to comply, she was asked "Do you believe in His only son our Lord Jesus Christ?"

Katarzyna responded "God had neither wife nor son, nor does He need this; for only mortals need sons. We are His children, and all who walk in His ways are His children." Why didn't she just comply?

"You are my witnesses," declares the LORD, "and my servant whom I have chosen, that you may know and believe me and understand that I am he.
Before me no god was formed, nor shall there be any after me. I, I am the LORD, and besides me there is no savior. I declared and saved and proclaimed, when there was no strange god among you; and you are my witnesses," declares the LORD, "and I am God."
(Isaiah 43:10-12, ESV)

That's why! Not even Plaintiff has the audacity to object to the fact, that not Jesus of Nazareth, but The LORD God the Father is clearly identified as the Speaker in Isaiah 43!

"For I desire loving-kindness, and not sacrifices, and knowledge of God more than burnt offerings." (Hosea 6:6, Chabad.org)

Inquisitions had been going on in Poland, officially, since May 1, 1318, when Pope John XXII appointed Dominican and Franciscan friars as inquisitors for the dioceses of Wroclaw and Kraków. Bishop Gamrat was promoted to

Archbishop of Gniezno and Primate of Poland in 1541.
We're going to find out what bishops and cardinals are
promoted for today.

Like Job, Abraham, and Noah did before the word Jew was
invented, Katarzyna chose The LORD alone. Like
Abraham, Moses, Ruth, and Obadiah, she was raised in
idolatry. Like them, she rejected idolatry and turned back to
The LORD God of Abraham, Issac, and Jacob (Exodus
3:15). "Turn back to Me and I'll turn back to you"
(Zechariah 1:3).

Chapter 2

Turning Back

Plaintiff Counsel: Your honor, Defense is misleading the jury down an extremely dangerous path. Since she was raised Catholic, presumably by Catholic parents from birth; logic dictates that her mother wasn't a Jew. Therefore, she wasn't a Jew. Therefore, Zechariah's invitation to turn back wasn't to her. Zechariah was speaking to Jews of the Old Covenant before they were given the opportunity to accept the once and for all final sacrifice of Jesus Christ (Hebrews 8:8-10 & 10:8-10). We're supposed to turn forward to the New and Everlasting Covenant of Jesus precious blood.

"Now the God of peace, that brought again from the dead our Lord Jesus, that great shepherd of the sheep, through the blood of the everlasting covenant, Make you perfect in every good work to do his will, working in you that which is well pleasing in his sight, through Jesus Christ; to whom be glory forever and ever. Amen." (Hebrews 13:20-21, KJV)

Defense Counsel: "Lord Jesus, that great shepherd of the sheep." Remember that when we get to Zechariah 13:7.

Plaintiff: Indeed, Jesus is the great shepherd of the sheep. Unfortunately, Mrs. Weiglowa rejected him. She didn't turn back to anything. All she did was subject herself to 613 commandments she had no chance of keeping anyway (Romans 3:10). It's unfortunate she was executed. Even worse, and this needs to be said, "He that believeth and is baptized shall be saved; but he that believeth not shall be damned." (Mark 16:16, KJV)

Defense: Damned for what? For following God's instructions! Think! If you were Buddhist, you could say you don't care what Moses and Isaiah say. But you can't, neither could Gamrat, nor any inquisitor.

Plaintiff: The Inquisitions were a stain on the church that Pope John Paul II apologized for in AD 2000. However, their purpose was not to torture or kill Jews, apostates, or Marranos. Many Jews received the good news of the gospels and saved their souls by accepting Jesus' final sacrifice for our sins. Unfortunately, some new converts to Christianity were insincere; troublemakers of the worst kind, insulting our Lord, deceiving souls to the eternal fires of hell, much like Defense's been doing. God is not mocked!

Defense: She went from worshipping a dead Jewish rabbi to worshipping the same God that Jesus worshipped. She started praying to the same LORD God 'the Father" that Jesus fell on his face and prayed to in Matthew 26:39-42. But you don't do what Jesus did. Instead, you get down on your knees before idols of a man who was a member of another religion. Eating his body and drinking his bl...

Plaintiff: Heresy! Your honor, please for all of our sakes, put a stop to this. Blasphemy of the Holy Spirit is the unforgivable sin, as we're told by Jesus Christ according to Matthew 12:31-32 and Mark 3:28-30 in the Holy Bible.

Judge: Noted. I'm going to address the jury. First, because this is the last thing anyone should be confused about: God's invitation to turn back is not limited to His adopted firstborn. It's for every single one of His children, regardless of race, color, gender, religion, whatever terrible things you may have done, etc. If you're alive, God's invitation to turn back is to you.

Next, since neither attorney's bothered to explain the basics of contract law; I'm going to. From a legal perspective, we have two entirely different types of evidence being presented. Contracts are to be interpreted based on what's found within the four corners of the original document. The original document is the Torah: the first five books in all Jewish and Christian Bibles.

Claims that we're in the New Covenant, and covenants in the Torah are obsolete, are based on parol evidence. That's the legal term for evidence found outside the four corners of any original document. Parol evidence is highly disfavored in the law. Offering anonymously written parol evidence, in this case, the Letter to the Hebrews, attempting to sever a covenant/contract made millennia earlier as recorded by Moses in the Torah, with an estimated 2.5-3 million people at Mount Siani as witnesses, is even more disfavored.

The Torah is neither anonymous nor hearsay. The generation in which it was given witnessed events recorded in it. They heard God's voice and experienced the Exodus together as a nation (Exodus 19-20:1). Subsequent generations were challenged to ask their fathers and grandfathers what they witnessed (Deuteronomy 4:9, 32:7).

You've not brought forth any evidence of a severance clause from within the four corners of the original contract. Deuteronomy 4:2, 13, etc. do not allow for parol evidence to supersede a word of the Torah. God does not break covenants regardless of if the other party breaks them, as made clear in Deuteronomy 4:31, 4:40, and Jeremiah 31:35-37. Therefore, your repeated objection that the Torah is no longer binding is overruled.

Defense: We'll get to know the man responsible for adding the Greek New Testament to the Hebrew Bible when we arrive on October 1, 366 on the timeline. Context will help us see the big picture.

Plaintiff: Pardon, your honor, Jeremiah, along with the rest of the Old Testament after the Torah is every bit as much parol evidence as...

Judge: Indeed, every word in the Jewish Bible after Deuteronomy is parol evidence regarding the Torah. If Jeremiah contradicted a word of it that would be a serious credibility problem for Jeremiah. However, there's no contradiction. If we were given the same message in the New Testament, there would be no disagreement, and this trial wouldn't be necessary.

Defense Counsel: "Not with our fathers did the LORD make this covenant, but with us, who are all of us here alive today." (Deuteronomy 5:3, ESV)

"Not" means not only; that's undisputed. Moses is speaking to the children of Israel, and all of their descendants in all generations, forever. Katarzyna went from worshipping The LORD God and Jesus; to The LORD God alone. No more mediator...

Plaintiff: Objection! "For there is one God, and there is one mediator between God and men, the man Christ Jesus" (1 Timothy 2:5, ESV)

Defense: "Your first father sinned, and your mediators transgressed against me." (Isaiah 43:27, ESV)

Paul's 1st letter to Timothy 2:5 is a classic example of the truth mixed with the lie. Paul concedes the obvious, there is one God; and Jesus was a man. That right there ends this trial (Numbers 23:19). We can go all the way back to Job 9:33 to know there's never been a mediator between God and man. Or we could simply read the 1st sentence of God's 2nd commandment (Exodus 20:3). The LORD God "the Father" desires a direct personal relationship with all of us, and forgiveness comes from direct repentance with no mediator (Deuteronomy 4:39, 5:7, Isaiah 40-46, Ezekiel 18, 33).

There are really only 2 entities in Rome's trinity: God and Jesus. God is Spirit. God's Spirit is Holy. The LORD God the Father and the Holy Spirit are the exact same indivisible entity; not separate "persons" (Numbers 23:19, Deuteronomy 6:4, Isaiah chapters 40-46). Even Rome's New Testament concedes the obvious, that God is Spirit (John 4:24).

Plaintiff: OBJECTION! Defense is misrepresenting the Holy Trinity. God the Father and Jesus the Son are two separate but equal persons consubstantial IN ONE BEING! Nobody divided or tried to divide God's Spirit. The Holy Spirit flows from the blessed union of Father and Son.

Judge: Where was the Holy Spirit before the union of Father and Son?

Plaintiff: With the Father. Jesus said, "But when the Helper comes, whom I will send to you from the Father, the Spirit of truth, who proceeds from the Father, he will bear witness about me." (John 15:26, ESV) The Holy Spirit is the Helper.

Judge: Defense is using language of Roman councils that confirmed the trinity. As Pope Eugene IV stated "Father is not Son... Son is not Father." In John 15 that you just quoted, Jesus is identifying "the Father" separately.

Plaintiff: The yolk, white, and shell are separate but comprise one egg...

Judge: There's no question that "God the Father" clearly identifies Himself as the Speaker in Exodus 20, Deuteronomy 4, 5, 6, Isaiah 42, 43, 44. Overruled.

Defense: The Hebrew word "ruach" first appears in the Torah in Genesis 1:2. God's Ruach was hovering over the waters. Ruach is accurately translated to spirit, wind, or breath. You can't see wind, but you know it's there. Like they saw no image at Mount Siani, but there was no question God was there (Exodus 19:9-20:20, Deuteronomy 4:9-20, 32-39, 5:3-5).

In Psalm 51:11, David's asking The LORD God to please not take away His "HaKodesh" (Holy Spirit). There's no difference whatsoever in saying God or God's Spirit was with David. Men on a Roman council unanimously voting to divide God's Spirit into 2 "separate but equal persons" and insert Jesus of Nazareth in the middle didn't change the Creator of heaven and earth.

Since a man who refuses to keep God's 1st and 2nd brought up 613. Nobody's ever been subject to anywhere even close to 613 commandments. Many are only for men; others for women and priests. Many only apply when there's a temple; which there hasn't been since Rome destroyed the 2nd Temple 1,953 years ago. Contrary to Plaintiff and Paul's opinion, The LORD God said, yes, we are capable of keeping all His commandments (Deut. 30:10-18).

Judge: Before you go any further, respond to Plaintiff's prior objection. Since she was raised Catholic, and presumably her mother wasn't Jewish. How could she turn back to something that she never was to begin with?

Defense: First, what didn't happen. She didn't open an email from ancestory.com, find out her mother was 1 percent Jewish, and run to the nearest synagogue. To be crystal clear, Katarzyna turned back to The LORD God of Abraham, Issac, and Jacob alone before she converted to Judaism.

Most rabbis even try and talk people out of converting, explaining it's not necessary, nor is it a gatekeeper for going to heaven. Turning back is not breaking God's 1st and 2nd commandments anymore. It doesn't require converting to or identifying as anything. Happens the second anyone decides to do it. Conversely, converting to Judaism involves keeping more commandments and becoming part of the community. Unlike Plaintiff, I'm not recommending anyone convert to anything, nor threatening hell if they don't. What I am highly recommending is that people stop perpetually breaking God's 1st and 2nd commandments.

In the last days before the Messianic Age, many more will realize that the written invitation to return to The LORD God of Abraham, Issac, and Jacob ALONE in Deuteronomy 4:29-30, Jeremiah 16:19-21, Zechariah 1:2, 9:9, 13:8-9, and 2 Chronicles 7:14 is to them.

That doesn't mean they'll convert to Judaism or any other organized religion. Some will convert for various reasons, such as restoring the covenant their ancestors broke, for them and their descendants. Others will have had more than enough religion. They'll turn back to an even older and far simpler covenant that God made with Noah and all his descendants forever. Every single man and woman on this jury, black, brown, red, white, yellow, Muslim, Christian, Jew, Hindu, Apache, Irish, etc., is a son or daughter of Noah.

They'll serve the same God as the Jews. Same God identified in the Sh'ma (Jewish Creed of Extreme Monotheism- Deuteronomy 6:4) that Jesus quoted as the greatest commandment in Mark 12:28-30. Same God that Jesus was prostrate on his face begging to in the garden according to Matt. 26:39.

Most of them already do. The big difference is they won't serve any god besides The LORD God. They'll start keeping God's 1st commandment, stop breaking His 2nd, and keep 5 more for a total of 7. God gave 6 commandments to Adam and Eve; 1 more was given to Noah and all his descendants. We'll get to those simple, basic, common-sense commands.

That said, the deeper answer to your question is Deuteronomy 4:27-31. 4:27-28 is what happened, it's also the timeline of the 4th Beast that terrified Daniel. 4:29 is what Katarzyna did about it. No matter what we've done, or how long ago our ancestors broke the covenant, God still honors covenants with our ancestors, through us (Deuteronomy 4:31). Moses is addressing the children of Israel and all their descendants in all generations forever:

"And the LORD will scatter you among the peoples, and you will be left few in number among the nations where the LORD will drive you. 28 And there you will serve gods of wood and stone, the work of human hands, that neither see, nor hear, nor eat, nor smell. <u>29</u> But from there you will seek the LORD your God and you will find him, if you search after him with all your heart and with all your soul." (Deuteronomy 4:27-29, ESV)

We're going to find out how the children of Israel became few in number. Currently, less than 16 million, scattered over the world, 0.2% of the global population. While Christianity (31% of global pop.) and Islam (25%) became the world's 2 largest religions (over 4 billion combined). Ironically, Native Americans decreased to 0.2% of U.S. pop. Besides most being Christianized in the name of Rome's trinity, we're going to find out why that's relevant.

The Torah teaches that idolatry results in violence and injustice. History teaches that the Torah is accurate. The timeline is the who, what, when, where, and how of Deuteronomy 4:27-28. Plaintiff told you that the New Testament fulfills the Old Testament. Oh, it does; but not how he claims. It's far more interesting. It was all foretold by the Prophets of Israel.

Muslims make their pilgrimage to the Grand Mosque in Mecca and kiss the black stone they say fell from heaven. Jesus was 1 of 120,000-200,000 Jews crucified on wood in the 2nd temple period. According to Josephus, Rome crucified so many Jews that they ran out of wood. Protestants' only idol is a wooden cross without Jesus' body. Long before the word Jew was invented, who exactly was Moses informing that their descendants would worship gods of wood and stone if they broke God's 2nd commandment?

Moses: "You are standing today, all of you, before the LORD your God: the heads of your tribes, your elders, and your officers, all the men of Israel, your little ones, your wives, and the sojourner who is in your camp, from the one who chops your wood to the one who draws your water, so that you may enter into the sworn covenant of the LORD your God, which the LORD your God is making with you today, that he may establish you today as his people, and that he may be your God, as he promised you, and as he swore to your fathers, to Abraham, to Isaac, and to Jacob. It is not with you alone that I am making this sworn covenant, but with whoever is standing here with us today before the LORD our God, and with whoever is not here with us today." (Deuteronomy 29:10-15, ESV)

Rabbi Moses teaches that there's not an extra word in the Torah (Deut. 32:47). Maybe Katarzyna figured the words "It is not with you alone... and with whoever is not here with us today" applied to her. Maybe not. Either way, regardless of what religion her mother was, she accepted The LORD's repeated invitations for everyone to turn back. It's not complicated.

"He has told you, O man, what is good; and what does the Lord require of you but to do justice, and to love kindness, and to walk humbly with your God?" (Micah 6:8, ESV)

This might help millions residing in Spain, Portugal, Italy, Turkey, Greece, Brazil, U.S.A., Mexico, understand the relevance of Deuteronomy. 4:27-28:

"Today, some 200 million people may be descendants of the Spanish and Portuguese communities forced to convert to Christianity. On July 31, 1492, practicing Jews living in Spain had to make a decision: Convert to Christianity or leave. If conversos – converted Jews – stayed and continued to keep their faith in secret, but were found out by members of the Inquisition or exposed by neighbors, they would be tortured brutally into admitting their "sin" and later be burned, all of which was ordered by the Church... almost 100 years before, in 1391, over half of Spain's Jews had converted to Christianity as a result of religious persecution... Genetic research released earlier this year [2019] found that 25% of Hispanics and Latinos have Jewish DNA... "Those who had been forcibly converted, which is possibly up to half of the whole Jewish population, were not allowed to leave, they did not have that choice." (Jerusalem Post, Spanish Inquisition: 527 years ago, Jews in Spain made an impossible choice, Ilanit Chernick)

"Of those Jews who chose to flee Spain in 1492, large numbers went to Morocco, Italy and to the Ottoman Empire... perhaps half of the total went to Portugal... condition upon their entry, all the boys, and young men and girls of the Jews be taken into captivity. After having them all turned into Christians... Unlike Spain, where many converted or were forced to leave, the Portuguese Jews were not allowed to leave when Portugal closed the exit doors in 1497... The Portuguese, mostly roman Catholic, are estimated to be 80% of Jewish admixture..." (HALPID, Volume V, Winter 1997, Volume 4, THE FORCED CONVERSION OF THE JEWS OF PORTUGAL 1497)

What religion were your ancestors 2,000 years ago before Christianity was invented? Or 1,400 years ago before Islam?

"Thus says the LORD: "Where is your mother's certificate of divorce, with which I sent her away? Or which of my creditors is it to whom I have sold you? Behold, for your iniquities you were sold, and for your transgressions, your mother was sent away." (Isaiah 50:1, ESV)

Rabbis teach that nobody really converts to Judaism; they always had Jewish soul and finally figured it out. Those numbers are based on incomplete DNA testing. Using math, based on birthrates, the numbers are much higher...

Judge: Nobody needs DNA testing to know that we're all related to Noah. Or a mathematician to calculate 2.5-3 million people who heard God's voice at Mount Siani 3,316 years ago have more than 16 million living descendants. The reason you're not capable of counting the children of Israel with DNA results or math is God's promise to Abraham.

"I will make your offspring as the dust of the earth, so that if one can count the dust of the earth, your offspring also can be counted." (Genesis 13:16, ESV)

Chapter 3

God's 2nd Commandment

Defense Counsel: Among the great ironies of life, is sometimes when a Christian follows instructions of the Great Commission in Matthew, Mark, Luke, John, and Acts to convert people to Christianity, "first to the Jew then to the Gentile" (Romans 1:16): The Jew does what they're supposed to
(Isaiah 43:10-12).

For example, a Christian explains to a Jew that Jesus is the suffering servant of Isaiah 53. Then the Jew shows the Christian, in their own Bible, in the 4 Servant Songs leading up to Isaiah 53, where we're explicitly told 8 times by The LORD God that the suffering servant (plural) is Israel (Isaiah 41:8-9, 43:10-12, 44:1, 44:2, 44:21, 45:4, 48:20, 49:3). Additionally, we're explicitly told the servant is Israel in Psalm 136:22, Jeremiah 30:10, 46:27-28.

God designated the children of Israel as His firstborn before freeing them from slavery (Exodus 4:22) They were given responsibilities as servant and witness (Isaiah 41:8-13). Witness to what?

"Thus says the LORD, the King of Israel
and his Redeemer, the LORD of hosts:
"I am the first and I am the last;
besides me there is no god.
Who is like me? Let him proclaim it.
Let him declare and set it before me, since I appointed an ancient people.

Let them declare what is to come, and what will happen.
Fear not, nor be afraid; have I not told you from of old and
declared it? And you are my witnesses!
Is there a God besides me?
There is no Rock; I know not any." (Isaiah 44:6-8, ESV)

Witness to the miracles of the Exodus and Oneness of
God (Exodus 19-20:2, Deuteronomy 5:1-6, 6:4). The
LORD God is clearly identifying Himself in the 1st
commandment:

"And God spoke all these words, saying, "I am the LORD
your God, who brought you out of the land of Egypt, out of
the house of slavery" (Exodus 20:1-2, ESV)

Moses, Isaiah, Jeremiah, almost all the prophets, warned
the children of Israel and all their descendants to stop
breaking God's 2nd more than all other commandments
combined. Deuteronomy chapter 4 is no exception, in
verse 23 we're told breaking the 2nd is breaking the
covenant.

"Is there a God besides me? ... I know not any." (Isaiah
44:8) Do you know God's 2nd commandment? We're
going to find out that the 2 most relevant sentences of this
Trial of the Trinity are God's 1st commandment and first
sentence of the 2nd: "Do not have other gods besides me."
(Exodus 20:3, CSB) "Besides" is a more accurate
translation than "before" such as "Thou shalt have no other
gods before me." (Exodus 20:3, KJV) Most accurate is:

"You shall not have the gods of others in My presence."
(Exodus 20:3, Chabad.org)

When we get to Zechariah 13, we'll find out what The
LORD God is going to do about being designated an equal

person with a man from Nazareth in Rome's trinity. But we must go through the timeline to understand why the shepherd will be struck and the sheep will scatter.

"I am the Lord, that is My Name; and My glory I will not give to another, nor My praise to the graven images."
(Isaiah 42:8, Chabad.org)

I didn't edit out the words except Jesus.

"I, I am the Lord, and besides me there is no savior."
(Isaiah 43:11, ESV)

I can't help but wonder if Katarzyna Weiglowa ever asked her priest: Which "separate but equal person" of the Trinity is speaking in Isaiah 42:8-43:11?

After the Roman Catholic Church converted Jews by getting them to break it, they did their best to hide the 2nd commandment from their great great grand-children and taught them how to break it.

God's 2nd commandant is Exodus 20:3-6; not a word more or less (Deuteronomy 4:2). But not a word of "You shall not make for yourself a graven image or any likeness which is in the heavens above, which is on the earth below, or which is in the water beneath the earth. You shall neither prostrate yourself before them nor worship them..."
(Exodus 20:4-5) appear anywhere in the Catholic 10 commandants. The 2nd commandment Catholics are taught is the 3rd commandment Jews and Protestants are taught.

Judge: How'd they remove a commandment and still end up with 10?

Defense: Officially since 1215, during Pope Innocent III's reign of terror: The Roman Catholic Church, split God's 10th commandment which is Exodus 20:14 in Jewish Bibles and Exodus 20:17 in Christian Bibles. The 10th became 9 and 10. That fills the space of the omitted 2nd commandment. The only graven image that Protestants break God's 2nd commandment by kneeling before is the cross...

Plaintiff Counsel: OBJECTION! Jesus is the image of God! Worshipping Jesus is absolutely not breaking the second commandment! "He is the image of the invisible God, the firstborn of all creation." (Colossians 1:15, ESV)

Defense: "Therefore watch yourselves very carefully. Since you saw no form on the day that the LORD spoke to you at Horeb out of the midst of the fire, beware lest you act corruptly by making a carved image for yourselves, in the form of any figure, the likeness of male or female," (Deut. 4:15-16, ESV)

Are figures in the likeness of male Jesus exempted?

Plaintiff: Objection! You can't use Deuteronomy against Jesus! Jesus is our God and Savior! "Simeon Peter, a servant and apostle of Jesus Christ, To those who have obtained a faith of equal standing with ours by the righteousness of our God and Savior Jesus Christ..." (2 Peter 1:1, ESV)

Judge: Paul's letter to the Colossians and Peter's second letter do not supersede or negate what God said recorded by Moses in Exodus 4:22, 20:1-6, Deuteronomy 4:2, 15-19, 23-40. God not wanting to be associated with any image of anything couldn't have been made clearer. In Deut. 4:31, and 4:40 it's reinforced that God's commandments will never change. Overruled.

"Know therefore today, and lay it to your heart, that the Lord is God in heaven above and on the earth beneath; there is no other." (Deut. 4:39)

Chapter 4

Song of Moses and Eve of Peace

We're in the year 5784 (2023). Until the coming of the Messiah, we're given every opportunity to cease idolatry and turn back. The entire Jewish Bible points to the Messianic Age when all idolatry and resulting violence comes to an end. We're supposed to look forward to it like we look forward to the Sabbath each week. Now is Erev Shabbat, 'The Eve of Peace.' When changing the year and the calendar, Rome knew the Messiah's to come before 6000 (2240), or sooner if enough people turn to The LORD God alone. Psalm 90...

Plaintiff: Objection! Jesus said, "But concerning that day and hour no one knows, not even the angels of heaven, nor the Son, but the Father only." (Matthew 24:36, KJV)

Defense: How can Jesus be God, and the Messiah, yet not know when the Messiah's coming? Either Jesus is God or equal to God; or he's not. If not, then your trinity's absolute idolatry. The Creator of heaven and earth whom nobody is equal to, knows exactly when the Messiah's coming:

"remember the former things of old; for I am God, and there is no other; I am God, and there is none like me, declaring the end from the beginning
and from ancient times things not yet done, saying, 'My counsel shall stand, and I will accomplish all my purpose,' (Isaiah 46:9-10, ESV)

Plaintiff: Your honor, the following verse from within the four corners of the Torah itself proves that the contract was severed, and the Jews are no longer God's chosen people.

"They have acted corruptly toward Him, They are not His children, because of their defect; But are a perverse and crooked generation." (Deuteronomy 32:5, ESV) The Jews were disowned for their repeated failures to keep God's commandments. Christianity is the new Israel. The blood of Christ Jesus is the new and everlasting covenant.

Defense: This trial should be extremely simple. Should've been over with God's 1st commandment and the first sentence of the 2nd! God's Name forever (Numbers 23:19)! God shares glory with no other (Isaiah 42:8)! Jesus is Not anyone's savior (Isaiah 43:11, 45:21-22, Hosea 13:4)! Every Christian concedes that every one of those verses is the word of God. Any of them, on their own, should end this trial immediately. Yet, instead of accepting the first three-quarters of his own Bible, Plaintiff uses the last quarter add-on to try and negate it.

Plaintiff: You've argued for literal interpretation of the text all trial. The Bible says, referring to the Jews "They are not His children." That's the plain and simple meaning of the text. Welcome to the New Covenant.

Defense: Another disgraceful context altering mistranslation. The accurate translation is: "Destruction is not His; it is His children's defect you crooked and twisted generation." (Deuteronomy 32:5, Chabad.org)

The point of the verse is free will. The children of Israel don't get to blame God for bad behavior or the consequences of it. It's that simple.

Judge: Overruled. Be aware, I'm past the point of aggravation with context altering mistranslations being offered as evidence in my courtroom.

Defense: Mistranslations that Plaintiff's used to try and deceive you are motivated by replacement theology: trying to replace Israel with Jesus. The monumental problem with that, is it's made crystal clear that we're never to change, add, remove, or contradict any word of the Torah and God's covenants are forever (Deuteronomy 4:2, 31, 40, 13:1, 28:28, 32:47).
"I will not violate my covenant or alter the word that went forth from my lips." (Psalms 89:24, ESV)

The last mistranslation Plaintiff cited is from the "Song of Moses" which comprises almost the entire chapter of Deuteronomy 32. It's the song Moses taught the children of Israel before he died. The song warns of terrible things that will happen if they break the 2nd commandment by serving other gods. Compared to the timeline we'll get to, here's a relatively minor example:

1008 CE Fatimid Empire: Caliph Al-Hakim bi-Amr Allah ordered Jews to wear a heavy wooden "golden calf" around their necks, Christians to wear a large wooden cross around theirs, and both groups to wear black hats.

Had God's 2nd commandment (Exodus 20:3-6) been followed, and people didn't worship images and idols of golden calves and crosses, that, and whole lot much worse, wouldn't have happened. Everyone involved had free will. The Song of Moses ends with justice, promising those who escalate idolatry into violence that they're going to get it even worse. Why?

"Because you cherished perpetual enmity and gave over the people of Israel to the power of the sword at the time of their calamity, at the time of their final punishment, therefore, as I live, declares the Lord God, I will prepare you for blood, and blood shall pursue you; because you did

not hate bloodshed, therefore blood shall pursue you"
(Ezekiel 35:5-6, ESV))

It's important to remember that foreknowledge is not the
same as predestination. Every negative prophecy in the
Torah could've been, and future ones still can be avoided.
Unlike covenants that are irrevocable throughout all
generations (Deuteronomy 4:31, 40). The importance of
free will cannot be overstated. Choices result in a blessing
or a curse (Deuteronomy 4,5,27, 28, 29, 30, 31, 32, etc.).
Without free will, everything, every relationship, including
with our Creator, would be meaningless.

Chapter 5

"Every Knee Shall Bow" To Who?

Defense: Was Jesus of Nazareth, who admits he doesn't know what God knows (Matt.24-36); and referred to himself as a man or son of man, which is the same thing, 82 times in Rome's New Testament, a man? Yes, or no?

"God is not man, that he should lie, or a son of man, that he should change his mind. Has he said, and will he not do it? Or has he spoken, and will he not fulfill it?" (Numbers 23:19, ESV)

Plaintiff: Objection! Jesus always was God, but later became man. "And the Word became flesh and dwelt among us, and we have seen his glory, glory as of the only Son from the Father, full of grace and truth." John (1:14, ESV)

Defense: According to Plaintiff, Jesus is God, a separate but equal person with God the Father, God's only son, the Messiah, the great shepherd of the sheep, and the word. The longest chapter in the Bible is Psalm 119. It's David's love letter to the word, to the Torah. Jesus' name isn't mentioned. Nor is Jesus' name mentioned anywhere else in the same Jewish Bible where Moses' name appears over 700 and David's name over 1,000 times.

"My soul melts away for sorrow; strengthen me according to your word!
Put false ways far from me and graciously teach me your law!

I have chosen the way of faithfulness; I set your rules before me." (Psalm 119:28-30, ESV)

"But the word is very near you. It is in your mouth and in your heart, so that you can do it." (Deuteronomy 30:14, ESV)

Plaintiff: Jesus isn't mentioned in the Old Testament because it was only "a shadow of the things to come, but the substance belongs to Christ" (Colossians 2:17, ESV). And yes, Deuteronomy 30:14 is correct. Jesus is the word who lives in us. Saint Paul further explains: "But when it pleased God, who separated me from my mother's womb and called me through His grace, to reveal His Son in me..." (Galatians 1:15-16, ESV)

Defense: The "word" says God is not a man, God does not change, God will never be a man, and God does not lie because God is not a man (Numbers 23:19)! Paul doesn't get to change that (Deut. 4:2, 32:47)! How do you disregard what the "1st person" of your trinity in your own Bible? Does God want people calling Him Jesus? Does God plan on changing His Name?

"God also said to Moses, "Say this to the people of Israel: 'The Lord, the God of your fathers, the God of Abraham, the God of Isaac, and the God of Jacob, has sent me to you.' This is my name forever, and thus I am to be remembered throughout all generations." (Exodus 3:15, ESV)

Forever means throughout all generations. Symbolic parallelism is when the prophet repeats the exact same message twice in the same sentence. Such as "This is my name forever, and thus I am to be remembered throughout all generations." And "God is not man... or a son of man"

(Numbers 23:19). Should Moses have repeated himself 3 times in the same sentence, so you...

Plaintiff: Nobody will be saved in any other name than Jesus Christ!

"let it be known to all of you and to all the people of Israel that by the name of Jesus Christ of Nazareth, whom you crucified, whom God raised from the dead... there is salvation in no one else, for there is no other name under heaven given among men by which we must be saved." (Acts 4:10-12, ESV)

Defense: AGAIN! "I, I am the Lord, and besides me there is no savior." (Isaiah 43:11, ESV)

"For thus says the LORD, who created the heavens... "I am the LORD, and there is no other." (Isaiah 45:18, ESV)

Do you have the gall to claim that's the 2nd person of your trinity is speaking and not the 1st? Does The LORD God say no other except Jesus?

Plaintiff: The Bible says Jesus' name is above EVERY other name! And at the name of Jesus every knee shall bow!

"And being found in human form, he humbled himself by becoming obedient to the point of death, even death on a cross. Therefore God has highly exalted him and bestowed on him the name that is above every name, so that at the name of Jesus every knee should bow, in heaven and on earth and under the earth, and every tongue confess that Jesus Christ is Lord, to the glory of God the Father." (Philippians 2:9-11, ESV)

Defense: What Paul wrote in his letter to the Philippians does not negate, change, overrule or supersede what The LORD God says, ancient words recorded 2,700 years ago about what happens at the end of this age:

"Assemble yourselves and come; draw near together, you survivors of the nations! They have no knowledge who carry about their wooden idols, and keep on praying to a god that cannot save.

Declare and present your case; let them take counsel together!
Who told this long ago? Who declared it of old? Was it not I, the LORD?

And there is no other god besides me, a righteous God and a Savior; there is none besides me.

"Turn to me and be saved, all the ends of the earth!

For I am God, and there is no other.

By myself I have sworn; from my mouth has gone out in righteousness a word that shall not return: 'To me, every knee shall bow, every tongue shall swear allegiance."
(Isaiah 45:20-23, ESV)

Part 2

Timeline of the 4th Beast that Terrified Daniel

Chapter 6

Daniel Warns of the 4th Beast

Defense Counsel: Daniel chapters 7 thru 12 are apocalyptic visions of past, present, and future empires that would subjugate the servants God chose to preserve, protect, and share the Torah with the world. Daniel's visions reflect the relationship between these empires and their heavenly counterparts.

Summary of Daniel Chapter 7: Verses 1-8 begin with Daniel having terrifying visions of beasts. 7:9-10 are about the Ancient of Days taking his seat in the heavenly court to open the books for judgment. The 4 beasts are judged and convicted. 7:11 one of those beasts (the 4th) is killed. 7:12 the other 3 beasts lose their power. 7:13 is indeed about the messiah; and God. God is the Ancient of Days. The Messiah is "one like a son of man."

"I saw in the night *visions, and* behold, with the clouds of heaven there came one like a son of man, and he came to the Ancient of Days and was presented before him."
(Daniel 7:13, ESV)

It's beyond me, how Plaintiff can quote Daniel 7:13 without Numbers 23:19 ringing a bell in his head. It's undisputed that 'son of man' and 'man' mean the exact same thing. The phrase son of man is used to make sure there's no confusion about the fact that the messiah will be a man, conceived the way men have been getting women pregnant since Adam and Eve figured it out. The very next sentence after verse 13 in Plaintiff's own Bible, beginning with the word "And" reads:

"And to him was given dominion and glory and a kingdom, that all peoples, nations, and languages should serve him; his dominion is an everlasting dominion, which shall not pass away, and his kingdom one that shall not be destroyed." (Daniel 7:14, ESV)

Notice the same language is used in Daniel 7 verses 6 and 14. 7:6 the beast is given dominion. 7:14 the son of man is given dominion. Neither the beast nor son of man is giving dominion. The LORD God is the giver of dominion. Kings David, Hezekiah, and Solomon were given dominion in their time.

7:15: Daniel didn't understand the beasts. 7:16 the Angel Gabriel explained the beasts to Daniel. "One who stood there," refers to 'standing one' meaning an angel or messenger. Angels are referred to as standing ones because angels don't have free will like we do. Therefore, angels are who they are, forever. As opposed to being given the opportunity to grow which comes with free will.

Continuing with Daniel 7, in verses 17-22 it's foretold, not predestined, that the beasts are the 4 kingdoms who will subjugate God's witnesses. The 4 beasts are the Babylonian, Medo-Persian, Greek, and Roman Empires. Daniel's most interested in the 4th beast that absolutely terrifies him. The 4th and last beast will be much worse than the others (Daniel 7:7-8, 23-25).

"He shall speak words against the Most High, and shall wear out the saints of the Most High, and shall think to change the times and the law; and they shall be given into his hand for a time, times, and half a time." (Daniel 7:25, KJV)

Sure enough, centuries later, the church in Rome tried to change the times and do away with God's law. They even punished people for celebrating the same Jewish holidays the man they turned into a god celebrated according to Luke 2:7,8,14,15.

What about the first part, how could the 4th Beast wear out the saints when Rome put themselves in charge of deciding who's a saint? We'll find out.

"But the court shall sit in judgment, and his dominion shall be taken away, to be consumed and destroyed to the end. And the kingdom and the dominion and the greatness of the kingdoms under the whole heaven shall be given to the people of the saints of the Most High; his kingdom shall be an everlasting kingdom, and all dominions shall serve and obey him." (Daniel 7:26-27, ESV)

Notice that after the 4th Beast is completely destroyed, the kingdom is given to the messiah in Daniel 7:14, and given to the people in Daniel 7:27. The Messiah is God's king on earth, a God-fearing ruler in the Messianic Age, a king from the Davidic line. A man of the same people who fear the same LORD as everyone else will.

"For the children of Israel shall dwell many days without king or prince, without sacrifice or pillar, without ephod or household gods. Afterward the children of Israel shall return and seek the Lord their God, and David their king, and they shall come in fear to the Lord and to his goodness in the latter days. (Hosea 3:4-5, ESV)

Plaintiff Counsel: Objection! Rome was sacked in AD 410 and the empire completely fell by 476. Daniel's prophecy of the fourth beast being destroyed has already been fulfilled.

Defense Counsel: The 4th Beast wasn't destroyed. It spilt up, morphed, turned over. Historical facts on the timeline prove they were just getting warmed up by 476. Still the largest landowner in the world; we're going to find out how they acquired it. Pope Francis' meetings with Klaus Schwab to plan our future, transhumanism... Judge: Overruled.

Defense: 1523-1313 BCE (Jewish year 2238) Jacob and his children left what is modern day Israel, Canaan....

Plaintiff: Objection. Defense has already made an unusually long closing argument. The Exodus of 3,336 years ago is not relevant to this trial.

Defense: Jury, the last thing the church wants you to find out is your history. In the USA, children are taught their ancestors came to the New World fleeing religious persecution. True, yet graduates of Central Catholic High, their mascot a crusader on horseback wielding a sword and "Shield of the Trinity" don't know how many crusades... Judge: How many pages?

Defense: 417. A timeline summarizing terrorism done falsely in the name of God by the 4th Beast would be millions of pages. Just to give you an idea: 500,000 pages of subpoenaed records from the Catholic Church's "secret archives" was condensed to an 884-page unanimously issued grand jury report; reduced to a paragraph; similar reports from Philadelphia 2005 and 2011 cut entirely. Forced baptism of entire communities throughout Europe for over a dozen centuries and "liquidation" of same cities during the Holocaust were removed for no other reason than reducing word count.

Judge: I agree with the Attorney Generals of Pennsylvania, Illinois, and the Prime Minister of Spain, victims deserve to have their stories told. Bringing it into the light is a step that cannot be skipped if the scourge is to be stopped. 417-pages is too long to be read in closing. Shorten it by at least 90 percent.

Defense: Fine. I'll skip most of it and abbreviate the rest.

c. 827-957 BCE, Mount Moriah Jerusalem: King Solomon built the 1st Temple according to plans the Prophet Nathaniel gave his father King David. King Solomon invited non-Jews to pray there and urged The LORD God to pay particular attention to their prayers.

"Thus all the peoples of the earth will know Your name and revere You, as does Your people Israel; and they will recognize that Your name is attached to this House that I have built" (1 Kings 8:43, Jewish Virtual Library)

Chapter 7

Timeline of the 4th Beast that Terrified Daniel: 753 BCE thru Sunday and Christmas 336 CE

Defense Counsel: Before we get to 2023, we'll understand why this ancient Roman history is as relevant today as it was 2,739 years ago.

753-716 BCE: After winning battles resulting from the capture and "Rape of the Sabine Women." **Romulus,** founder and 1st king of Rome **vowed to build a Temple to Jupiter in Rome.** Jupiter was the "sky god," symbolized by the eagle, thunder, lightning, and oak tree. **Jupiter, ancient Rome's king of pagan gods** is the Egyptian equivalent of Amun, **Babylonian equivalent of Baal**, Persian- Ahura Mazda, Greek-Zeus, Norse-Thor, and Hindu-Brihaspati.

To be clear: The LORD God of Abraham, Issac, and Jacob has no equivalent.

716-672 BCE: Most of Rome's religious and political traditions were started by the 2nd king of Rome, Numa Pompilius, including Vestal Virgins and the office of Pontifex Maximus. **The main responsibility of the Pontifex Maximus is to carry on the traditions of the ancient Roman cults.** According to Roman tradition, Pompilius negotiated with Jupiter to establish principles of the Ancient Roman religion, such as offerings and sacrifices to pagan gods, authority over public and private religious institutions, supervision of funds, funerary rites, etc. The instructions were written, sealed, and passed on to the first Pontifex Maximus, Numa Marcius. From 382 CE until today, the Pope, Bishop of Rome, and Pontifex Maximus have been the same person. Currently that's Jorge Mario Bergoglio AKA Pope Francis.

Mount Moriah Jerusalem, 423 BCE according to Jewish Sources, 586 BCE according to secular sources: the 1st Temple was destroyed. King Nebuchadnezzar exiled 10,000 Jews thought to be the brightest and have the most potential, including the Prophet Daniel. Construction of the 2nd Temple in 353 BCE or 516 BCE... Judge: Why the difference in dates?

Defense: If secular scholars concede the dates, they're admitting that Jeremiah and Daniel accurately prophesied destruction and rebuilding of the Temple. They have a hard enough time not being able to explain how stones weighing up to 400 tons, with no mortar, fit so perfectly that a piece of paper won't fit between them. That's just for the retaining wall of the Temple Mount which is the size of 6 football fields...

Plaintiff: Pardon. For the record, we would like to note that in addition to Old Testament Prophets, Jesus also predicted the destruction of the Temple.

Defense: Most Christian historians date the anonymously written accounts of Mark, Matthew and Luke to after the Temple was destroyed. It's like predicting September 11, 2001, in 2030. Judge: Continue the timeline.

475 BCE: Haman, advisor to King Ahasuerus (Xerxes I) 4th king of kings of the Achaemenid Empire. Mordecai refused to bow to him; so Haman ordered every Jew in Persia killed. The festival of Purim, celebrated to this day, commemorates Queen Esther's courage in saving Persian

Jews from extinction. During the Inquisitions, Queen Esther became the unofficial Patron Saint of "New Christians."

167 BCE Jerusalem: "The Abomination of Desolation" Antiochus IV Epiphanes slaughtered thousands of Jewish men; their wives and children sold into slavery. He tried to completely obliterate the Jewish religion. Circumcision was banned. He ordered every Torah scroll burned. After looting the Temple, he set an idol of Zeus and sacrificed a pig on the alter, forced priests to eat it. Surviving Jews were ordered Hellenized, to abandon their faith and traditions in favor of Greek ideas and idols. They were forced to build altars and sacrifice pigs on them in every village, daily. Noncompliers "were whipped with rods, and their bodies torn to pieces, then crucified while they were still alive, and breathed. They also strangled those women and their sons whom they had circumcised." (Josephus, Antiquities of the Jews XII.5.4)

167 BCE: "Hannah and her 7 Sons" were among those rounded up by Antiochus IV Epiphanes for keeping kosher, brought before the king and ordered to eat pork. The oldest brother refused, his tongue was cut out, skin peeled back as his brothers and mother watched. While still breathing, he was thrown into a large hot cauldron. After her next 5 sons were scalped and peeled for refusing to eat pork, the king urged her to make her youngest comply. She urged him to follow his brothers' example instead; then threw herself into the fire (2 Maccabees 7). Their remains were interred in a synagogue that was later converted into a Catholic church in Antioch.

63 BCE: The Siege of Jerusalem was led by Pompey. Roman forces conquered Judea, ending Jewish independence, beginning Roman occupation. In Rome,

Julius Caesar became Pontifex Maximus. The 4th Beast officially begins:

6 CE: Already under Roman occupation, Roman Emperor Augustus officially incorporated Judea into the Roman Empire. Coponius was appointed the 1st prefect (governor) of Judea. According to Josephus, he "had the power of life and death." Rome imposed a census and more taxes. Judas of Galilee led the "4th Philosophical Sect" AKA "Zealots" in resistance to Roman occupation.

27-34 CE: Judea (present day Israel): Jesus of Nazareth was crucified. He was 1 of approximately 120,000-200,000 Jews crucified by Rome during the 2nd Temple Period. Pontius Pilate was Judea's 5th Roman prefect (governor). Pilate had the same power over life and death in Judea as Coponius had.

49-68 CE: Saul of Tarsus AKA Paul wrote letters; some while being detained with privileges under Roman Governor Felix' protection (Acts 24:23).

66 CE: Roman soldiers killed about 50,000 Jews in the Alexandria riot.

66-73 CE: The First Jewish-Roman War resulted in Roman victory. Judea, Samaria, and Edom were incorporated by the 4th Beast into Roman Palestine AKA Syria Palaestina. Out of the 1st Jewish-Roman War also came the Jewish Diaspora. This exile of the Israelites from their ancient homeland (bigger than modern day Israel) was the last, and according to the prophets, will be the last time the children of Israel are exiled. This final exile started coming to an end in 1948.

April 14, 70 Jerusalem: Titus seized Jerusalem. According to Josephus, Jerusalem was ravaged with murder, famine, and cannibalism.

August 30, 70 Jerusalem: On the Jewish fasting day of Tish B' Av, Roman Emperor Nero sent General Vespasian, his son Titus and 60,000 Roman soldiers to slaughter the Jews and burn down the 2nd Temple in Jerusalem. According to Josephus, over a million Jews were killed in Jerusalem and another 97,000 were enslaved.

Present Day Jerusalem, the Jews are still waiting for the messiah to begin construction of the 3rd and Final Temple according to the blueprints found in the final 8 chapters of Ezekiel.

April 16, 73: The Siege of Masada pretty much brought the first Jewish-Roman War to an end. According to Josephus, 3 days before Passover, the Roman Army ravaged Jerusalem with murder and cannibalism. Rome sent the X Legion and Jewish POWs, totaling 15,000 men. After entering with battering rams, they found 960 men, women, and children who committed mass suicide rather than face Roman soldiers. *Today, swearing-in ceremonies of IDF Armoured Corps soldiers on top of Mount Masada end with "Masada shall not fall again." (Moshe Dayan, IDF Chief of Staff 1953-58)*

66-76 CE: Roman occupied Judea: The anonymously written gospel later named Mark was written.

80-95 CE: Roman occupied Judea: The anonymously written gospels later named Matthew and Luke were written.

88-107 CE: Ignatius, early church father and Bishop of Antioch wrote "Your bishop presides in the place of God."

90-110 CE: Roman occupied Judea: The anonymously written gospel later named John was written.

132-135 CE: The Bar Kokhba revolt was a bloodbath. According to Cassius Dio, 580,000 Jews were killed.

165 CE: "Pay attention, all families of the nations, and observe! An extraordinary murder has taken place in Jerusalem, in the city devoted to God's law, in the city of the Hebrews, in the city of the prophets, in the city thought of as just. And who has been murdered? And who is the murderer?

I am ashamed to give the answer, but give it I must... The one who hung the earth in space, is himself hanged; the one who fixed the heavens in place, is himself impaled; the one who firmly fixed all things, is himself firmly fixed to the tree. The Lord is insulted, God has been murdered, the King of Israel has been destroyed by the right hand of Israel... Why was it like this, O Israel? You forsook the Lord; you were not found by him. You dashed the Lord to the ground; you, too, were dashed to the ground, and lie quite dead." Melito, Bishop of Sardis who coined calling the Jewish Bible the "Old Testament."

155-220 CE: Tertullian's been called "father of Latin Christianity," "founder of Western theology" and first "church father" to coin the term "Trinity."

December 25, 274 Rome: Pontifex Maximus Aurelian dedicated Rome's "4th Temple of the Sun" to the pagan sun-god "Sol Invictus" on "Dies Natalis Solis Invicti" or "Birth of the Invincible Sun."

286 CE: Roman Empire split into Eastern and Western Empires by Diocletian. Theodosius I was the last Emperor to rule both. The Western Roman Empire included Rome; its primary capital was Mediolanum (Milan). Eastern Roman Empire's capital was Nicomedia, later Constantinople (modern-day Istanbul).

October 28, 312 Rome: Roman Emperor Constantine won the battle of Milvian Bridge, attributing victory to "Sol Invictus" (the unconquerable god of the sun). Sol is the pagan god of the sun. Cults of Sol Invictus and Mithra were popular among Roman army soldiers who spread these religions throughout the empire. Constantine became the first Christian Roman Emperor. More importantly, Constantine was the first Pontifex Maximus to identify as Christian.

February 313: The Edict of Milan made Christianity a preferred religion, granting legal status to Christians. A good example of how Rome did not convert to Christianity; rather Christianity converted to Rome. Christianity was allowed, preferred, then became official religion of Rome in 380.

318 CE Alexandria: Christians rioted in the streets shouting "There was a time when Christ was not!"

March 7, 321 Rome: Pontifex Maximus/Emporer Constantine decreed "On the venerable day of the Sun let the Magistrates and the people residing in the cities rest, and let all workshops be closed" (Edict of Constantine). He passed the first "Sunday law" making Sol's Day the official day of rest.

"You may read the Bible from Genesis to Revelation, and you will not find a single line authorizing the sanctification of Sunday. The Scriptures enforce the observance of Saturday, a day which we [Catholics] never sanctify." (James Cardinal Gibbons, The Faith of Our Fathers, p. 11)

"From this same Catholic Church, you have accepted your Sunday, and that Sunday, as the Lord's Day, she had handed down as a tradition: and the entire Protestant world has accepted it as tradition, for you have not an iota of Scripture to establish it. Therefore that which you have accepted as your rule of faith, inadequate as it of course is, as well as your Sunday, you have accepted on the authority of the Roman Catholic Church." (D.B. Ray, The Papal Controversy, 1892, p. 179)

Plaintiff: Objection! Jesus is Lord of the Sabbath. Jesus was given ALL Authority over Heaven and Earth. Jesus passes that authority on to his disciples to lead everyone to the peace and love of the body of Christ.

"And Jesus came and said to them, "All authority in heaven and on earth has been given to me. Go therefore and make disciples of all nations, baptizing them in the name of the Father and of the Son and of the Holy Spirit" (Matthew 28:18-19) That's what the Bible says! That's the Holy Trinity: Father, Son, and Holy Spirit!

Defense: Because Rome added it! And that's exactly what they did! Mass-murder and forced baptism in the name of the Trinity! Here's more Catholic sources, 17th, 18th, 19th century priests mocking Protestants for worshiping on Sunday, bragging about... Judge: Unnecessary. Move on.

325 CE: Constantine convened the Council of Nicaea for 2 main purposes:

Get Eastern and Western churches to come to an agreement on the Trinity. Unsuccessful, they couldn't agree as to whether Jesus was God or not.

From the 2nd century until 325, the date of Easter was based on the date of Passover which is calculated based on instructions in the Oral Torah. Constantine wanted an end to Rome's dependance on the Jewish calendar. Since then, Easter's been the first Sunday after the first full moon, on or after the spring equinox according to the lunar calendar. Bishops continued fighting about how to calculate the date of Easter for 7 centuries.

325 Rome: The 4th Beast banned Jews from Jerusalem.

325: The Nicene Creed explicitly affirmed the Father as the "One God." Jesus as "the Son of God begotten" Therefore "consubstantial with the Father" and "of the same substance." The Holy Spirit was not declared "God" or "consubstantial with the Father."

"Who has measured the Spirit of the LORD, or what man shows him his counsel? Whom did he consult, and who made him understand?" (Isaiah 40:13-14, ESV)

After 56 years more fighting, they changed their mind and the Nicene Creed declaring God's Holy Spirit equal to God once again in 381 at Constantinople

December 25, 336 Rome: The 1st Christmas was celebrated by order of Pontifex Maximus Constantine on the birthday of the pagan sun-god Sol. Sol's birthday followed "Saturnalia" (December 17-23) where they sacrificed a pig to Saturn at the Temple in the Roman Forum.

"Saturnalia, the most popular of Roman festivals.
Dedicated to the Roman god Saturn, the festival's
influence continues to be felt throughout the Western
world... it was the liveliest festival of the year. All work and
business were suspended... The influence of the
Saturnalia upon the celebrations of Christmas and the New
Year has been direct. The fact that Christmas was
celebrated on the birthday of the unconquered sun...
connected with (January 1, the Roman New Year) when
houses were decorated with greenery and lights, and
presents were given to children and the poor. Concerning
the gift candles... human sacrifices, but, according to
legend, Hercules advised using lights (phos means "light"
or "man" according to accent) and not human heads."
(Encyclopedia Brittanica, Saturnalia)

Ironically, the Catholic Encyclopedia's an interesting
source: "Mithra is the Mediator (Mesites) between God and
man... Sunday was kept holy in honour of Mithra, and the
sixteenth of each month was sacred to him as mediator.
The December 25th was observed as his birthday,
the natalis invicti, the rebirth of the winter-sun... "(New
Advent Catholic Encyclopedia, Mithraism)

Is Sunday "kept holy" and Christmas 'turned over' from
worshipping Sol or Mithra? We'll understand how it's both
when we get to the turning over according to Leviticus. It
should be clear that neither Sol, Mithra, or Christmas have
anything to do with any of The LORD God's holidays. And
Sunday is not the Sabbath.

"Hear the word that the Lord speaks to you, O house of
Israel. Thus says the Lord: "Learn not the way of the
nations, nor be dismayed at the signs of the heavens

because the nations are dismayed at them, for the customs of the peoples are vanity.

A tree from the forest is cut down and worked with an axe by the hands of a craftsman. They decorate it with silver and gold; they fasten it with hammer and nails so that it cannot move.

Their idols are like scarecrows in a cucumber field, and they cannot speak; they have to be carried, for they cannot walk. Do not be afraid of them, for they cannot do evil, neither is it in them to do good."

There is none like you, O Lord; you are great, and your name is great in might." (Jeremiah 10:1-6, ESV)

Chapter 8

The Holy Spirit or Pope Damasus I?

353 CE: Roman Emperor Flavius Julius Constantius made it official that if any Christian converted to Judaism their property would be confiscated.

To see the big picture, understand that the 4th Beast adding anonymously written Greek texts to the Hebrew Bible was about as perverse a mockery as adding German texts to the Hebrew Bible after the Holocaust would've been. Keep in mind, the Greek Empire was the 3rd Beast preceding Rome.

Plaintiff Counsel: OBJECTION! Not only is saying the Fourth Beast added the New Testament to the Bible, BLASPHEMY! It's a mockery of these proceedi...

Judge: What's your specific objection: That Rome is identified by the Angel Gabriel and Prophet Daniel as the Fourth Beast. Or do you dispute that councils in Rome decided what gospels and letters would comprise the New Testament; then added it to the Jewish Bible?

Plaintiff: It's called the Old Testament because we're in the New Covenant now. The Holy Spirit inspired every word in the New Testament of the Holy Bible! To say otherwise is blasphemy against the Holy Spirit.

Defense: I don't know how anyone could even attempt to make an honest assessment that Jeremiah 31:34 has been fulfilled.

Judge: We've been over this. Jeremiah 31:33-37, Isaiah 11:9, Habakkuk 2:14, and Zechariah 14:9 have been admitted. Those verses and more, along with current events prove beyond any doubt that the New Covenant has not yet begun. If it had, there'd be no wars, ideologically driven or otherwise anywhere in the world. There would be disagreements over religion. As we're told repeatedly, knowledge of God would cover the entire earth. This trial wouldn't be necessary if we were in the New Covenant. Continue.

Defense: Pope Damasus I was not referred to as the "Holy Spirit." He was referred to as "the ladies' ear-scratcher" and "Damasus of Rome." He was in charge when Greek texts were added to the Hebrew Bible, anonymously written gospel accounts and letters, letters written by Paul...

Plaintiff: OBJECTION! The Holy Spirit inspired the New Testament which was added to the Old Testament to complete the Holy Bible!

Defense: Your honor, would you please make a ruling on the following statement: The Holy Spirit was a man born in Rome in 305 CE who was often accused of murder, adultery, womanizing, and bribery. The Holy Spirit twice paid mercenaries to storm into Catholic Churches to slaughter every man and woman inside. He ordered another massacre of Catholics hiding in a cemetery. The Holy Spirit died on December 11, 384. Would you allow that statement to be used as evidence in your courtroom? Judge: No.

Defense: That's what Plaintiff's effectively claiming, when he shouts: The Holy Spirit added the New Testament to the Bible. Substitute Pope Damasus I for Holy Spirit and his statement becomes accurate.

Pope Damasus I added the New Testament to the Hebrew Bible in 382 CE. A fact conceded by Christian scholars and historians. Quoting the Oxford Dictionary of the Christian Church, "Held at Rome in 382 under Damasus gave a complete list of the canonical books."

October 1, 366: "Damasus of Rome" murdered and bribed his way into the papacy. He was either the 35th or 37th Pope depending how many "antipopes" are counted. Undisputedly, Damasus I took the papacy to unprecedented levels of power. Damasus was thought by most of the clergy to be an illegitimate pope, and Ursinus as the rightful successor to the deceased Pope Liberius. They were both voted in, 2 different elections simultaneously, in 2 churches: each winning 1 election. Most of the clergy supported Ursinus. Wealthy families (of which Damasus came from) supported Damasus. The Gesta portrays Ursinus as the rightful successor to Pope Liberius and vilifies Damasus as a follower of Anti-Pope Felix.

Here's how Damasus solved the problem: The first massacre ordered and paid for by Damasus resulted in a 3-day killing spree at the Basilica Giulia. Damasus then exiled his remaining opponents. They held up at the Basilica of Sicininus, now the Basilica Santa Maria Maggiore. The following is an account of the massacre at the Basilica Sicininus, the 2nd of 3 massacres carried out in quick succession by mercenaries hired by Pope Damasus I.

"Then Damasus and his unfaithful following summoned the gladiators, charioteers, gravediggers, and all the clergy, and with hatchets, swords, and clubs they besieged the basilica, inciting a great battle, beginning at the second hour of the day... broke down the doors and set fire underneath it, then rushed in and ransacked the building... when they were destroying the roof of the basilica, were killing the faithful congregation with the tiles. Then all of Damasus' supporters rushed and killed a hundred and sixty of the people inside, both men and women." (Gesta, AD 368)

Following that massacre, Damasus sent another squad to hunt down and kill Ursinian supporters who fled to the cemetery of Saint Agnes. These massacres, along with Damasus' bribing of officials, including paying off a city judge named Viventius, solidified his position as pope.

The books of the Jewish Bible are still out of order in "Old Testaments" of Christian Bibles today. That happened under Pope Damasus I. He also made Latin the official language of the church and had Jerome translate the New Testament from Greek into Latin.

Plaintiff: Objection! Damasus is literally a Saint. His feast day is celebrated on December 11. He was exonerated by 44 bishops. Heretics who falsely accused him were excommunicated. The most trustworthy source we have is Saint Jerome, who blamed Ursinus for instigating the massacres: "Damasus is ordained 35th bishop of the Roman church, and after a not very long interval Ursinus was appointed bishop by some people, and with his partisans invaded [the church of] Sicininum, in which, coming together with some people from the supporters of Damasus, very cruel slaughters were committed" (Jerome).

Defense: Jerome was on Damasus' payroll as his personal secretary. Damasus funded Jerome's other writings. A letter Jerome sent to Pope Damasus I opens with "Yet, though your greatness terrifies me..." He was influencing Jerome's writings, evidence written by Jerome himself in 409 CE: "A great many years ago when I was helping Damasus, bishop of Rome with his ecclesiastical correspondence, and writing his answers to the questions referred to him by the councils of the east and west..." Every source speaking favorably of Damasus cites Jerome. The church canonizes a man with a reputation for mass-murder, bribery, adultery... Judge: Overruled. Continue.

February 27, 380 Rome: "Cunctos populos" AKA Edict of Thessalonica issued by Theodosius I made Nicene Christianity AKA Trinitarian Christianity the official State Church (religion) of the Roman Empire. It condemned all Christian creeds besides the Nicene Creed. Everyone who didn't support Rome's Trinity and Nicene Creed was labeled a heretic. The earliest Torah-observant Christians, such as the Nazarenes and Ebionites were murdered, their books burned, and they were almost erased from existence and memory in the following years.

Chapter 9

"The Decide" thru Banning Deuteronomy 6:4

381 CE: Roman Emperor Theodosius I convened the First Council of Constantinople. The doctrine of the Trinity was made official after 56 years of debate. Jesus was officially declared to be equal to The LORD God.

381 CE: "The Decide" or "Jewish Decide" Although Roman soldiers crucified Jesus under Pilot who had the same power over life and death in his jurisdiction other governors. The anonymously written curse of the Jews: "His blood be upon us and our children" (Matthew 27:25) was used to hold Jews responsible for killing the man Jesus of Nazareth. About 300 years after Matthew was written, the trinity became official, making Jesus officially God or equal to God. This escalated Matt. 27:25 to mean the Jews were now officially responsible for deciding that God would be killed. The 4th Beast apologized for the Decide 1,584 years later at the Second Vatican Council.

"The Jews are slayers of the Lord, murderers of the prophets, adversaries of God, haters of God, men who show contempt for the law, foes of grace, enemies of their father's faith, advocates of the devil, brood of vipers..." (Saint Gregory of Nyssa (335-394) chief defender of Doctrine of the Trinity)

"Observe here the infatuation of the Jews; their headlong haste, and destructive passions will not let them see what they ought to see, and they curse themselves, saying, "His blood be upon us", and even entail the curse upon their children. Yet a merciful God did not ratify this sentence, but accepted such of them and of their children as repented; for Paul was of them, and many thousands of those who in Jerusalem believed." (Saint John Chrysostom (347-407 CE) quoting Mathew 27:25)

Chrysostom was a bishop and "Doctor of the Church." He's recognized as a Saint in many churches, including the Catholic, Eastern Orthodox, Lutheran, Anglican, and Oriental Orthodox. Many of Bishop Chrysostom's homilies targeted "Judaizing Christians" who were keeping the Sabbath and participating in Jewish holidays that are actually found in the Bible, common practice among Christians at that time. He claimed synagogues were full of Christians, especially women who loved the solemnity of the Jewish liturgy. Christians taking part in Rosh Hashanah, which we'll explain when we arrive at 1553 CE, particularly infuriated him. Chrysostom was asked why Jews were so hateful; he said it was because of their "odious assassination of Christ." The Nazi Party used Chrysostom and Luther's homilies quoting the anonymously written gospel of Matthew to justify the Holocaust.

381: Under Pope Damasus I, the Nicene Creed from 325 CE was revised to support the revised Trinity.

382: For the first time, the ancient Roman Cult title Pontifex Maximus was given to the Pope. When Eastern Roman Emperor Theodosius made Christianity the official religion of the empire, Western Roman Emperor Gratian refused the title of Pontifex Maximus. Gratian granted the title to Pope Damasus I. Since King Numa Pompilius established the position prior to 672 BCE, the chief duty of the Pontifex Maximus has been maintaining sacrifices to pagan gods and carrying on the traditions of ancient Roman cults that were "turned over" from the ancient Babylonian cults.

Present Day Rome, engraved into big doors at an entrance to the Vatican, "BENEDICTUS XVI PONT. MAX ANNO DOMINI MMV PONT. I" or "Benedict XVI, Pontifex Maximus in the year of our Lord, 2005, in the first year of his pontificate." As we're going to find out, traditions of the ancient cults are being carried on under the Pontifex Maximus, including one that's so disgusting it's the only thing we're told never crossed The LORD's mind.

Plaintiff Counsel: Objection! False and slander. "Gratian (375-383) was the first emperor to sever the official bond linking paganism to the imperial
power, by refusing to accept the insignia of Pontifex Maximus (chief priest of paganism). 'Such a garment,' he said, 'is not becoming to a Christian." (Philip Hughes, A History of the Christian Church, 1934)

Judge: If Gratian rejected it because he thought it was unbecoming a Christian, then why did Pope Damasus I accept it?

Defense: To carry on the traditions of ancient Babylonian cults that evolved into Roman cults. That's been the chief job description long before there was a pope. Pontifex Maximus Francis is actually doing his job. We'll understand after we get through 'turning over' and the end of the timeline.

Judge: Plaintiff, if the responsibility of the office ended, then why does Pope Francis still hold the Pontifex Maximus title today?

Plaintiff: It's merely symbolic. Pontifex Maximus means "Greatest Pontiff." It's also translated as "Bridge Builder" symbolic of the bridge between God and man. Judge: Overruled. Continue.

382 CE Rome: The Council of Rome reporting to Pontifex Maximus/Pope Damasus I voted on what would comprise the New Testament. It would be tacked on to the already completed Jewish Bible to comprise the Catholic Bible. A dozen centuries later, Protestants removed several books from the Catholic canon to make up their own Christian Bible.

389 and 391 CE Rome: "Theodosian decrees" banned all worship, temples, holidays, of any kind except for Trinitarian or Nicene Christianity.

391 CE Alexandria: "busts of Serapis which stood in the walls, vestibules, doorways, and windows of every house were all torn out and annihilated..., and in their place, the sign of the Lord's cross was painted in the doorways, vestibules, windows, and walls, and on pillars." (Christianizing The Roman Empire AD 100–400, Ramsay MacMullen)

415 CE: "The Alexandria Expulsion" an estimated 100,000 Jews were expelled. Their property was seized.

438 Jerusalem: Theodosius II's wife arranged for Jews to visit and pray at the ruins of the Temple Mount. Jews were stabbed and stoned by monks. Monks were put on trial, claimed the stones fell from heaven, and were acquitted.

451: Roman Emperor Marcian convoked the Council of Chalcedon to stop remaining internal opposition to the Trinity. The "hypostatic union" of the Trinity was made official. If you think hypostatic union is complicated, just remember it took Rome 125 years of debate (325-451) to hammer it out.

465: The Council of Vannes banned Christian clergy from participating in Jewish holidays. This next one might best sum up this entire trial:

April 7, 529: Eastern Roman Emperor Justinian banned the Sh'ma because it "denies the Trinity."

שְׁמַע יִשְׂרָאֵל יְיָ אֱלֹהֵינוּ יְיָ אֶחָד

In Hebrew, it sounds like: Sha-ma Israel Adoni Elohenu Adoni Ehad. "Hear, O Israel: The Lord is our God; the Lord is one." (Deuteronomy 6:4, Chabad.org)
Notice the same prayer is 6 words in Hebrew, but 12 words in English. How ironic is it that Justinian, a Christian, banned the verse in his own Bible that Jesus quoted when asked what the greatest commandment was?

Was banning the Jewish Creed of extreme, indivisible, absolute monotheism foundational to the Jewish Bible and faith. And replacing it with the Nicene Creed, Christianity "fulfilling" Judaism, or was it the exact opposite?

Chapter 10

Baptized Catholic "by force if necessary"

531 CE: Eastern Roman Emperor Justinian censored Jewish liturgy for being "anti-trinitarian." He banned all prayers in Hebrew. Conversion to Judaism officially became punishable by death. Jews were not permitted to testify against Christians. New laws restricted citizenship to Christians. Those laws would determine the status of Jews for centuries. Entire Jewish communities chose Catholic baptism over death. Many synagogues were converted into churches. "They shall enjoy no honors" -Justinian (482-565 AD)

576: Clermont: Bishop Avitus gave Jews a choice: Get baptized Catholic or leave. Most of the Jews in Clermont immigrated to Marseilles.

582 Merovingian Kingdom (present day Germany, France, Switzerland, and Austria): All Jews living there were ordered to be baptized Catholic.

589: The 3rd Council of Toledo reiterated the mutual ban on intermarriage and ruled that children out of those marriages be raised Christian.

598 Palermo: Bishop Victor converted synagogues into Catholic churches.

610 CE: Islam grew out of the Roman Empire. One of 3 major "successor states" that emerged in the 600s:

1. Arabic speaking Islamic Empire which controlled the Middle East, North Africa, and Spain.

Greek speaking Orthodox Christian Byzantine Empire, which controlled Southeast Europe.

Latin speaking Catholic Carolingian (Frankish) empire controlled most of Western and Central Europe. During the Early Middle Ages (600-1100) these 3 empires were enemies. What they had in common was converting Jews.

Islam spread via Conversion by the Sword much like Christianity. This timeline doesn't include those examples because Muslims weren't forced baptized in the name of Rome's trinity.

614: The Fifth Council of Paris decreed that all Jews holding military or civil positions, and their entire families get baptized Catholic.

615: The "Juramentum Judaeorum" or "Jewish Oath" meant no Jew could be believed in court against a Christian. This oath became standard throughout Europe in 1555.

626: The Council of Clichy declared every Jew who accepts public office must convert to Christianity.

632: Eastern Roman Emperor Heraclius decreed forced baptism of all Jews living in the Byzantine Empire.

653 Toledo: Jews were given the choice: convert to Christianity or leave.

692: Visigothic King Edward enacted 28 anti-Jewish laws. All Jewish and Christian holidays supervised by a Catholic priest to prevent "backsliding."

692 Constantinople: The Quinisext Council threatened Christians with excommunication for so much as talking to any Jew.

November 9, 694 Visigothic Kingdom (present day parts of Spain, Portugal, and France): King Ergica presided over the 17th Council of Toledo which focused on punishing Jews. He ordered Jewish property confiscated, all Jews be enslaved to Christians, all Jewish children over 7 years old separated from their parents and raised Christian.

A quick summary of the 700s and 800s: Jews were banned from worshiping. Christians were banned from socializing with Jews. Jews were forced to obtain travel permits from Catholic priests. Throughout the Western world, Jews were given one of the two following choices:

1. Convert or leave.

2. Convert or die. Orders from various popes, kings, and bishops to baptize every Jew "by force if necessary." The next centuries were an especially brutal period for Jews who were marked for extermination simultaneously by Muslim and Catholic empires both arising out of the 4th Beast. In Morocco, Jews were forced to provide virgins for refusing to attack other Jewish communities.

722: Eastern Roman Emperor Leo III forcibly converted all Jews in the empire to Christianity.

740 York: Archbishop Ecgbert banned Christians from eating with Jews.

October 13, 787, Iznik Turkey: The 2nd Council of Nicaea reintroduced worshiping idols. A flagrant rebellion against God's 2nd Commandment (Exodus 20:3-6): "cross...

everywhere set up as a symbol... images of Jesus Christ,
the Virgin Mary... exhibited on the walls of churches...
homes, and in all conspicuous places, by the roadside and
everywhere, to be revered by all who might see
them." (Second Council of Nicaea, 7th Session)

782: Charlemagne killed an estimated 4,500 Saxons trying
to Christianize them at the Massacre of Verden.

The 8-900s are marked with Jewish expulsions. Entire
Jewish neighborhoods destroyed. Synagogues burned
with people locked inside. More land seizures. Throughout
Europe, orders to convert Jews to Christianity continued.
Here's just 1 example from each century:

874: Eastern Roman Empire: Basil I ordered all that all
Jews in the Byzantine Empire be baptized Catholic "by
force if necessary."

932-942: Eastern Roman Emperor Romanos I Lekapenos
decreed that all Jews must convert to Christianity.

Chapter 11

Blood Libel

July 16, 1054: The "Great Schism" resulted in the separation of Roman Catholic and Eastern Orthodox churches.

November 27, 1095: Pope Urban II called for the 1st official Crusade.

1099: Crusaders started a Catholic Military Order called the Order of Knights of the Hospital of Saint John of Jerusalem, claiming the purpose was to support the Hospital of Saint John of Jerusalem. They crusaded, conquered, stole land, controlled armies and navies, and enforced laws from popes and kings. Several popes were knights.

February 15, 1113, Rome: Pope Paschal II issued "Pie postulatio voluntatis" formally recognizing the Knights Hospitaller as an independent sovereign entity. Several successor organizations emerged. Currently, all are under the Sovereign Military Order of Malta headquartered in Rome. As of 2023, they're recognized as sovereign by 104 nations.

1146: Radulph, a Cistercian monk and preacher to Crusaders, instructed crusaders to avenge themselves on "those who had crucified Jesus." He wasn't referring to the Romans.

1155 Rome: Pope Adrian IV (only English born pope) gave King Henry II of England permission to invade and govern Ireland: "... spread abroad the glorious name of Christ on earth... enlarge the boundaries of the Church, to reveal the truth of the Christian faith to peoples still untaught and barbarous, and to root out the weeds of vice from the Lord's field... That Ireland, and indeed all islands... belong to the jurisdiction of blessed St. Peter and the holy Roman church is a fact beyond doubt... enter this island of Ireland, to make that people obedient to the laws... payment to St. Peter and the holy Roman church of an annual tax of one penny from every household." (Laudabiliter)

Blood Libel accusations became popular throughout Europe in the 12th century. Accusations varied, but pretty much had the same theme: A Jew, or multiple Jews kidnapped and murdered a Christian child. For example, Jews allegedly killed a child and drained him of blood to make matzoh for Passover or drank the blood as Passover wine. Or Jews tortured Christian children by inflicting the wounds of Jesus, thorns in their heads, whippings, crucifying them during Holy Week. Often, testimony of Jews was not allowed. Land and property of convicted Jews were forfeited, and debts were canceled.

Typically accusations were made around Easter which was around the same time as Passover. The following are examples of Jews burned for what the Jewish Encyclopedia calls "Blood Accusations" and "Ritual Murder." Entire communities were massacred for 1 anonymous accusation against 1 person.

1144 AD Norwich England "William of Norwich" – 1168 Gloucester England - 1179 Pontoise France "Richard of Paris" - 1181 St. Edmunds - 1182 Saragossa Spain - 1183 Bristol England - 1192 Winchester - 1235 Fulda Germany - 1255 Lincoln England "Little Saint Hugh" - 1267 Pforzheim - 1270 Weissenburg - 1286 Oberwesel Germany - 1294 Bern - 1303 Weissensee - 1329 Savoy - 1462 Rinn - 1475

Trento Italy "Simon of Trent" - 1490 Toledo Spain - 1494 Tyrnau Hungary - 1505 České Budějovice Czech Republic -1529 Bosing Hungary – 1833 "Dolorous Passion" - 1840 Damascus Syria - 1844 Tarnow Galicia - 1891 Corfu - 1891 Rhenish Prussia – 1899 Polna Bohemia – etc.

Most of the recorded confessions are beyond ridiculous. For example, in 1247 Valreas France, Jews confessed that they wanted the child's blood to drink with Catholic communion on Easter Sunday. Nonsensical confessions shouldn't be a surprise considering torturers didn't stop until a confession was given. After confessing, sometimes they were given an opportunity to renounce their faith and break the covenant with God by getting baptized Catholic in exchange for not being burned at the stake.

Plaintiff: Objection. Blaming Rome or Christianity for blood libel is unfair and misleading. Jews weren't the only victims of blood libel. During this same period, Christians were falsely accused of eating their own children. Furthermore, popes had no tolerance for blood libel accusations. This behavior was never ordered, sanctioned, or condoned by any pope. Popes Innocent III, Innocent IV, Gregory X, and others expressly forbade beating, torturing, and killing of any Jews over blood libel. Popes offered Jews protection. They even ordered to cease vandalism of Jewish cemeteries.

The following is an excerpt from an official letter written by Pope Gregory X on October 7, 1272, titled "PAPAL PROTECTION OF THE JEWS" they weren't technically called Papal Bulls until about a century later:

"Gregory, bishop, servant of the servants of God... Since it happens occasionally that some Christians lose their children, the Jews are accused by their enemies of secretly

76

carrying off and killing these same Christian children and of making sacrifices of the hearts and blood of these very children. It happens, too, that the parents of these very children, or some other Christian enemies of these Jews, secretly hide these very children in order that they may be able to injure these Jews, and in order that they may be able to extort from them a certain amount of money... And most falsely do these Christians claim that the Jews have secretly and furtively carried away these children and killed them, and that the Jews offer sacrifices from the heart and the blood of these children, since their law in this matter precisely and expressly forbids Jews to sacrifice, eat, or drink the blood, or to eat the flesh of animals having claws. This has been demonstrated many times at our court by Jews converted to the Christian faith: nevertheless very many Jews are often seized and detained unjustly because of this... no one shall dare to devastate or to destroy a cemetery of the Jews or to dig up human bodies for the sake of getting money..." (Pope Gregory X)

Judge: Raises more questions than provides answers. Nonetheless, Pope Gregory X was defending Jewish people from false accusations. Sustained.

Defense: We'll get to Pope Innocent III's doublespeak when we arrive at Host Desecration Trials in the 1200s. Once we understand that, all of this will be put into better perspective. Besides the land grabs, and debt forgiveness resulting from the accused being killed. The deeper motivation for the hatred necessary for such evil comes from the same anonymously written Matthew 27:25 that along with the trinity motivated "The Decide."

"The first literary reference to it is made about this time in the following passage from the writing, "Bonum Universale de Apibus," ii. 29, § 23, by Thomas of Cantimpré "It is quite certain that the Jews of every province annually decide by lot which congregation or city is to send Christian blood to the other congregations." Thomas also believes that since the time when the Jews called out to Pilate, "His blood be on us, and on our children" (Matt. xxvii. 25), they have been afflicted with hemorrhages.." (Jewish Encyclopedia, Blood Accusation)

1171 "Many Masters of the Torah died at the stake, the death of the saints was accompanied by a solemn song resounding through the stillness of the night, causing the Churchmen who heard it from afar to wonder at the melodious strains, the like of which they had never heard before. It was ascertained afterwards that the martyred saints had made use of the Aleinu as their dying song." (The Vale of Tears, a 16th-century martyrology, Joseph Ha-Kohen describes the persecution of the Jews in Blois France)

1182 France: After the expulsion of all Jews from France, many synagogues were converted into churches, including the Synagogue of Orleans which was turned into St. Sauveur Chapel.

1184 Rome: Pope Lucius III ordered bishops to begin inquisitions regarding alleged heresies in Southern France.

1184-1230s: The Medieval Inquisitions were what they sounded like.

1189-1192: The 3rd Crusade AKA Kings Crusade was to capture Jerusalem from the Muslims and convert or kill non-Christians along the way.

One final point about blood libel accusations. After 34 people were tortured then burned at the stake over lies in

Fulda Hesse Germany in 1235, Emperor Frederick II tried to put an end to blood libel accusations. He declared that if the Jews at Fulda could be proven guilty, every Jew in the kingdom would be put to death. If not, they'd be publicly exonerated. The report: "There is not to be found, either in the Old or the New Testament, that the Jews are desirous of human blood. On the contrary, they avoid contamination with any kind of blood... also a strong likelihood that those to whom even the blood of permitted animals is forbidden, cannot have a hankering after human blood. Against this accusation stand its cruelty, its unnaturalness, and the sound human emotions which the Jews have also in relation to the Christians. It is also unlikely that they would risk their life and property."

1184-1230s: Episcopal Inquisitions; technically part of the Medieval Inquisitions "Ad abolendam" meaning "For the purpose of doing away with all forms of heresy."

1200 Paris: Disagreements over the Trinity led Bishop Eudes de Sully to threaten excommunication to anyone except qualified clergy caught discussing theology.

Chapter 12

Pope Innocent III, Crusades, and Host Desecration Trials

Defense Counsel: The Conti di Signi family produced 4 Popes, 9 cardinals, many dignitaries, lords, dukes, and generals.

February 22, 1161, Papal States: Lotario dei Conti di Signi was born. His father was Count Trasimondo Conti di Signi. His uncle was Pope Clement III.

From January 8, 1198, until his death on July 16, 1216, Lotario dei Conti di Signi ruled over the Papal States and beyond as Pontifex Maximus, Pope, and Vicar of Christ. He claimed supremacy over all Europe's kings. He ordered 3 crusades: the 4th, 5th, and Albigensian Crusades AKA Cathar Crusades. His rhetoric incited 2 more crusades. He was an expert in using anonymously written New Testament verses, especially Matthew 27:25, to instigate massacres, killing at least hundreds of thousands, by some estimates, well over a million people. His church reforms still stand today.

August 15, 1198, Rome: Pope Innocent III issued "Post miserabile" to revive crusading. He appointed cardinals to preach and organize crusades: Surmised that prior crusades failed due to lack of funding, poor leadership, too many non-combatants taking part. Solutions included setting up donation chests at churches all over Europe to fund the massacres. He made clear that motivation for crusading must be spiritual rather than increasing wealth. He informed everyone of what spiritual privileges (indulgences) crusaders and fundraisers would receive in heaven.

"…that land on which the feet of Christ stood and where God, our King, had deigned before the beginning of time to work out salvation…Still the Apostolic See cries out, and like a trumpet, it raises its voice, eager to arouse the Christian peoples to fight Christ's battle and to avenge the injury done to the Crucified One." (Pope Innocent III, Post Miserabile)

1199: Pope Innocent III declared that the Bible contained lessons too profound for laypeople to grasp, and they should wholly rely on clergy to interpret scripture for them. That remains Catholic tradition to this day. Conversely, rabbis teach that the Torah was written so children can understand it. Sure, it most definitely has deep mysteries; but the plain meaning of the text, which is never superseded, couldn't be simpler.

 1202-1204: 4th Crusade: On their way to recapture Jerusalem from Muslims, massacres got out of control. "There was never a greater crime against humanity than the Fourth Crusade." (historian Sir Steven Runciman, 1954)

Nov. 13-24, 1202, Zara Croatia: Part of the 4th Crusade, first time a Catholic community was massacred by Catholics during the Crusades. Crusaders with a navy of 60 ships, each with capacity for 600 infinity sacked Zara.

1203: Pope Innocent III excommunicated crusaders that participated in killing Christians at Zara. In the same year, he rescinded those excommunications.

1203 Siege of Constantinople: The Jewish quarter was burned to the ground. Catholics were also slaughtered by Crusaders.

1205: Jews were expelled from Spain, this time by Muslims.

1208: "Shield of the Trinity" was invented. The inverted triangle flow chart served 2 purposes: 1. An attempt to explain what logic can't. Like most Christians today, they couldn't clearly articulate the trinity. 2. The "Heraldic Arms" of God was painted on Crusaders shields so when "Soldiers of Christ, Ruler of All" spread the "Glory of Christ" converting non-Christians by "any means necessary" massacring communities, there was no mistaking why.

The Cathars called themselves "Good Christians." Basically, they were dualistic Gnostics; vegetarians who abstained from sex. Rejected the symbol of the cross, considering it a material instrument of torture. Viewed Jesus' resurrection as metaphorical to reincarnation. Rejected Rome's Trinity, viewing Jesus as an Angel, but not God. Like Catholics, they believed in transubstantiation of the Eucharist. However, this was the big problem: They believed everyone had the power to transform bread into Jesus' body, and wine into his blood for human consumption; not just Catholic priests.

1209 Rome: Pope Innocent III called for a crusade against the Cathars in southern France. It's known as the Albigensian or Cathar Crusades. It lasted 20 years. Estimates of the slain vary between 200,000 -1,000,000. The Cathars ceased to exist. Some historians refer to it as the first ideological genocide. According to the Torah, all wars and genocides are ideological.

July 22, 1209, Beziers France: The famous saying "Kill them all and let God sort them out" was inspired by Paul's 2nd Letter to Timothy. Pope Innocent III's representative Arnaud Amalric's response "Kill them. The Lord knows those that are his own" to Crusader Simon de Montfort when he couldn't tell who to kill based on how they looked. He promised crusaders they could keep the property of heretics they killed. Amalric was quoting 2 Timothy 2:19 from the Vulgate. The Vulgate is the Greek New Testament of the Catholic Bible translated (mostly by Jerome) into Latin.

"But the sure foundation of God standeth firm, having this seal: the Lord knoweth who are his; and let everyone depart from iniquity who nameth the name of the Lord." (2 Timothy 2:19, Vulgate)

"…The city was put to the sword. So did God's vengeance give vent to its wondrous rage…Béziers was taken. Our men spared no one, irrespective of rank, sex or age, and put to the sword almost 20,000 people. After this great slaughter the whole city was despoiled and burnt…" (Amalric's letter to Pope Innocent III in August 1209)

"Kill them all for the Lord knoweth them that are His" (2 Tim. ii. 19) and so countless number in that town were slain…"(Papal legate's official recording of the massacre citing 2 Timothy 2:19) The following anonymously written New Testament verses were cited as justification for attempted genocide by Pope Innocent III, Hitler… Plaintiff: Objection! False! He didn't call for genocide. Pope Innocent III specifically forbade wiping out the Jews.

"Although in many ways the disbelief of the Jews must be reproved, since nevertheless through them our own faith is truly proved, they must not be oppressed grievously by the faithful as the prophet says: "Do not slay them, lest these be forgetful of Thy Law," [Ps. 58 (59):12] as if he were saying more openly: "Do not wipe out the Jews completely, lest perhaps Christians might be able to forget Thy Law, which the former, although not understanding it, present in their books to those who do understand it." (Pope Innocent III, Constitution for the Jews, AD 1199) Judge: Explain that last sentence.

Plaintiff: He was expanding on the teachings of Saint Paul. Despite the Jew's veil over their hearts of stone causing them to reject and crucify God; they still have a purpose in this world to teach the Old Testament and remind Christians of the former law.

Defense: Got it. Pope Innocent III didn't order the code red. He cited Matthew 27:25 in 2 of his 3 official calls for crusades. Both encyclicals would be cited by future Popes and Bishops to order more massacres.

"The Son's blood still cries out to the ears of the father." (Pope Innocent III, Etsi non displiceat, 1205 CE)

Imagine misappropriating a story from the Jewish Bible to incite hatred against Jewish people: "Just as Cain was a murderer and an untouchable, despised and rejected by humanity because he killed his brother Abel, the Jews, guilty of murdering their Lord, are vagabonds on the face of the earth; their perpetual exile punishes and recalls their crime. But just as the sign of God prevented Cain from being killed, so we must let Jews live among us. The Jews are the enemies of Christ and utter blasphemies against his name." (Pope Innocent III, Ut esset Cain, 1208)

1210 England: King John imprisoned all Jews in his kingdom. He released them if they paid 66,000 marks.

1212 Toledo: Jews were given a choice: Get baptized Catholic or die.

The Children's Crusades of 1212 are the first recorded European youth movement. Who provoked them?

"Pope Innocent III anxiously attempted to mobilize the prayers of Christians on behalf of the threatened Spanish church by holding processions in Rome on May 16, 1212. It is likely that similar processions were held at Chartres on May 20. In all probability, a shepherd boy, Stephen of Cloyes, and some of his fellow workers took part in them. The enthusiasm generated by these processions gave birth to a popular Crusading movement whose aims were summed up in acclamations shouted out by the pueri: "Lord God, raise up Christendom!" and "Lord God, return to us the True Cross!" (Encyclopedia Britannica, Children's Crusade)

June 1212 Children's Crusade France: A 12-year-old shepherd Stephen of Cloyes claimed to have received a message from Jesus instructing him to lead a crusade to the Holy Land. He delivered a letter, allegedly given to him by Jesus disguised as a poor pilgrim, addressed to King Phillip II of France; who told Stephen to go home. Instead, Stephen preached, amassing 15,000-30,000 followers, mostly teenagers. Many claimed to be miracle workers from God. Most wound-up starving to death on the journey or were captured by Muslims and sold into slavery. None reached Jerusalem.

July 1212 Children's Crusade Germany: A shepherd boy Nicholas of Cologne claimed a vision from Jesus instructing him to lead a crusade to recapture Jerusalem from Muslims and convert them to Christianity. Most died on the journey. The remaining 7,000 made it to Genoa. Nicholas told them the Mediterranean Sea would part as the Red Sea parted in the Exodus. It didn't. Most stayed in Genoa. Others went to Rome to see Pope Innocent III.

Stephen and Nicholas essentially made the same claim as Paul. All 3 claimed to receive a special message directly from Jesus that others were supposed to follow. All 3 claimed divine inspiration. Nobody who listened to The LORD's explicit instructions in Deuteronomy 13 was fooled by Stephen of Coyes, Nicholas of Cologne, Paul of Tarsus, or anyone else who claims to have any message that contradicts so much as 1 word of the Torah.

April 1213 Rome: Pope Innocent III issued the "Quia maior" stating that crusading is a moral obligation for all Christians. Copies were sent all over the empire, France, Germany, Ireland, Poland, etc.. It was one of 3 crusade themed letters he issued that month. The opening invokes Matthew 16:24 calling followers of Jesus to "take up the cross." He said crusading is an "ancient expedient of Jesus Christ for the salvation of his faithful which he has designed to renew in these days." Priests were ordered to recite the crusade themed prayer Deus quis admirabili at every Mass.

1215: Rome: "I have decided...to convoke a general council, by means of which evils may be uprooted....morals reformed, heresies wiped out, the Faith strengthened princes and people won to the cause of aiding the Holy Land..." (Pope Innocent III calling for the 5th Crusade)

Troubadours were Christians who considered themselves Catholics, at least at for a time They've been called the front-runners of secular music. Most of their music was love songs. They resided in southern France and Italy from the 11th century until the 13th century when they were imprisoned then burned at the stake. They were completely annihilated because the Catholic Church decided their music was sinful. In 1229 Guilhem Figueira, a famous Troubadour, wrote the following song referring to Crusades ordered by Pope Innocent III. It was sung to the melody of a Roman Catholic song about Mary. The word Saracens means Muslims.

"Deceitful Rome, avarice ensnares you, so that you shear the wool of your sheep too much. May the Holy Ghost, who takes on human flesh, hear my prayer and break your beak, O Rome! You will never have a truce with me because you are false and perfidious with us and the Greeks…Rome, you do little harm to the Saracens, but you massacre Greeks and Latins. In hell-fire and ruin you have your seat, Rome."

That hymn was so popular the Office of Inquisition in Toulouse banned it. It was still being condemned over 50 years later. Figueira supported the crusades for a time. He also called Rome the "Mother of Fornication."

November 11, 1215, Lateran Palace Rome: Pope Innocent III convened the 4th Lateran Council. Besides coming up with more language still trying to articulate Rome's trinity. The 4th Council had 3 main objectives: crusading, "combatting heresy," and church reform. Annual confession to a priest in private, eating Jesus' transubstantiated body and drinking his blood were mandated. Tithing, taxes, elections, and dress codes for Jews were addressed. On the last day of the council 71 canons were drafted, not debated, then made official. Most scholars conclude that Pope Innocent III drafted all 71 himself.

All Jews in all Christian countries were ordered to wear an identification badge called the "Badge of Shame" at all times. Nazis will give the same order 7 centuries later with the Jüde Star Badge.

Mandatory confession and communion during Lent would become an opportunity to anonymously report noncompliant "New Christians" to local inquisitors.

"His body and blood are truly contained in the sacrament of the altar under the forms of bread and wine, the bread and wine having been transubstantiated, by God's power, into his body and blood." (4th Lateran Council) Transubstantiation is what allows Catholic's to eat and drink bread and wine that's been transformed into the body and blood of Jesus of Nazareth, by the authority granted to the priest by the 4th Beast. We've proved that ritualistic human cannibalism "vile abomination" prohibited...

Plaintiff: Objection! A new low of insults to our Lord and 2 billion...

Defense Counsel: Perhaps we should read the definition of transubstantiation according to Innocent III's Papal Bulls or the U.S. Council of Catholic Bishops website 2023. And ritualistic, human, and cannibalism from the Merriam Webster Dictionary. Judge: Unnecessary. Move on.

Defense Counsel: The Torah teaches that all sin begins with idolatry, gets worse, results in violence and injustice. How can ritualistic human cannibalism possibly get worse?

For over 480 years, Host Desecration allegations typically began with a Catholic accused of stealing the transubstantiated host from church and selling it to a Jew.

Usually, the accused Jew was owed money. From there, the stories went in one of the following directions: Allegedly, the Jew stabbed the host until blood came out. Sometimes a little bit of blood came out. Sometimes, especially in Germany, Jesus' blood gushed out of the wafer. Sometimes the blood frightened the Jew, and/or splashed a mark on their forehead to remind them that their ancestors decided that Roman soldiers would crucify Jesus. Or Jews burned the host in their oven, causing angels and doves to fly out. Or buried the host in fields and the host transformed into butterflies, flying around healing the crippled and blind. If that ever actually happened maybe more people should've done it.

Allegedly, the reason why Jews stabbed communion wafers "by crucifying the host they imagine they are crucifying Jesus anew." The accused were tortured until they confessed. Entire communities, all persons and homes, were searched after the church bells rang summoning people to be informed of a missing or stolen host. Groups of people, entire Jewish communities at once were ceremoniously burned at the stake because 1 person was accused, often anonymously, of Host Desecration.

It wasn't uncommon for the same people who murdered their parents to try and force surviving children over 6 years old to eat pork. If they complied, they were baptized Catholic. If not, they were sold into slavery.

The following entire communities were ravaged because of a single Host Desecration Allegation: 1243 Beelitz Germany - 1264 Bolsena Italy - 1290 Paris - 1294 Laa Austria - 1298 Koneuburg and Rottingen Germany - 1299 Ratisbon - 1325 Krakow Poland - 1330 Gustrow - 1337 Deggendorf - 1367 Barcelona - 1370 Enghien Belgium - 1388 Prague - 1399 Posen - 1401 Glogau - 1453 Breslau -

1478 Passau - 1492 Sternberg Bavaria - 1510 Berlin -
1514 Mittelberg France - 1558 Sochaczew Poland – Alcoy
Spain 1568 - 1671 Lisbon Portugal - 1761 Nancy France -
1836 Bislad Romania etc. A few specifics:

Easter Sunday, 1338 Pulkau Austria: Allegedly, a bleeding
host was found in front of a Jew's house. It spread that the
host started performing miracles. Jews in Pulka were
burned at the stake. Jews in 27 other communities as far
as Bohemia massacred because of the story in
Pulkau. Catholic Church "Zum Heiligen Blut" or "The Holy
Blood" was built on site of one of the massacres.

1556 Poland: Somebody started a rumor that a poor
Catholic woman named Dorothy sold 3 Jews the host she
received during communion. They then stabbed the "Body
of Christ" until it bled.

"We have never stabbed the host, because we do not
believe that the host is the Divine body, knowing that God
has no body nor blood. We believe, as did our forefathers,
that the Messiah is not God but His messenger. We also
know from experience that there can be no blood in flour."
(One of those Jews, before they were burned at the stake
along with Dorothy Lazhentzka)

May 22, 1370, in Brussels, is a good example of how
Catholic and Jewish sources record the same Host
Desecration massacres. First, we'll go to the Jewish
Encyclopedia starting with why Jews were in Brussels in
the first place. Then we'll get the Catholic Encyclopedia
version:

"They followed the Roman legions in their path of
conquest. In the wars of Vespasian and Titus a
considerable number of Jewish captives found their way

either willingly or unwillingly to Gaul and the Iberian peninsula. The defeat of Bar Kokba completed the dispersion of the Jews in the West... The chronicles of the times abound with many tales of arbitrary and cruel deeds. ... always the wealth of these unfortunates that constituted their sole crime... The clergy, too, who looked upon them as decides, threw the weight of their influence against them...more than once the whole of a Jewish population was held responsible for the crime of an individual... In 1321 the Jews were again expelled from France, and for a second time sought refuge within the borders of Belgium... Jews of Belgium at this time were, like their brethren all over Europe, persecuted on charges of having desecrated the host, of having killed infants, and of having poisoned wells. The storm that swept over the Jews of Belgium annihilated them; and so completely was the work of destruction done that scarcely a trace of their existence has remained.

Brussels massacre of 1370... carrying red crosses wherewith to inflame the people against the Jews... to the Jewish quarter, destroyed the houses of the Jews, dragged their unfortunate victims through the streets, and without distinction of age or sex massacred them. Five hundred, it is said, perished on this occasion. Nor was the duke's treasurer spared. Taken alive and put to the torture, he was made to confess that he was engaged in the plots to poison the wells and to defile the consecrated host. He was burned alive. Similar butcheries occurred in other towns in the duchy, more particularly at Louvain, where the Jews were all delivered to the flames (1349 and 1350) ...massacre at Brussels on May 22, 1370... signalized as the miracle of St. Gudule... representative of the various incidents of the piercing of the host and of the miracle of the blood spurting forth, were painted for the church, and are to this day an evidence of the blind fanaticism which wrought such dreadful havoc among innocent men, women, and children… accused of profaning the host and adjudged to die. Many, however, saved themselves by conversion; and their descendants are still to be found numerously in that country." (Jewish Encyclopedia, Belgium)

Here's the Catholic account of one of those events: "On Good Friday, in 1370, the merchant and his group of friends drew their knives and began stabbing the hosts. Unexpectedly, the broken hosts started to bleed before their eyes causing the thieves to drop to their knees in horror. Blood flowed from the Hosts uncontrollably, and feeling great guilt, they gathered them up and returned them and confessed to a local priest before turning themselves in. The hosts were enshrined in the Cathedral of St. Michael and remained there until World War II. Over the centuries the miracle has remained a vital part of local devotion. It was a reminder of the reality of Jesus' presence in the Eucharist and connects the Blessed Sacrament to Good Friday, when a soldier pierced the side of Jesus, a torrent of blood and water poured out." (uCatholic.com 2023)

1410: Segovia Spain: Jews were accused desecrating the host, and that host desecration caused an earthquake. They were executed, property confiscated, and their synagogue was turned into Corpus Christi Church.

Chapter 13

Baptized or Die in Europe

1217 Toulouse France: Alix de Montmorency gave Jews a choice: Get baptized Catholic or go to jail. All Jewish children six years old and younger were taken to be raised Catholic.

1218 Toledo: Honorius III demanded enforcement of the 4th Lateran Council's order that Jews pay tithes to Catholic churches. Jews were also given a dress code to distinguish them from Christians.

1217-1271: The 5th Crusade was a series of Crusades to recapture Jerusalem by first conquering Egypt.

1223 Pope Gregory IX condemned all public controversy of Rome's trinity.

After his edict proved ineffective, King Louis IX instructed: "I tell you that no one, unless he be a very learned clerk, should dispute with them; that the layman, when he hears the Christian Law mis-said, should not defend it, unless it be with his sword, with which he should pierce the mis-sayer in the midriff, as far as the sword will enter." (King Louis IX). He led the 7th and 8th Crusades; and was canonized Saint Louis by the 4th Beast in 1297.

1227: Pope Gregory IX appointed Dominican and Franciscan friars as inquisitors, granting them authority over everyone except bishops.

1227-1229: The 6th Crusade was known as the Crusade of Frederick II. Many were killed. Many were baptized Christian.

1229: Pope Gregory IX ordered that no Jewish child baptized Catholic by his converted father was permitted to stay with their mother so long as she remained Jewish.

1229: Decree of the Council of Toulouse "We prohibit also that the laity should be permitted to have the books of the Old or New Testament; but we most strictly forbid their having any translation of these books."

1238: Nicholas Donin, Preacher to Crusaders, presented Pope Gregory IX with 35 accusations. Donin told King Louis IX that if he wanted to get rid of the Jews once and for all, the only way was by destroying every Torah.

Many Gothic cathedrals have statues of 2 females representing "the Church Triumphant; and the Synagogue, with blindfolded eyes, Defeated."

The 1230s are stained with the Papal Inquisitions.

June 9, 1239: Pope Gregory IX teamed up with the church's "strong right arm" and "eldest son" King Louis IX of France. They ordered the 7 western kingdoms: France, England, Leon, Portugal, Aragon, Navarre, and Castille to simultaneously seize every copy of the Talmud on the 1st Saturday of the following Lent.

Before the printing press, on the first Sabbath during Lent, March 3, 1240, throughout France: The Roman Catholic Church seized 24 cartloads of Talmuds. Then King Louis IX organized the famous debate. The Talmud's defense counsel was Rabbi Yechiel of Paris, and Rabbi Moshe the

Count of Coucy. The prosecution was led by Jewish apostate Donin La Rochelle, a student of Rabbi Yechiel before converting to Christianity and changing his name to Nicholas Donin.

"Lady, I beg of you, do not oblige me to reply. The Talmud is a holy book of venerable antiquity in which no one until the present has been able to discover a fault. Jerome, one of your Saints, was familiar with all of our Law; if he had found the least blemish in it, he scarcely would have allowed it to remain. No prelate, no apostate even, has ever reproached us our belief.
Your doctors, and you have had many more learned than Nicholas these last fifteen hundred years, have never attacked the Talmud. They have recognized it as fitting that we should have a commentary on the Scriptures" (Rabbi Yechiel to Queen Blanche). King Louis IX was in charge: Saying anything critical of the church or Christianity was strictly forbidden.

1241 Frankfurt: "Judenschlacht" or "Slaughter of the Jews" They were given the Catholic choice: baptism or death. 180 chose death. 24 chose baptism.

June 17, 1242, Place de Greve Place by Notre Dame Cathedral, Paris: King Louis IX oversaw the sentence for the Talmud being found guilty. Priests in robes danced around the fire as about 12,000 handwritten Talmunds were burned.

1242 Aragon: King James I "James the Conqueror" ordered Jews to attend conversion sermons in church. Orders from Rome gave friars permission to enter synagogues whenever they wanted.

1248-1254: The 7th Crusade, known as the "Crusade of Louis IX to the Holy Land" first of 2 Crusades led by "Saint Louis" and his army of 30,000.

1251 France: The 1st Shepherds Crusade

How did the Vatican become the largest landowner in the world?

May 15, 1252: Pope Innocent IV issued "Ad extirpanda" a Papal Bull officially authorizing torture by Inquisitors.

1254: King Louis IX expelled all Jews from France. Their land, property, and synagogues were given to the Roman Catholic Church.

1267 Vienna: Jews were forced to wear cones on their heads in addition to the yellow badges they were already mandated to wear.

1269: King Louis IX invented the "rouella" aka" little wheel" aka "mark of humiliation" for Jews to wear for 500 years.

1271-1272 The 9th Crusade was the last Crusade to reach the Holy Land. There were more than a dozen other crusades.

1287 England: King Edward I ordered Jews arrested and released if their communities paid 12,000 pounds.

July 18, 1290, England and Ireland: Veteran of the 9th Crusade, King Edward I issued the "Edict of Expulsion." Many Jews were drowned. The rest were allowed to take only what they could carry. Everything else was confiscated.

1291: Jewish refugees from England were expelled from France upon arrival.

1292 present day Italy: Jews were given a choice: Get baptized or leave.

April 20, 1298, Germany: Starting in Rottingen, accusations of Jews desecrating the host resulted in entire Jewish communities throughout the region being given the choice: Get baptized Catholic or die.

A German Knight named Rintfleisch claimed to have received a mission from God to finish off "the accursed race of the Jews." 146 entire Jewish communities were destroyed. Approximately 100,000 people were killed. Most burned at the stake.

August 1, 1298 Nuremberg, Germany: Rabbi Mordechai ben Hillel, age 48, his wife, and 5 children were 7 of 628 people who chose to die that day rather than break their covenant with God by getting baptized.

The 1300s were even more violent. In Egypt and Baghdad, Muslims gave Jews a choice: Convert to Islam or die. Synagogues were converted into Mosques. In the "Holy Roman Empire" Christians gave Jews a choice: Get baptized Catholic or die. In Spain, it was "by all means convert them to Christianity." Jews were expelled multiple times from Germany, France, Milan, Poland, Hungary, and Bulgaria. For example, in France, Jews were expelled in 1305, allowed to return in 1315, expelled in 1322, returned, expelled again in 1394. Entire Jewish communities were massacred by Crusaders in Germany, France, Spain, and Prague. In Sicily and Castile, Jews were forced to wear the yellow badge. Jewish prayers were banned in France. Host Desecration Trails were held resulting in Jews baptized or burned at the stake in Germany, Austria, Spain, Poland, Brussels, Zurich, etc.

1305: King Philp IV expelled about 100,000 Jews, all property except the clothes they were wearing was confiscated.

Friday, October 13, 1307: French Templar Knights were arrested and tortured until they confessed to devil worshiping, desecrating the cross, homosexuality, etc. Dozens burned at the stake. Pope Innocent II gave them special privileges in 1139, including not paying taxes. They set up a vast network of banks that allowed deposits in their home countries and withdraws in the Holy Land. They became wealthy by confiscating property of their victims. After the knights were burned at the stake, their property was confiscated by the largest landowner in the world.

1306-1319 Rhodes: The Hospitaller Crusade

1309 England, France, Germany: The Crusade of the Poor

1320 France: The 2nd Shepherds Crusade

1321 Central France: After slaughtering over 5,000 Jews accused of "ordering lepers to poison the wells" King Philip V admitted they were innocent.

1343: Pre-Easter massacres of Jews started in Germany and spread throughout Europe. Many survivors fled to Poland.

1349: The Basel Massacres, part of the Black Death persecutions encouraged by Catholic Bishops: 600 Jews were burned at the stake; the rest were expelled. Except for 140 children of the slain who were baptized Catholic.

Their cemetery was destroyed, and synagogue turned into a Catholic church.

During the bubonic plague or "Black Death" it was noticed that less Jews contracted it. Instead of noticing that they didn't eat pigs, bats, or rats, and washed their hands before eating as instructed in the Torah; they were blamed.

1378 Seville: Archdeacon Ecija Ferrand Martinez called on "all good Christians" to destroy the 23 synagogues in Seville, lock the Jews in a ghetto, and "by all means convert them to Christianity."

1391 AD: "The Massacre of 1391" or "Pogroms of 5151" Jewish calendar. An estimated 50,000 Jews were killed in the Iberian Peninsula. An estimated 100,000 Jews in the Aragon chose to be baptized Catholic rather than be executed. By 1391 over half the Jews in Spain were baptized Catholic.

The 1400s continued with Jews burned alive in Germany, Austria, Spain, and Italy. Host Desecration Trials in Germany, Austria, and Poland resulted in Jewish children given a choice to eat pork then being baptized Catholic or refusing to eat pork and being sold into slavery. Synagogues throughout Europe were burned; Catholic Churches were built on the ashes. All Jews were expelled from Trier, Lyon, Zurich, Cologne, Jihlava, Bern, Fribourg, Dusseldorf, Augsburg, Utrecht, Passau, Verona, and Nuremberg. In Lithuania, Jews were given a choice: Get baptized Catholic or forfeit all property. In Portugal and Bavaria Jews were given a choice: Get baptized or be expelled. In Germany and France, Jews were given a choice: Get baptized or die.

Chapter 14

Baptized or Die in the New World

1413 Spain: Pope Benedict XIII gave Jews the choice: get baptized Catholic or die. By 1415 approximately 50,000 more Spanish Jews were baptized Catholic.

1421: "Wiener Gesera" or "Viennese Decree" ordered Jew's property confiscated and forced conversion of their children. This led to 280 adults burned at the stake. The rest were expelled. Their children became Christian.

1422: Pope Martin V decreed no more violence against Jews in a Papal Bull reminding Christians that Christianity is derived from Judaism.

1423: Pope Martin V's decree was reversed.

1430 Aix-en-Provence France: Jews were given the choice: Get baptized Catholic or die.

1450 Bavaria: Duke Louis IX gave Jews a choice: Convert to Catholicism or leave.

June 18, 1452 Rome: Pope Nicholas V issued the Papal Bull "Dum Diversas" declaring Catholic nations should condemn any enemy of Christ to eternal slavery. He granted King Alfonso of Portugal authority to enslave any non-Christian, making it his "Christian duty." This was the first international edict to promote and enforce transcontinental slave trading.

January 8, 1455 Rome: Pope Nicholas V expanded Alfonso's power: "... granted among other things free and ample faculty to the aforesaid King Alfonso — to invade, search out, capture, vanquish, and subdue all Saracens and pagans whatsoever, and other enemies of Christ wheresoever placed, and the kingdoms, dukedoms, principalities, dominions, possessions, and all movable and immovable goods whatsoever held and possessed by them and to reduce their persons to perpetual slavery... and to convert them to his and their use and profit... these islands, lands, harbors, and seas, and they do of right belong and pertain to the said King Alfonso and his successors..." (The Bull Romanus Pontifex (Nicholas V)

1456: Pope Caliextus III issued a Papal Bull that prohibited Jews from testifying against Christians. Christians were still allowed to testify against Jews. This ruling would prove devastating to Jews accused of Blood Libel.

Feast of the Assumption, August 15, 1474, Modica Sicily: Catholics ran through the streets yelling "Viva Maria! Morte ai Giudei!" in English "Hurrah for Mary! Death to the Jews" killed 360 Jews and demolished synagogues.

1478-1834: The Spanish Inquisition was founded by King Ferdinand of Aragon and Queen Isabella of Castile with approval of Pope Sixtus IV. Infamous for torture by the rack, rope, water, and slow fire. Slow fire was smearing someone's feet with flammable material and holding them at a distance where they wouldn't burn too fast. The rack pulled people apart past the point of multiple joint dislocations. Inquisitors sailed to the New World. Estimates vary significantly, the consensus is that 54-60 million Native Americans were killed during the Spanish Inquisition.

June 21,1481 Rome: Pope Sixtus IV issued the Papal Bull "Aeterni regis" granting Portuguese more power to take slaves from Africa to the Indies.

1482 Rome: Pope Sixtus IV issued "Numquam dubitavimus" which empowered Ferdinand of Aragon to appoint inquisitors to prevent Torah observance of those who had been converted to Christianity.

March 31, 1492: The "Edict of Expulsion" or "Alhambra Decree" was signed by King Ferdinand and Queen Isabella. All Jews living in Spain had until the end of July to either get baptized Catholic or leave the country. Houses were exchanged for mules, and other assets sold for a fraction of their value.

July 25, 1492, Rome: Pope Innocent VIII died drinking blood of young boys.

August 2, 1492: The last Jews left Spain. Christopher Columbus was supposed to set sail but was delayed because the harbor was full of fleeing Jews.

May 4, 1493, Rome: Pope Alexander VI issued the papal bull, "Inter Caetera" giving Spain and Portugal more power to go into other people's native lands to conquer, colonize, convert to Christianity, and enslave. "…the Catholic faith and the Christian religion be exalted and be everywhere increased and spread, that the health of souls be cared for and that barbarous nations be overthrown and brought to the faith itself." (Inter Caetera)

"When Alexander VI promulgated the bull Inter caetera on May 4, 1493, granting Spain a large part of the new world, there seems to have been no doubt that the natives who dwelt in the 'very remote islands and mainlands' would be willing and able to accept the teachings of the Catholic church. For Alexander had been informed that in those far off lands... were very many peoples living in peace... these very peoples... believe in one God the Creator in heaven and seem sufficiently disposed to embrace the Catholic faith and be trained in good morals..." (Francis G. Davenport, ed., European treaties bearing on the history of the United States and its dependencies to 1648, Washington, D.C., 1917, p 76)

The old Cherokee's response to being asked how many Indians were converted by the sword: "This is what you need to understand. Before the land was divided, the peoples were scattered, and the languages confused; we all came from Jerusalem... Yes, we serve the same God as the Jewish people. But don't think for one second that The Great Spirit is the same as the Christian god that my people were killed in the name of... Of course we had sacred writings. They were burned by Christianizers. You were taught wrong about Natives by white Christians. Any Indian worshiping any god except the One Great Spirit with no human form has lost his way. They brought troubles upon us all. Once proud people became drunks, dependent on the government because they lost their way, not the other way around. Our only chance is to turn back to the source... The great confusion started years before the languages were confused and the nations were scattered. That's why the languages were confused, because of seeking other gods; not the other way around... I'm warning you, if you give the lesser gods power, the One Great Spirit will no longer walk with you... That's how it started at the Tower of Rebellion. The Tower of Nimrod. You call it the Tower of Babel. Nimrod means to rebel. Babel means to confuse. Confused means worshiping the sun instead of the One Great Spirit that created the sun... Our spirit wasn't created to worship the sun, moon, stars, buffalos, eagles. Not any man either. If we worship the sun, we get big trouble. Only if we respect the Spirit that made the sun, we can be a strong people. There's only One Great Spirit... Yes, that's what I've been trying to explain to you. The Hebrews call the Great Spirit Yahweh. We call the Great Sprit Ye-ho-waah. We sing Ye-ho-waah-O, Ye-ho-waah, ah way, O... Hebrews say the God who is not a man. Cherokee say One Great Spirit with no human form. (David in Oklahoma)

1493 Portugal: King João II ordered 2,000 children of Jewish exiles from Spain taken from their parents, forcibly baptized Catholic, then shipped to São Tomé Island. 1493: Approximately 37,000 Jews were expelled from Sicily.

1500s: African slaves arrived in the Caribbean and Haiti. More Host Desecration Trails in Germany, Austria, etc. Synagogues converted into Catholic churches in Italy, Bavaria, etc. Jews expelled from Naples, Puglia, Genoa, Bologna, Ratisbon, etc. New Christians expelled from Calabria. Ottomans raped, beat, killed, looted homes of Jews. Jews were burned alive in Slovenia, Austria, Poland, Rome, Berlin, etc. In Russia and Lithuania, Jews are given a choice: Become Russian Orthodox Christian or Die. Jewish books were burned and/or banned including the Torah in Venice.

1511 Puglia Italy: Jews not killed were expelled. Synagogues were converted into Catholic churches.
May 7, 1516: Spanish Inquisitor-General, Cardinal Ximenes de Cisneros ordered Fray Juan Quevedo, Bishop of Cuba to hunt down and exterminate "New Christians" who were "Fugitive Jews" fleeing to America.

1519: All Jews in Ratisbon Bavaria were expelled. Their synagogue converted into a Catholic church. Their gravestones were taken and used for buildings.

May 25, 1520: King Charles V, with permission of Dutch Inquisitor and future Pope Cardinal Hadrian, issued an edict ordaining inquisitors for the New World to deal with New Christians fleeing Europe.

1530 Malta: The Knights of Malta (Sovereign Military Order of Malta) emerged from the Order of Knights of the Hospital of Saint John of Jerusalem (1099). They were the Knights of Rhodes from 1309-1522. Now headquartered in Rome, they're recognized as sovereign by 104 nations.

1536: The Portuguese Inquisition, infamous for torture, led by King John III.

1536: William Tyndale was burned at the stake was for translating the Bible into English. According to Tyndale, the Church forbade owning or reading the Bible to control, restrict teachings, and enhance their own power.

1536 Mexico: According to Franciscan Missionary Fray Toribio de Motolinia who arrived in "New Spain" in 1524, 5 million Indians were baptized Catholic during that period.

June 1, 1537, Rome: Pope Paul III issued the Papal Bull "Altitudo divini consilii" declaring Friars had not sinned by forcing baptism "in the name of the Father, and of the son, and of the Holy Spirit."

Chapter 15

Replacing the Spouse and Conquering the Firstborn

Prophets taught that the worst form of Idolatry is worshiping both The LORD God the Father and any other god at the same time. Idolatry is often compared to adultery because it's the worst form of it. Would a woman expect her husband to be ok with bringing another man into the marriage? The LORD God is our Father and our Husband. Why is that made so clear?

"And in that day, declares the Lord, you will call me 'My Husband,' and no longer will you call me 'My Baal." (Hosea 2:16, ESV)

"For your Maker is your husband, the Lord of hosts is his name; and the Holy One of Israel is your Redeemer, the God of the whole earth he is called." (Isaiah 54:5, ESV)

Lord of hosts does not mean Lord of Catholic communion. Adonai Tsvaot (יְהוָה צְבָאוֹת) in English: Lord of hosts appears 284 times in the Jewish Bible, referring to the exact same LORD God whose Name we're told is forever in Exodus 3:15. Lord of hosts is a title, also known as: Supreme Commander of the Angel Armies of The LORD God.

The 4th Beast didn't just try to replace Israel with Jesus. Or replace a direct relationship with God by designating Jesus as mediator. They tried to replace every aspect of the relationship.

"We must put aside all judgment of our own, and keep the mind ever ready and prompt to obey in all things the true spouse of Christ our Lord, our holy mother, the hierarchical church" (Jesuit Rule 1) "…rules are about belonging to the church, about being a part of it. This is why Rule 1 is as much a rule as it is the end of the rules: They help us to "keep our minds disposed and ready to be obedient to the true Spouse of Christ our Lord, which is our holy Mother the hierarchical Church…" (Father George Ganns, SJ-Jesuits.org)

Plaintiff: Objection! The Jesuits are correct. The resurrection changed everything. Jesus conquered death at calvary. Therefore, the blessings of the firstborn son belong to Jesus and his followers. The church is indeed the bride of Christ. "For the husband is the head of the wife even as Christ is the head of the church, his body, and is himself its Savior" (Ephesians 5:23, ESV)

"The one who conquers will have this heritage, and I will be his God and he will be my son." (Revelation 21:7, ESV)

Defense: If someone murdered your firstborn son, would you adopt the killer and give him your son's inheritance? Justice is a major theme...

Judge: Plaintiff, open the Bible of your choice and read aloud Joel 3:1-3.

"For behold, in those days and at that time, when I restore the fortunes of Judah and Jerusalem, I will gather all the nations and bring them down to the Valley of Jehoshaphat. And I will enter into judgment with them there, on behalf of my people and my heritage Israel, because they have scattered them among the nations and have divided up my land, and have cast lots for my people, and have traded a boy for a prostitute, and have sold a girl for wine and have drunk it." (Joel 3:1-3, ESV)

Judge: Who is speaking in Joel 3:1-3? Plaintiff: God the Father.

Judge: Who is speaking in Revelation 21:7? Plaintiff: John of Patmos, inspir...

Judge: Explain how Revelation is the fulfillment of Joel 3, Deuteronomy 4, 32, Numbers 23, Jeremiah, Isaiah and everywhere else where we're explicitly and repeatedly told that God never breaks covenants/promises even if we do, never forgets, never changes His mind.

Plaintiff: Revelation was inspired by the Holy Spirit. That's why it's in the Bible. Jesus came to fulfill the law. Through his death and resurrection...

Judge: Revelation 21:7 is parol evidence that utterly opposes every single one of God's eternal promises/covenants. Overruled.

Defense: 1539 Paris: Ignatius of Loyola, Peter Faber and Francis Xavier formed the Society of Jesus AKA the Jesuits. The Jesuits set up educational systems at all levels throughout Europe, Asia, and the New World, which they control to this day. They set up international trade routes to transport goods and people throughout Asia and the Americas.

Jesuits were colonizers, Christianizers, politicians, involved in the same activities as the Knights in 1099, except educational and missionary work was at their forefront rather than hospitals. Jesuits have been referred to as the first globalists. The "Black Pope" Is the unofficial title of the

"Father General" who's the highest-ranking Jesuit. Today, that's Arturo Sosa, who's described the gospels as "relative... written by human beings... accepted by human beings." In 2018 he argued the doctrine of the Church is in "continuous development", and "never in white and black." Pope Francis is the first Jesuit pope. Joe Biden is the first Jesuit President of the USA. Anthony Fauci is not the first Jesuit doctor to recommend forcing pharmaceuticals on millions.

Early Jesuits named themselves "The Company of Jesus," and were nicknamed "God's Marines" for their willingness to go anywhere and do anything at the pope's command. Jesuit "Rules for Thinking with the Church" were established.

Jesuit Rule #13 "To be right in everything, we ought always to hold that the white which I see, is black, if the Hierarchical Church so decides it, believing that between Christ our Lord, the Bridegroom, and the Church, His Bride... Finally, we must praise all the commandments of the church, and be on the alert to find reasons to defend them, and by no means in order to criticize them... If we wish to proceed securely in all things, we must hold fast to the following principle: What seems to me white, I will believe black if the hierarchical church so defines."(Ignatius of Loyola)

1540 Rome: Pope Paul III approved the Jesuit Order and made Ignatius of Loyola its Father General AKA Superior General: "they [Jesuit Priests] acted as royal confessor to all French kings for 2 centuries, from Henry III to Louis XV; to all German emperors after the early 17th century; to all Dukes of Bavaria after 1579; to most rulers of Poland and Portugal; to the Spanish kings in the 18th century; to

James II of England; and to many ruling or princely families throughout Europe." (New Catholic Encyclopedia)

"Between 1555 and 1931 the Society of Jesus [i.e., the Jesuit Order] was expelled from at least 83 countries, city states and cities, for engaging in political intrigue and subversion plots against the welfare of the State, according to the records of a Jesuit priest of repute [i.e., Thomas J. Campbell]. Practically every instance of expulsion was for political intrigue, political infiltration, political subversion, and inciting to political insurrection." (Historian J.E.C. Shepherd)

"It is my opinion that if the liberties of this country, the United States of America are destroyed it will be by the subtlety of the Roman Catholic Jesuit priests, for they are the most crafty, dangerous enemies to civil and religious liberty. They have instigated MOST of the wars in Europe." (Marquis de LaFayette French General who served under George Washington)

"Like you, I disapprove of the restoration of the Jesuits, for it means a step backwards from light unto darkness." (Thomas Jefferson)

"I learned much from the Order of the Jesuits. Until now, there has never been anything more grandiose, on the earth, than the hierarchical organization of the Catholic Church. I transferred much of this organization into my own party" (Adolf Hitler)

"The S.S. organization had been constituted by Himmler according to the principles of the Jesuit Order. Their regulations and the Spiritual Exercises prescribed by Ignatius of Loyola were the model Himmler tried to copy exactly. Himmler's title as supreme chief of the S.S. was to be the equivalent of the Jesuits' 'General' and the whole structure was a close imitation of the Catholic Church's hierarchical order." (Walter Schellenberg, former Chief of Nazi counterespionage)

"We came in like lambs and will rule like wolves. We shall be expelled like dogs and return like eagles." (Francesco Borgia, Third Jesuit Superior General) By 1556, Jesuits founded 74 colleges in Ireland, Germany, Poland, Japan, Egypt, and India. Today, they control 189 colleges worldwide, 28 in the United States.

July 21, 1542: The "Supreme Sacred Congregation of the Roman and Universal Inquisition" was organized by Pope Paul III

September 9, 1553, Rome, Rosh Hashanah in the Jewish year 5314: Inquisitors completed a 9-day search confiscating what they claimed was every Talmud in Italy. They were burned in the Campo dei Fiori. It would be more than 50 years before a Talmud could be found anywhere in Italy.

A little taste of what's been stolen from so many people: Rosh Hashanah is the New Year for people whose ancestors weren't converted by the sword. It's usually in September or October. It begins a 10-day period of introspection of the past year, ending on Yom Kippur. It's meant to call to mind times we've hurt others and think about how to do better in the coming new year. In Hebrew, tashlich means "casting off." Anyone who chooses to participate fasts for 25 hours, not because the health benefits are excellent; but because God instructed us to in Leviticus 23:27. Then before sunset, they gather outside by some flowing water. The rabbi reminds gatherers of the tradition of "casting off your sins." Letting go of everything that may have hurt you during the past year which could include negativity, toxic relationships, self-destructive behavior, etc. They then go to a quiet place by the water, individually, just them and God; and call to mind whatever should be let go. Symbolically casting away anxiety along with little pieces of bread into flowing water; exhaling as they watch the bad from the previous year float away. After letting go, they shift their focus on doing their best in every aspect of life in the coming New Year.

October 31, 1553, Venice Italy town square: The 4th Beast burned every Torah and Talmud they could find.

1543: Martin Luther wrote "On the Jews and Their Lies." Highlights from the famous Protestant Reformer's 8-point plan to exterminate the Jews: "set fire to their synagogues or schools... their houses also be razed and destroyed... their prayer books... all cash and treasure of silver and gold be taken..."

1545-1563: The Council of Trent convoked by Pope Paul III issued condemnations of Protestant heresies, decisions about Bible canon, original sin, veneration of saints, etc. Ironically, they decided that the grace of God can be forfeited through mortal sin. In support of the trinity "Holy Mary, Mother of God, pray for us sinners" was added to the Holy Mary prayer.

1546: In his "Admonition against the Jews, Martin Luther accused Jews of ritual murder, black magic, and poisoning the wells.

1555 Rome: Pope Paul IV issued Papal Bull Cum nimis absurdum. He renewed anti-Jew legislation and locked up the Jewish ghetto in Rome, nightly. Jewish men were ordered to wear a yellow hat, banned from practicing medicine and buying property. Women and girls are mandated to wear a yellow scarf.

113

Chapter 16

Inquisitions Across the Pond and the Slave Bible

May 23, 1556: Pope Paul IV ordered more Inquisitions in Portugal to deal with "New Christians" that fled from Spain. Hitler wasn't the first person to define "Blood Purity." Inquisitors called it "Limpieza de sange" or "cleanliness of blood" during the Spanish and Portuguese Inquisitions.

"It appears utterly absurd and impermissible that the Jews, whom God has condemned to eternal slavery for their guilt, should enjoy our Christian love." (Pope Paul IV reminding of "The Decide" according to Matt. 27:25)

1563: After Russian troops took Polotsk from Lithuania; Jews were given a choice: Become Russian Orthodox Christian or die. 300 Jewish men, women, and children were thrown alive into ice holes of the Dvina River...

Plaintiff: Objection! Enough is enough. Your honor, it's apparent that members of the jury are visibly upset. It's unfair to my client that the jury be unnecessarily and intentionally put under duress before deliberation.

Defense: Your religion became the largest because of decisions made under duress. Your honor, may we have a rabbi explain that when moved to weeping for The LORD's saints and martyrs, repentance is triggered and they're forgiven sins? He also talks about a 2nd century rabbi who had his skin ripped off. *"Christian: Don't Jews believe in Vicarious Atonement? Rabbi Tovia Singer Responds."* *(YouTube) played in court.*

"Precious in the sight of the Lord is the death of his saints."
(Psalm 116:15)

1569: Pope Pius V issued Papal Bull Hebraeorum Gena
Sola, mandating expulsion for all Jews refusing to convert
to Catholicism.

1569: Pope Pius V expelled all Jews from Bologna. He
confiscated their cemetery and ordered all Jewish
gravestones destroyed.

 "The Jewish people fell from the heights because of their
faithlessness and condemned their Redeemer to a
shameful death. Their godlessness has assumed such
forms that, for the salvation of our own people, it becomes
necessary to prevent their disease...We order that, within
90 days, all Jews in our entire earthly realm of justice - in
all towns, districts, and places - must depart these
regions." (Pope Pius V, Papal Bull "Hebraeorum gens"
(The Jewish Race) He was canonized Saint Pius V.

1570-1820: 29 Auto de fes were celebrated during
Inquisitions in the "New World." An "Auto de fe" or "Act of
faith" was burning "New Christians."

November 4, 1571: The Inquisition in Mexico officially
began.

1571 Berlin: Jews were expelled. Their property was
confiscated.

"If we wish to wash our hands of the Jews' blasphemy and
not share in their guilt, we have to part company with them.
They must be driven from our country and we must drive
them out like mad dogs." (Martin Luther).

1573: All Jews in Germany were expelled. Their property was confiscated.

1573-1966 Rome: "Index Librorum Prohibitorum" (Index of Forbidden Books) Thousands of books were banned, anything and everything deemed heretical by the "Sacred Congregation of the Index."

1573-1826: This included books critical of slavery.

1600s: More Inquisitions and Auto-da-fe's. Convert or be expelled in France. Convert or die in Germany. Host Desecration Trails by Jesuits in Belarus. People being put on trial, then put to death simply for being Jewish. People praying the Sh'ma while being burned at the stake. Jews sold into slavery in Austria. Africans and Native Americans continued being sold into slavery and "Christianized." Witch hunts and trial ramped up in the 1700s. Estimates vary significantly, from 60,000 to over 2 million women killed for being witches.

1614 Frankfurt Germany: Vincent Fettmilch aka "the new Haman of the Jews" led a raid on synagogue, then destroyed the entire Jewish community.

1615 France: King Louis XIII gave Jews a choice: Leave the country within 1 month or die.

1618-1648: The 30 Years War: 6-8 million Protestants and Catholics killed each other over which version of worship better served the 4th Beast.

January 23, 1639, Lima Peru: 72 Jews and "New Christians" aka "Conversos" were burned at the stake in an Auto-da-fe.

1648-1656: The Ukrainian Cossacks led by Bohdan Chmielnicki AKA "Chmiel the Wicked" Jews massacred, drowned by the hundreds, tortured, murdered in synagogues with butcher's knives. Synagogues and Torahs were destroyed. About 100,000 people, 300 entire communities were wiped out.

1650: "Council of the 4 Lands" Jews in towns by Belorussia were massacred.

1691 Palma Majorca: Jews chose to jump into the fire rather than be baptized Catholic.

Jewish prayers were banned in Germany. Jews were expelled from Poland, Gibraltar, and Russia. In Austria, Jewish families were limited to having 1 son. In Berlin, Jews were banned from getting married. Synagogues and Jewish people's homes were burned to the ground in Poland, Spain, Prague, etc. Jews and New Christians were burned at the stake in Portugal.

May 18, 1721, Madrid: Maria Barbara Carillo was the oldest known person to be executed for heresy during the Spanish Inquisitions. She was 95 or 96 years old when she was burned at the stake for secretly practicing Judaism.

1742: Elizabeth I re-ordered the expulsion of the Jews from Russia. This time they were given a choice to convert to Russian Orthodox or leave.

1775 Rome: Pope Pius IV issued "Editto sopra gli ebrei" (Edict over the Hebrew) 24 rules against Jews stood for 25 years, including: Death to any Jew who spends the night anywhere besides a ghetto. All neighborly relations between Christians and Jews were forbidden, including Jews inviting Christians to synagogues.

December 9, 1804, Russia: Alexander I introduced "Regulations Regarding the Jews." 200,000-300,000 Jews were expelled from the Pale Settlement.

1807: The Slave Bible was published by Beilby Porteus and "The Incorporated Society for the Conversion and Religious Instruction and Education of the Negro Slaves in the British West India Islands." Stories such as the Exodus, the children of Israel being freed from slavery along with about 90% of the rest of the Jewish Bible were removed from the "Select Parts of the Holy Bible for the use of the Negro Slaves in the British West-India Islands."

About 50% of the Christian New Testament was removed. Verses written by Paul, the anonymous author of Ephesians, and Peter instructing slaves to be obedient even when their masters were cruel remained.

July 15, 1834: The Spanish Inquisition officially ended.

June 23, 1858, Italy: Pope Pius IX ordered the Carabinieri (police) to take 6-year-old Edgardo Mortara from his family's apartment. Anna Morisi, a Catholic, worked as a housekeeper for the Jewish family. Post employment, she told Bologna's Inquisitor Father Pier Feletti that 6 years prior she sprinkled water on the infant's head saying: "I baptize you in the Name of the Father, and of the Son, and of the Holy Ghost." According to the rules of the Supreme Sacred Congregation of the Roman and Universal Inquisition, that made the boy Catholic. Therefore, he could not be raised by his Jewish parents. This became an international issue. The Catholic Church controlled the press. The family tried everything to get their child back.

Pope Pius IX spent a lot of time with the child, practically raising him; he became a priest.

"Of these dogs, there are too many of them at present in Rome, and we hear them howling in the streets, and they are disturbing us in all places." (Pope Pius IX regarding Jews)

Russia: Increasing since 1805, Blood Libel accusations became rampant in the 1870s-80s, much of it instigated by anti-Jewish propaganda in the press.

1870: Established in 1555, the Jewish Ghetto in Rome was abolished.

1881-1883 Russia: Under Alexander II, violence against Jews was reported in more than 200 of the settlements they were previously forced into.

August 15, 1868, Franklin Tennessee: Samuel Bierfield was the first Jew lynched by the KKK, murdered alongside his black clerk Lawrence Bowman.

May 1882-1917 Russia: "May Laws" forbade Jews to settle, build or buy houses, outside of the Pale. Over 500,000 Jews fled Russia, 90% to the U.S.A.

1922 Yemen: An ancient Islamic Law requiring Jewish orphans under age 12 to be forcibly converted to Islam was reintroduced.

Chapter 17

Leading up to the Holocaust thru Vatican's Apology for "The Decide"

"War is a place where the young kill one another without knowing or hating each other, because of the decision of old people who know and hate each other, without killing each other." (Erich Hartmann, Ace German pilot WW2)

1903: Portions of the "Protocols of the Elders of Zion" blaming Jews for the world's problems and conspiracy to rule the world were first published in a Russian Newspaper. In the following decades, editions were translated into many languages and circulated all over the world.

1918 Michigan: Henry Ford purchased the Dearborn Independent. From 1920-1922 the newspaper had a wider circulation than The New York Times.

1919 Munich: The Nazi Party was established.

1920 Detroit: Based on the "Protocols of the Elders of Zion" Henry Ford wrote 91 issues of "The International Jew: The World's Foremost Problem" They were published in the Dearborn Independent until 1927. Every Ford dealership in the USA was required to distribute to every customer. They were translated into several languages and distributed internationally.

July 29, 1921 Munich: Adolf Hitler became chairman of the Nazi Party.

August 17, 1921: The London Times provided evidence that the Protocols of the Elders of Zion were entirely fraudulent. Turned out to be forgeries prepared in cooperation with Russian Secret Service. Mostly plagiarized from French political satire Maurice Joly's "Dialogue in Hell Between Machiavelli and Montesquieu" (1864) that never even mentioned Jews.

1924: Heinrich Himmler wrote Henry Ford is "one of our most valuable, important, and witty fighters." 1925: "Only a single great man, Ford, [who], to [the Jews'] fury, still maintains full independence [from] the controlling masters of the producers in a nation of one hundred and twenty million." (Adolf Hitler, Mein Kampf) Hitler distributed Ford's books throughout Germany and had a life size portrait of Henry Ford behind his desk.

1926 Detroit: Father Charles Coughlin started a radio ministry which would be nationally broadcasted in the USA. At the height of his popularity, the parish priest received more mail than President Roosevelt.

February 11, 1929, Rome: Benito Mussolini, Pope Pius XI, and King Victor Emmanuel III signed the Lateran Treaty that would establish Vatican City as a fully sovereign nation.

1930: Cardinal Pietro Fumasoni Biondi asked Bishop of Detroit Michael Gallagher to tone down Father Coughlin's blaming the Jews for causing the world's problems. "I made no mistake and have never doubted my judgment in putting him before the microphone..." (Bishop Gallagher)

1930 Germany: The Nazi Party was up to 18% of the vote. By 1932, up to 37% of the vote, the Nazi Party became the largest political party in Germany.

"The Fuhrer had come to power, thanks to the votes of the Catholic Zentrum [Center Party overseen by Jesuit Ludwig Kaas], only five years before 1933, but most of the objectives cynically revealed in Mein Kampf were already realized; this book... was written by the Jesuit controlled Father Bernhardt Stempfle and signed by Hitler... it was the Society of Jesus which perfected the famous Pan-German programme as laid out in this book, and the Fuhrer endorsed it." (Edmond Paris, The Secret History of the Jesuits, p 138)

Recall, the SS was constituted by Himmler according to the principles of the Society of Jesus (1540-1542 CE on the timeline).

January 1933 Linz: Austrian Bishop Gfollner issued an official letter stating it's the duty of all Catholics to adopt a "moral form of antisemitism."

-
February 27, 1933: Nazi's burned down the Reichstag, blamed it on Communists, and took power.

April 26, 1933: Adolf Hitler met with Bishop Wilhelm Berning of Osnabrück and Monsignor Steinmann representing the Roman Catholic Church in Germany. Hitler claimed he's only doing what the Catholic Church did to the Jews for 1,600 years. He reminded the prelates that the Church has regarded the Jews as dangerous and pushed them into ghettos. Hitler said his anti-Jewish actions were "doing Christianity a great service." Bishop Berning and Monsignor Steinmann later described the talks as "cordial and to the point."

Heinrich Himmler's SS set up Concentration Camps. Jewish lawyers banned from practicing law. Kosher slaughter of animals banned. Jewish books burned. Non-Jews given loans as incentive to get married. Hitler made up new regulations for journalists. Nazi Party banned all opposing parties.

July 1, 1933: The German government stated, "Reich Chancellor Hitler still belongs to the Catholic Church and has no intention of leaving it."

July 1933 Kaiser Wilhelm Memorial Church Berlin: Pastor Joachim Hossenfelder preached a sermon on Paul's letter to the Romans 13:1-2, reminding worshipers the importance of obedience to authority. The word of Paul, especially Romans 13, and Martin Luther were preached ad-nauseam throughout the 3rd Reich. Including by Otto Dibelius who reminded Germans that Christians must not fail to support the state, "even when [the state] acts hard and ruthlessly."

July 14, 1933: Germany enacted law for the "Prevention of Offspring with Hereditary Diseases" sterilization of "unfit" parents and potential parents, as well as euthanasia of the "defective" and "useless eaters."

July 20, 1933, Rome: The "Reich Concordat" was signed by Cardinal Secretary of State Eugenio Pacelli (future Pope Pius XII) and the Nazi controlled German government. Article 16 stated Bishops are required to take an oath of loyalty to the Reich. This treaty helped legitimize the 3rd Reich.

January 1, 1934: Nazis removed Jewish holidays from the German calendar.

1934: Jews and other non-Aryans were restricted from enrolling in schools; working in farming, journalism, art, literature, music, broadcasting, theater, politics, having health insurance, and voting. The Volksgericht (People's Court) was established to deal with enemies of the state. No trial by jury. No right of appeal. "Aryan heritage" as a prerequisite for military service. Additional 25% tax imposed on all Jewish assets. In Germany and Austria Jews forced to forfeit businesses. Jewish children were prohibited from using playgrounds. Pro-Nazi rallies in NYC. Anti-Jewish riots at Polish universities.

1935 Rome & Detroit: Apostolic Delegate Amleto Cigognani tried to stop Fr. Coughlin's radio broadcasts. Bishop Gallagher continued to protect him.

1935 Detroit: General Motors agreed to build a new plant near Berlin to manufacture "Blitz" trucks. They would be used to invade Russia, France, and Poland. General Motors and Ford Germany were first and second largest truck producers for the Nazis.

November 15, 1935, Germany: Churches collaborated with the Nazi's by furnishing records of who was a Christian, and who was not.

February 10, 1936, Germany: The Nazi Gestapo was placed above the law.

February 29, 1936: Cardinal Hlond, head of the Catholic Church in Poland and strict Vatican policy follower, issued an official letter advocating discrimination against Jews "so long as they remain Jews."

August 1936 Rome: Pope Pius XI and Bishop of Detroit Gallagher agreed that Father Coughlin should continue his radio broadcasts.

October 25, 1936: Hitler and Mussolini formed the Berlin-Rome Axis.

March 14, 1937, Rome: Pope Pius XI issued a reminder of the Jew's crime of "The Decide" (Matthew 27:25). He also accused the Nazis of violating their concordat with Rome by attempting to control Catholic Education.

April 24, 1937: Protestant Pastor Martin Niemoller, one of the most outspoken Germans against Hitler, preached that it's unfortunate God permitted Jesus to be born a Jew. In 1961 he became President of the World Council of Churches. He came up with the famous quote "First they came for the Communists, and I did not speak out because I was not a Communist. Then they came for the Socialists, and I did not speak out because I was not a Socialist. Then they came for the trade unionists, and I did not speak out because I was not a trade unionist. Then they came for the Jews, and I did not speak out because I was not a Jew. Then they came for me, and there was no one left to speak out for me."

March 12, 1938: The German Army entered Vienna. Austria was annexed and immediately subject to all Nazi laws in effect in Germany.

May 30, 1938: Adolf Hitler announced that it's his "unalterable decision to destroy Czechoslovakia."

June 15, 1938, Germany: "Asocial Action" All Jews previously convicted of anything including parking tickets were arrested and taken to death camps.

July 30, 1938: Henry Ford accepted the highest medal Nazi Germany could award to a foreigner, the Grand Cross of the German Eagle. The next month, senior executive for

General Motors, James Mooney accepted the Order of Merit of the German Eagle medal for his "distinguished service to the Reich."

August 17, 1938, Germany: All Jews were ordered to change their first and last names by January 1, 1939. Males were ordered to add "Israel" to their names; and females to add "Sara."

1938: Catholic priest Jozef Tiso became prime minister of Slovakia and established ties to Nazi Germany. Shortly after, Slovakia declared itself an independent state under protection of Nazi Germany.

1938: Adolf Hitler told Minister of Justice Hans Frank that he came to fulfill the self-imposed curse on the Jews "And all the people answered, "His blood be on us and on our children!" (Matthew 27:25, ESV)

November 9-10,1938: "Kristallnacht" or "Night of Broken Glass" 30,000 Jews taken to camps, 267 Synagogues burned, 7,000 businesses destroyed...

November 11 1938: "No foreign propagandist bent upon blackening Germany before the world could outdo the tale of burnings and beatings, of blackguardly assaults on defenseless and innocent people, which disgraced that country yesterday." (The Times of London)

November 20, 1938, Detroit: Father Coughlin used Nazi documents to blame Jews for communism, WW2, and Germany's problems. *Coughlin lived in the largest mansion in Detroit (39,000 sq-feet). Along with all the furnishings, art, pottery tile, etc. It was paid for by the Fisher Brothers who were the main auto-body supplier for General Motors.*

January 30, 1939: Hitler threatened that if war breaks out, the result will be extermination of all Europe's Jews. He mocked the Western Allies' lack of humanitarian action in regard to the Jews. "It is a shameful spectacle to see how the whole democratic world is oozing sympathy for the poor, tormented Jewish people, but remains hard-hearted and obdurate when it comes to helping them." (Adolf Hitler)

February 10, 1939: Pope Pius XI died. His unpublished encyclical on racism and antisemitism were in line with the Vatican's traditional policy concerning Jews. His policy was based on doctrine written by Bishop Augustine of Hippo, that the Jews are Cains who must not be killed but must wander in suffering until they see the light and choose conversion to Roman Catholicism. Recall Pope Innocent III's encyclical Ut esset Cain (1208).

September 23, 1939, Poland: On Yom Kippur (Day of Atonement) The SS publicly humiliated Jews throughout Poland: shaving beards, forced dancing, beatings, etc. Jews in Piotrkow were compelled to defecate in synagogues then clean it up with holy books.

September 28, 1939 Pultusk Poland: The SS choose the first day of Sukkot to forcibly deport more than 8,000 Jews.

Remember Sukkot, we already went over Leviticus 23:34, and according to Zechariah 14:16 everyone alive after the Final War will be keeping Sukkot.

November 23, 1939, Poland: Jews were ordered to wear white armbands with a blue Star of David every time they appeared in public effective December 1. By this time, many synagogues, homes, and businesses had already been burned. And many Jewish cemeteries had already been destroyed in Germany, Austria, Poland, and Czechoslovakia.

April 30, 1940, Poland: Nazis sealed off the first ghetto in Lodz locking 230,000 Jews inside.

June 1940, Detroit: Henry Ford refused to help the Allied Forces win World War II by refusing a U.S. government request to manufacture Rolls-Royce engines for British fighter planes.

June 14, 1940, Oswiecim Poland: The first 728 political prisoners including non-Jewish teachers and Catholic priests were transported to Auschwitz. How many killed at Auschwitz is unknown. Adolf Eichmann estimated 2,500,000; other estimates are as low as a million people.

October 1940: Jews were forced to pay for and build a wall around the Warsaw Ghetto.

January 1941 Poland: The Warsaw ghetto grew to 400,000 people. Daily calorie restrictions imposed: Germans were allowed 2,310 calories per day. Foreigners 1,790, Poles 934, and Jews were allowed 183 calories per day.

June 22, 1941, Occupied Soviet Union: "Einsatzgruppen" were mobile killing squads ordered to kill Jews upon sight. They killed more than a million Jews, plus others. Most adults were killed with machine guns. Children were bound at the ankles before their heads were smashed against walls.

September 29, 1941, Babi Yar- the outskirts of Kyiv, Ukraine: "You are to appear by 7:00 am with your possessions, money, documents, valuables, and warm clothing at Dorogozhitshaya Street, next to the Jewish

cemetery. Failure to appear is punishable by death."
33,771 Jews were murdered.

December 1941 Rome: The Jesuit journal Civiltà Cattolica, published in Rome under strict Vatican supervision, reminded Catholics that the Jews are primarily responsible for murdering God, and the Jews repeat this crime by means of ritual murder "in every generation." This and the resulting violence and injustice was made possible by Matthew 27:25 and Rome's trinity.

December 8, 1941, Chelmno, Poland: 2,300 Jews were gassed. By 1944, at least 152,000 Jews plus an undermined number of Poles and Gypsies were gassed to death at Chelmno.

December 16, 1941: Hans Frank, governor-general of Occupied Poland, noted in his diary that 3,500,000 Jews in the region were under his control.

January 30, 1942, Berlin Germany: Adolf Hitler announced that the war would result in complete annihilation of Jews.

February 22, 1942: 10,000 Jews were transported from the Lódz Ghetto to the Chelmno extermination camp where they were gassed.

February 24, 1942: 30,000 more Jews from Lódz Ghetto to Chelmno.

March 1, 1942, Żłobek Duży Poland: The Nazis began the construction of a new death camp at Sobibór where approximately 250,000 Jews were murdered before October 1943.

March 2, 1941, Minsk Ghetto Poland: Children from a Jewish nursery thrown into a sandpit, tossed candy, buried alive. Over 5,000 adults were killed too.

June 27, 1942, Rome (technically Vatican City): Pope Pius XII founded the Vatican Bank AKA Institute for the Works of Religion.

April 8, 1942: It was reported that no Jews remained in Crimea.

April 20, 1942 East Prussia: At Hitler's birthday party, Hermann Göring said he was responsible for the Reichstag fire of February 27, 1933.

April 1942: 4,400 Jews died of starvation in the Warsaw Ghetto.

June 5, 1942: The SS reported that 97,000 persons have been "processed" in mobile gas vans.

June 13, 1942: British Ambassador to the Vatican Francis d'Arcy Osborne observed that Pope Pius XII "moral leadership is not assured by the unapplied recital of the Commandments."

June 16, 1942: The American chargé d'affaires in the Vatican, Harold Tittmann, reported to the State Department that Pope Pius XII is adopting "an ostrich-like policy towards atrocities that were obvious to everyone."

July 7, 1942: Himmler chaired a meeting to discuss sterilization and other gynecological procedures and experiments on Jewish women at Auschwitz. Procedures were to be conducted without the women's knowledge.

July 1942: The Jewish community of Gorodenka Ukraine was liquidated.

July 19, 1942, Occupied France: The Family Hostage Law was announced. "Terrorists" who do not surrender to German authorities were told their male relatives would be killed, females sent to work camps, and children sent to special schools for "political reeducation."

July 23, 1942: SS Colonel General Viktor Brack advised Heinrich Himmler that all healthy Jews should be castrated or sterilized, the remainder annihilated.

July 22-September 12, 1942: 265,000 Jews were transported from Warsaw to the Treblinka death camp to be exterminated.

July 27, 1942: The German government in the Occupied Eastern Territories ordered any Pole or Ukrainian, attempting to assist any Jew, be shot dead.

July 31, 1942, Poland: "At present, together with me, both of us get ready to meet and receive death. I wish my little daughter to be remembered. Margalith, twenty months old today...I don't lament my own life nor that of my wife. I pity only the so little, nice, and talented girl. She deserves to be remembered." (Israel Lichtenstein, written from the Warsaw Ghetto)

August 1-2, 1942: 81,000 Polish Jews from Warsaw were deported to Treblinka death camp. Aug. 9: Jewish community at Radun Belorussia was liquidated. Aug. 20: Jewish community of Falenica Poland was liquidated. Aug. 24, Lask Poland: Men, women, and children were locked in a church and killed.

Sept. 1942 Piatydni Ukraine: 14,000 Jews mowed down with machine-guns.

September 1942 France: The Vichy Ministry of Information urged the press to remember "the true teaching of Saint Thomas and the Popes...the general and traditional teaching of the Catholic Church about the Jewish problem."

September 1, 1942, Lodz Ghetto, Poland: Security forces raided 5 hospitals, slaughtering patients. Babies were thrown out of upper-story windows and bayoneted before they hit the ground.

October 1-2, 1942, Luboml Ukraine: 10,000 Jews were murdered.

October 3, 1942: The Polish Ambassador to the Vatican reminded Pope Pius XII that Germans have already gassed thousands of Jews.

Oct. 4: The last Jews in Germany were sent to Auschwitz.

Oct. 11-12: 11,000 from Ostrowiec-Swietokrzyski Poland killed at Treblinka.

October 1942: British Vatican Ambassador Francis d'Arcy Osborne wrote that Pope Pius XII only occasionally denounces moral crimes. But such rare and vague declarations "do not have... lasting force and validity... policy of silence in regard to such offenses against the conscience of the world must necessarily involve a renunciation of moral leadership."

November 1-6, 1942: Over 170,000 Jews were killed in a week at the Belzec, Auschwitz, and Treblinka death camps.

December 1942 Lithuania: Nazis locked 1,000 Gypsies in a synagogue until they starved to death.

Examples such as these continue for about 2 more years. An estimated 5,820,960 Jews were killed in the Holocaust.

Aug. 1942-Sept. 1943: Over 2 million killed in brutal combat as Russian forces turned the tide against the Nazis at the Battle of Stalingrad.

In the USA, teenagers lied about their age to volunteer, received a couple months training, then shipped off to fight combat seasoned Nazi soldiers. And they won. June 6, 1944: D-Day. December 16, 1944: Battle of the Bulge, etc. Thank you WW2 veterans, U.S.A., U.K., Soviet Union, and every other of the Allied Forces. WW2 officially ended on September 2, 1945.

5 Iyar 5708 (May 14, 1948): Declaration of the Establishment of the State of Israel. This was prophesied throughout the Jewish Bible in Genesis 12:2-3, 17:8; Leviticus 25:23; Deuteronomy 30:3-5; Isaiah 11:12, 43:5-6, 66:8; Jeremiah 12:15, 16:14-15, 30:1-31, 40, 31:23; Ezekiel 36:8, 37:1-28, 46:9-10; Hosea 3:5; Joel 3:1-21; Amos 9:14-15; Psalm 23:1-6, etc.

"Therefore say, 'Thus says the Lord God: I will gather you from the peoples and assemble you out of the countries where you have been scattered, and I will give you the land of Israel." (Ezekiel 11:17, ESV)

May 1949 (Jewish year 5709): "Operation Magic Carpet" nicknamed "Operation on Wings of Eagles" 45,000 of 46,000 Jews were allowed to leave Yemen. 380 flights brought them back to Israel. Imagine watching airplanes fly back and forth from Yemen to Israel, knowing God's promises made thousands of years before the airplane was invented.

"Who are these that fly like a cloud, and like doves to their windows? For the coastlands shall hope for me, the ships of Tarshish first, to bring your children from afar, their silver and gold with them, for the name of the LORD your God, and for the Holy One of Israel, because he has made you beautiful." (Isaiah 60:8-9, ESV)

"they shall come trembling like birds from Egypt, and like doves from the land of Assyria, and I will return them to their homes, declares the LORD." (Hosea 11:11, ESV)

August 12, 1952 Moscow: "Night of the Murdered Poets" "I was ready to confess that I was the pope's own nephew and that I was acting on his direct personal orders" (Joseph Yuzefovich, testifying about being tortured)

1965 Rome: Section 4 of the Vatican II statement on non-Christian religions, Nostra Aetate: The Roman Catholic Church forgave "The Decide." In other words, the 4th Beast officially exonerated Jews for deciding that Romans would kill God 1,584 years after they made the claim based on their own doctrine of the trinity and anonymously written gospel of Matthew 27:25.

-
June 5, 1967: The Arab States of Egypt, Syria, and Jordan attacked Israel, resulting in the 6 Day War from June 5-10 (Monday-Sabbath.) Israel won.

Chapter 18

1970s thru "The Stuff of Nightmares"

Defense Counsel: "... legal and historical sources speak about passing children to Moloch in fire. According to the rabbinic interpretation, this prohibition is against passing children through fire and then delivering them to the pagan priests... refers to an initiation rite... Leviticus 18 and 20. The common denominator of all these traditions is the understanding of Moloch worship as the transfer of Jewish children to paganism either by delivering them directly to pagan priests..." (Jewish Virtual Library, Cult of Moloch)

Child sacrifice was a big problem, especially sacrificing firstborn sons to Baal-Haddad-Moloch, long before Abraham's generation. God called Abraham to kill Issac and then stopped him, a test of Abraham, in more ways than one. It was also a reference for all generations, in a story sure to get our attention, that God does not want human sacrifice. Before Baal worshippers started doing it, such a disgusting thing never even crossed The LORD's mind, as we're told in Jeremiah 7:31, 19:5, 32:35.

According to the Roman Catholic Church's own records, clergy being sex offenders has been a widespread problem for more than 1,717 years.

306 CE Spain, Synod of Elvira: In addition to passing laws to divide Jews and Christians, including banning intermarriage, socializing, eating together: "CANON 18 Bishops, presbyters, and deacons, if—once placed in the ministry—they are discovered to be sexual offenders, shall not receive communion, not even at the approach of death, because of the scandal and the heinousness of the crime."

"CANON 33 BISHOPS, presbyters, as well as deacons and subdeacons having a position in the ministry are ordered to abstain completely from [conjugal relations with] their wives and not to have children. Whoever, in fact, does this, shall be expelled from the dignity of the clerical state." "CANON 71 Men who sexually abuse boys shall not be given communion even at the approach of death."

1139 CE Rome: Pope Innocent III's 2nd Lateran Council again mandated celibacy for clergy. By this time, clergy had reputations for womanizing. For example, Pope John XII known for concubinage, incest, simony, mutilation, forcing himself onto married women, widows, and virgins. He ordered eyes plucked out, hands and genitals cut off; and was compared to the devil.

June 24, 1967, Rome: Pope Paul VI issued "Sacerdotalis caelibatus" upholding celibacy as the church's "brilliant jewel" based on "the model of Christ's own celibacy."

When we find out who's paying for these crimes, who really allows this filth, we'll circle back to damning evidence from the 600's, 1051, and 1665 CE.

1819-1969 USA: "He said if I ever told anybody that I would go to hell"... From 1819 to 1969, tens of thousands of children were sent to more than 500 boarding schools across the country, the majority run or funded by the U.S. government. Children were stripped of their names, their long hair was cut, and they were beaten for speaking their languages... By 1900, 1 out of 5 Native American school-age children attended a boarding school. At least 80 of the schools were operated by the Catholic Church... "A national crime scene"... "rampant physical, sexual, and emotional abuse"...

Unlike children abused by priests at churches in Boston and other big cities while they were living at home, Native American children were put into the care of alleged abusers at remote boarding schools, sometimes hundreds of miles from home... employed at least one credibly accused priest, sister or brother for 91 consecutive years. At these schools, successive generations of students continuously lived among predators.

They can scream for help, but no one's going to hear them or believe them. It's a perpetrator's wonderland," said Patrick J. Wall, a former Catholic priest who once worked for the church as a self-described "fixer" settling child sexual abuse cases... "It happened to Native Americans, but the history belongs to everyone who's an American."... at St. Paul that "they would stuff flashlight batteries" in the children's mouths to punish them. "They would jam it there and hit them like that and make their mouth bleed," Chandler recounted. "If you cried, they would hit you all the harder... Before she would do these things, she'd make a sign of the cross."... when she was 9, she was raped by a priest on a kitchen table... a priest "would take me down to the basement and have me perform oral sex on him." He also showed her an area where coffins were stored. "One time he put me inside a coffin and I thought I would die,"... philosophy was: "Kill the Indian in him, and save the man.".... "They were stolen," ... altar boy and he was raped by the priests," she said. "He was sexually abused by the nuns. And his hands were beat black and blue." ... a rope and a strap used to lash children as punishment. The rope was four strands tied together... the "Jesus rope,"... The strap carried strands of razor-sharp metal strips. "This strap taught me not to feel," (The Washington Post, In the name of God, Sari Horwitz, Dana Hedgepeth, Emmanuel Martinez, Scott Higham, Salwan Georges, May 29, 2004)

"As a native Catholic the very faith you embrace is one that was used to destroy you, that collaborated with the government in cultural genocide.... This is the terrible irony of being Native American and Catholic." (Sister Marie-Therese Archambault) She's Lakota Sioux and a Catholic Nun.

1950-1974, St. John School for the Deaf, St. Francis Wisconsin: Father Lawrence Murphy raped over 200 deaf children during a 24-year period. He confessed in 1993. 575 victim reports detailed over 8,000 instances of criminal sexual assault by over 150 clergy in the Milwaukee Archdiocese during this time. A documentary about what happened is titled "Mea Maxima Culpa: Silence in the House of God" (2012).

An example of how predator priests are spread around by the 4th Beast:

St. Mary's Parochial Grammar School North Attleboro Massachusetts: 1960, Father James Porter was put in charge of Alter Boys. By 1963 at least 4 parents alleged abuse to his superiors. 1964, arrested for molesting a 13-year-old and sent to an institution. 1965, reassigned. 1967, admitted to another institution ran by priests. Declared cured; reassigned. Complaints continued. Transferred from parish to parish in Texas, New Mexico, and Minnesota. In 1973, Father Porter confessed to molesting children in 5 states in a letter to Pope Paul VI requesting his release.

1977-1982 Munich: Cardinal & Archbishop Joseph Ratzinger, former member of Hitler Youth, German Army WW2 veteran, and future Pope Benedict XVI, failed to act on 4 priests accused of child sexual assault.

June 22, 1983, Rome: Emanuela Orlandi, 15-year-old daughter of a Vatican official reported missing. In May 2012, Father Gabriele Amorth claimed that Orlandi was kidnapped by the Vatican police, forced into sexual servitude, then murdered. "Emanuela Orlandi 'was kidnapped for sex parties for Vatican police' "A teenage girl whose disappearance in Rome has remained a mystery for 30 years was kidnapped for sex parties by a gang involving Vatican police and foreign diplomats, the Roman Catholic Church's leading exorcist has claimed." (The Telegraph, UK, Nick Squires, May 22, 2012)

"This was a crime with a sexual motive. Parties were organized, with a Vatican gendarme acting as the 'recruiter' of the girls. The network involved diplomatic personnel from a foreign embassy to the Holy See. I believe Emanuela ended up as a victim of this circle." (Vatican Chief Exorcist, Father Gabriele Amorth, appointed by Pope John Paul II)

1987: The Archdiocese of Dublin was the first to take out insurance, renewed annually, to protect against legal costs and damages arising from child sex abuse litigation.

1992 Boston: "We call down God's power on our business leaders, and political leaders, and community leaders. By all means, we call down God's power on the media, particularly the Globe." (Cardinal Bernard Law infuriated with the Boston Globe informing the public that he was moving predator priests from parish to parish)

1993 Dublin Ireland: Unmarked graves of 155 women were found at one of hundreds of Magdalene Laundries run by the Roman Catholic Church. The Magdalen Asylum for Penitent Females was founded in 1765. Some operated for over 200 years. An estimated 30,000 women were confined to these institutions in the 19th and 20th centuries. Women were treated like criminals because they were unmarried and pregnant. No official history exists because of the Roman Catholic Church's "policy of secrecy." To this day requests for information have been denied.

1993 Archdiocese of Camden New Jersey: Racketeer Influenced and Corrupt Organizations Act charges were filed against the Roman Catholic Church. "The lawyers who have been involved in these cases have always thought that the church operated like a criminal enterprise... Those people need to be in jail," (Steve Rubino the lawyer who filed the first Civil Racketeering case against the Roman Catholic Church).

Top 3 reasons why there're not more RICO charges filed against the Roman Catholic Church: 1. The Federal RICO statute does not cover personal injury crimes. 2. RICO statues were designed to prosecute crimes that enrich the organization. Despite the Vatican's policy of secrecy regarding financials, it's proven they've paid out over 4 billion dollars in sexual assault claims so far. 3. "Every other institution in this country would be forced to be accountable to its members for this this kind of behavior, but the pope is accountable to no one." (David Clohessy National Director of SNAP)

2001: Boston magazine placed Cardinal Bernard Law 4th on its "Power List," behind Senator Edward Kennedy.

2002: "The Magdalene Sisters" inspired by "Sex in a Cold Climate." Survivor's accounts of the film said the reality was "a thousand times worse."

2002 Boston: After being caught repeatedly transferring rapist priests, Cardinal Law offered his resignation. Pope John Paul II refused it. After public backlash, he accepted it. Law was the first Cardinal to resign over these vile abominations, breaking a streak of more than 1,717 years.

2003: Massachusetts A.G. Thomas F. Reilly said up to 1,000 children were sexually abused by 250 priests in Boston. He offered evidence that Law knew of the problem before arriving in 1984 and covered it up the whole time.

2003: According to former Catholic Priest Richard Sipe's "Celibacy in Crisis" about 50% of priests are admittedly sexually active. According to DNA tests, Catholic priests have fathered over 20,000 illegitimate children. Many end up abused in orphanages run by the church. "The more children of priests I met and spoke with, I found all sorts of anecdotal stories about destroyed records and people knowing and systems within the church hiding the children of priests and documents going astray." (Brendan Watkins) "I can confirm that these guidelines exist," the Vatican spokesman Alessandro Gisotti wrote in response to a query from The New York Times. "It is an internal document." (Vatican's Secret Rules for Catholic Priests Who Have Children-New York Times, Jason Horowitz and Elisabetta Povoledo, Feb. 18, 2019)

2004: Two years after Cardinal Bernard Law resigned in disgrace, Pope John Paul II appointed him High Priest of the Basilica di Santa Maria Maggiore, 1 of 4 basilicas under direct jurisdiction of the Vatican. Law was 1 of 115 cardinals who elected Pope Benedict XVI. Pope Francis presided over Law's funeral.

May 20, 2009, Ireland: The Ryan Report, chaired by Judge Sean Ryan on "Reformatory and Industrial Schools

operated by the Catholic Church, funded and supervised
by the Irish Department of Education, demonstrated
beyond a doubt that the entire system treated children
more like prison inmates and slaves than people with legal
rights and human potential. Catholic officials encouraged
ritual beatings... amid a "culture of self-serving secrecy."
Government inspectors failed to stop the abuses...
beatings and rapes, subjection to naked beatings in public,
being forced into oral sex, and subjection to beatings after
failed rape attempts... described by some as Ireland's
Holocaust... "endemic" in the institutions that dealt with
boys..." the stuff of nightmares"...particularly chilling:
"systemic, pervasive, chronic, excessive, arbitrary,
endemic." (The Guardian, UK)

November 26, 2009, Ireland: The Murphy Report "the
Dublin Archdiocese's preoccupations in dealing with cases
of child sexual abuse... maintenance of secrecy, the
avoidance of scandal, the protection of the reputation of
the Church, and the preservation of its assets. All other
considerations, including the welfare of children and justice
for victims, were subordinated... archbishops, bishops, and
other officials cannot claim that they did not know that child
sexual abuse was a crime... they have the same
obligations as all other citizens to uphold the law and
report serious crimes to the authorities... no doubt that
clerical child sexual abuse was covered up" from January
1975 to May 2004 according to the 720-page report.

2010 Buenos Aires Argentina: Cardinal Jorge Mario
Bergoglio (future Pope Francis) commissioned a 4-volume,
2,000-plus page forensic internal study of the legal case
against convicted priest Julio Grassi. It concluded the
reverend was innocent and orphans from Grassi's "Happy
Children" homes were lying. Grassi was a convicted child
molester and repeat sex offender. The study was on the

legal investigation rather than the sex crimes; to be used internally to prevent future investigations from moving forward. May we play recorded survivor witness testimony of Pope Francis' protecting predator priests?

Judge: Proceed. Defense: We'll start it 2 minutes prior to survivor testimony, so we can listen to Pope Francis' advisor explain that might take 30 years for the Vatican to stop their employees raping children. *"Abuse in the Catholic Church: Priests Protected by the Vatican's Code of Silence" was fast-forwarded 38 minutes into the 54-minute video and played until the end. All video evidence played by Defense is free and easily accessible on YouTube.*

August 25, 2011, Boston: On August 25, 2011, Cardinal O'Malley released names of 159 of 250 of priests accused of sexually abusing minors.

2013 Ireland: A formal state apology was issued for sex crimes committed at the Dublin Magdalen Laundry from 1964 to 1968.

2015: The movie "Spotlight" based on the uncovering of 229 predator priests in the Archdiocese of Boston was released.

2017 USA: According to an internal survey conducted by the GCSRW of 4,374 people, 58.5% of women and 35.7% of men reported sexual abuse within the Methodist Church, 23% claimed local pastors were perpetrators, 15% claimed other local church leaders were the perpetrators.

2017: Walter "Robby" Robinson who led the investigation for the Boston Globe (played my Micheal Keaton in Spotlight) "This epidemic within the Catholic Church knew

no boundaries, neither state lines, or intentional boarders...
so heinous where the gulf between good and evil was so
evident, and the evil rests squarely with the Catholic
Church. The most iconic institution for 1.2 billion people
around the world. The church in which so many of us were
baptized, confirmed, married. The church I once assumed
would bury me... victims of priests in South Africa, Italy,
even India... New Orleans... Dallas... Fall River... Phil was
trying to tell them that the cardinal was involved in an
international criminal conspiracy. It turns out he actually
was... In 2003, the Massachusetts Attorney General...
found that nearly 250 priests in the Boston Archdiocese
had sexually molested children over a 60-year period...
**That is 10.75 percent of all the priests who served in
Boston over those 60 years. I'd like you to think about
those numbers for a moment.** Boston is the archdiocese
where there has been the fullest accounting of the extent
of the abuse. Believe me, there is nothing in the water in
Boston that made priests any more likely to molest
children, than say in Seattle or Denver or New York. Just
this year another grand jury in a small diocese in
Pennsylvania, the Johnstown Altoona diocese reported 9
percent of priests there abuse children. And there are a
couple of other diocese in the US where grand juries have
gotten ahold of all the churches files, and the percentage
of priests in those dioceses who abuse children is also in
the 9 to 10 percent range... we would have never asked
those questions had not Marty Baron arrived from Miami...
he had no allegiances, but for one, to his conviction that a
newspaper's primary mission is to hold powerful people
and institutions accountable...

John Geoghan was a pedophile and was accused of
molesting 84 children in 6 parishes over 30 years... the
archdiocese knew for all those years what Geohan had
done and simply transferred him from parish to parish...

the public had a right to know... Geoghan was the tip of the iceberg... hush money... mechanics of the cover up. For decades, Cardinal Law and his predecessors had routinely transferred priests whose sexual misconduct... In the 1970s, some priests were sent for treatment, then immediately sent off to new assignments...

There was also a lend-lease program. Cardinals and archbishops around the country would take particularly egregious offenders and send them to other dioceses. It worked like this: Here, you take one of my bad guys; I'll take one of yours... those settlements included confidentiality agreements. There was no record of the complaint; and no one, including the lawyers, could talk about it... incriminating files in the Geoghan case had mysteriously vanished from the Boston courthouse. The church's influence was apparent everywhere... the vast majority have yet to come forward... one thing we discovered when we started to work on this story is that we all had been raised Catholic... I will not go inside a Catholic Church unless it's for somebody's wedding... funeral. I still have my faith... you don't need the institution of the church to maintain your faith in God..." (Spotlight on the Church: How Sex Abuse Went Unnoticed for So Long, and What it Took to Expose It) YouTube

May 2018 Minnesota: The Archdiocese of St. Paul agreed to pay $210,000,000 in settlements to 450 sexual abuse victims.

August 14, 2018 Harrisburg: "Good afternoon, Josh Shapiro, honored to serve as Pennsylvania's Attorney General, and I'm here, finally, to announce the results of a two-year grand jury investigation into widespread sexual abuse of children within the Catholic Church, and the **systemic cover-up by senior church officials in**

Pennsylvania and at the Vatican... an intense legal battle has played out between my office and individuals who have concealed their identities through sealed court filings. These petitioners, and for a time some of the diocese, **sought to prevent the entire report from ever seeing the light of day**... Shamefully, these petitioners still don't have the courage to tell the public who they are... it happened everywhere... systematic cover-up by church leaders, the weaponization of faith, the failure of law enforcement... **abuse and cover-up in every diocese in Pennsylvania**... every diocese, the cover-up was sophisticated... from the diocese own secret archives... **organized cover-up by senior church officials that stretched, in some cases, all the way to the Vatican.** The term secret archives is not my term. It is how the church officials themselves referred to the troves... bishops had the key to the secret archives, which contained both allegations and admissions of the abuse and the cover-up... files on more than 400 priests... including rape, committed by grown men, priests, against children... the church showed a complete distain for victims... In the Diocese of Pittsburgh, the grand jury named 99 priests... groomed and violently sexually assaulted young boys. One boy was forced to stand on a bed in a rectory strip naked and pose as Christ on the cross for the priests. They took photos of their victim, adding them to a collection of child pornography which they produced and shared on church grounds... priests gave their favorite boys gifts, gold crosses to wear as necklaces. The crosses were markings of which boys had been groomed... raped a young girl, got her pregnant, and then that priest arranged for an abortion... The pattern was abuse, deny, and cover-up... the cover-up made it impossible to achieve justice for the victims... all of the victims were brushed aside in every part of the state... Priests were raping little boys and girls and the men of God who were responsible for them, not only did nothing, they hid it all, for decades, monsignors, auxiliary bishops, bishops, archbishops, cardinals have mostly been protected.

Many, including some named in this report have been promoted... Bishop Wuerl is now Cardinal Wuerl. Father Zubik is now Bishop Zubik... The grand jury found this report to law enforcement was another lie... sexually abused 5 sisters from the same family... the principle reported it to the diocese... high school principal was instructed to do nothing... never been able to tell their story until today. They were gagged from speaking by confidentiality agreement insisted upon by the diocese... **they paid for their silence**... Predators in every diocese weaponized the Catholic faith and used it as a tool of their abuse... Father Robert Moslener groomed his middle school students for oral sex by telling them how Mary had to lick Jesus clean after he was born... Father Ed Graff told a seventh-grader he abused that what they were doing was okay because the priest was an instrument of God... Monsignor Thomas Benestad made a nine-year old give him oral sex then rinsed the boy's mouth out with holy water... taught this abuse was not only normal, but that it was holy... District Attorney [Robert] Masters actually testified to the grand jury, that his reason for failing to investigate and prosecute the sexual abuse case against a priest was that he wanted the diocese support for his political career... young boy ran into a police station in Scranton after his priest attempted to assault him. He told the grand jury that the on-duty officer said I don't want to know anything about this. I just want you to get out of here ... speech problems... uncontrollable stuttering... many attempted suicide, sadly many were successful..." (Pennsylvania Catholic Church sexual abuse grand jury report: press conference) YouTube

August 22, 2018, Rome: "... we must have the courage to tear down the culture of secrecy and publicly confess the truths we have kept hidden. We must tear down the conspiracy of silence with which bishops and priests have protected themselves at the expense of their faithful, a conspiracy of silence that in the eyes of the world risks making the Church look like a sect, a conspiracy of silence not so dissimilar from the one that prevails in the mafia... how many other evil pastors is Francis still continuing to prop up... (Archbishop Carlo Maria Viganò) He called for several high-ranking Vatican resignations including Pope Francis. He also called out the "Deep Church" and "Deep State" in a letter retweeted by President Trump in June 2020.

January 24, 2019, Texas: 14 Catholic dioceses released the names of 286 priests credibly accused of sexually abusing children.

2019: According to a Houston Chronicle report, approximately 380 clergy and religious leaders within the Southern Baptist Convention were accused of sexually abusing over 700 people since 1998. Their leaders tried to cover it up, moving predator clergy around to different churches.

June 9, 2019: "As San Francisco District Attorney, Kamala Harris decided to cover up the files, which the previous DA had obtained... She was even informed by a victim that the priest who abused him was still working with children, yet she did nothing. She could have helped victims and maybe prevented additional abuse as California Attorney General, but she did not... San Francisco DA's office had files on clergy sex abusers. But Harris refused to share them with victims" (AS SAN FRANCISCO DISTRICT ATTORNEY, KAMALA HARRIS'S OFFICE STOPPED COOPERATING

WITH VICTIMS OF CATHOLIC CHURCH CHILD ABUSE,
Lee Fang)

2019 USA: "Nearly 1,700 priests... These priests, deacons,
monks, and lay people now teach middle-school math...
the same year the names over 5,100 credibly accused..."
(Nearly 1,700 priests credibly accused of kid sex abuse
face little oversight, AP probe finds, Associated Press,
October 4, 2019)

November 2020 England and Wales: "... once again
demonstrates that the Catholic church is not a safe place
for children... masturbation, oral sex, vaginal rape and anal
rape... sadistic beatings driven by sexual gratification...
deeply manipulative behaviour by those in positions of
trust... One child was abused hundreds of times between
age 11-15 by a priest... After each incident he was
required to make confession, and the priest concerned
made it plain that his sister's place at a local convent
school depended on his compliance...Their lack of
cooperation passes understanding...For decades, the
Catholic church's failure to tackle child sexual abuse
consigned many more children to the same fate.... Even
today, the responses of the Holy See appear at odds with
the pope's promise to take action on this hugely important
problem." (from the 162 page Independent Inquiry Child
Sexual Abuse report chaired by Alexis Jay)

"I offered my resignation to Pope Francis. His answer has
come back very clear, very unambiguous. He wants me to
stay in post, so I will stay because that's where my orders
come from, that's where my mandate comes from."
(Cardinal Vincent Nichols, head of the Roman Catholic
Church in England and Wales) That statement was made
after public outcry for his resignation.

May 31, 2020, Switzerland: 1,002 "situations of sexual abuse" 56% of cases involved boys, 39% girls. "The situations identified surely amount to only the tip of the iceberg," (Monika Dommann and Marietta Meier)

October 5, 2021 France: "Nuns used crucifixes to rape girls during decades of abuse carried out by clergy in France's Catholic Church that saw attacks on 330,000 children covered up 'by a veil of silence', damning report finds... independent commission, made up of 22 lawyers, doctors, historians, sociologists and theologians, worked for two-and-a-half years... number of victims the report identifies is a minimum... Some victims did not dare to speak out or trust the commission... We can see how systemic it was." (UK Daily Mail, by Clare Mccarthy and Peter Allen)

Your honor, may we play this 26-minute and 31-second video titled (Insider: Vatican Meeting in Secret to Discuss AI and Transhumanism) (This isn't on Youtube; banned most likely. Fortunately, It's free on banned.video) from October 29, 2021, discussing division of the Jesuit "Mafia of San Gallen" resulting from high-ranking Jesuits being killed by the "Covid shot." The "Scientists of the Church" including Pope Francis who "worships science; not God." (Leo Zagami) Judge: No.

January 6, 2022, Rome: Pope Francis denounced people spreading "baseless information" that's since been proven accurate regarding the COVID-19 vaccine. He lectured the world about everyone's "moral obligation" to comply with mandates, wear masks, and take the experimental mRNA injection.

November 13, 2022, Mount Sinai: Pope Francis issued a new set of 10 Commandments promoting the climate change agenda. Tablets representing the original 10 Commandments given by God were smashed in mockery.

As of February 3, 2023, the Catholic Church's paid 40 million euros ($43.5 million US) to victims of sexual abuse in Germany in over 1,809 cases so far.

2023 Illinois USA: "... contributed to the delay of releasing this report, during the pandemic... other unexpected challenges... we also dealt with a ransomware attack that temporarily crippled our office systems... 451 Catholic clergy abused 1,997 children... church leadership who covered up that abuse..." (Illinois A.G. Kwame Raoul)

2023 Baltimore Maryland: "... preyed upon by multiple abusers over decades...600 children... likely far higher." (Maryland A.G. Anthony Brown)

August 23, 2023: "Nicaragua's government announced... legal identity of the Society of Jesus in the country had been officially revoked... includes the seizure of all assets... expulsion of the order's members... Jesuit-run University of Central America in Nicaragua... on charges that the university was aiding terrorism and treason... fourth Catholic college in Nicaragua to be taken over by the country's government in recent months... the Society of Jesus in Nicaragua — now treated as enemies of the state, Jesuits " (Jesuits face crackdown, after long history with Nicaragua's Ortega, Edgar Beltran)

October 7, 2023, Israel: Hamas attacked, killing 1,200, taking 200 hostages.

October 27, 2023, Madrid: Spain's first official report on sexual abuse in Catholic institutions estimates that 440,000 people currently living in Spain have been abused by Roman Catholic clergy. "The cases were made possible by silence... representatives of the institution blamed them for the abuse... Some bishops scolded us, not only refusing to cooperate but also saying: 'What are you doing messing around with this?'... This is a necessary report... People have killed themselves because of this..." (from the 770-page report, following an 18-month investigation of 487 cases, 8,000 people interviewed, submitted to Spain's parliament by Ombudsman Angel Gabilondo who expressed disgust with the "church's common practice of transferring sexual abusers to other parishes, schools, and countries.")

"Today we are a little better as a country, because a reality has been made known that everyone has known for many years, but which no one spoke of." (Pedro Sánchez, Prime Minister of Spain)

Chapter 19

Funding the Terror

Defense Counsel: If after being made aware of more than $4,000,000,000, that's a billion with a b, not including sealed files, insurance schemes, lobbying, shell games with land and trusts, etc., that the Roman Catholic Church's spent on silencing survivors and spreading the scourge of child sexual abuse throughout the world. Even if a parishioner's intentions are charity or church maintenance, by putting money in the collection basket, are they making themselves a party to breaking the LORD God's 3rd Commandment?

Plaintiff's accused me of "Blasphemy of the Holy Spirit." According to Rome's gospels, Matthew 12:31-32, etc., it's an unforgivable sin. Is that true? What do the scriptures say? We're told repeatedly in the Original Testament that no matter what we've done, if we turn to The LORD alone, we'll be forgiven immediately; with 1 exception:

"You must not misuse the name of the LORD your God. The LORD will not let you go unpunished if you misuse his name." (Exodus 20:7, NLT)

That's the 3rd commandment that Jews and Protestants are taught. Catholics are taught that it's the 2nd. Most of the time, most rabbis focus their teaching on not taking false or pointless oaths. Most Christians focus on not taking God's Name in vain. Both are correct; but neither is the point here.

Some people use profanity. Maybe a toddler even uttered the word "shit." Maybe the toddler can't comprehend what that has to do with G-d's name. Frankly, neither can I. Nobody with an ounce of sense, in any religion, thinks God will forgive murder, rape, and adultery; but not profanity. If anyone wants a more detailed explanation of the 3rd commandment, there's a good article by Dennis Prager titled "There Is a 'Worst Sin': Evil in God's Name."

The Roman Catholic Church is by far the biggest breaker of God's first 4 commandments: 1st with the trinity. 2nd they omitted; and Mass, from start to finish, is an exercise in breaking it. 4th they changed the day in 336 CE.

Examples of the 4th Beast breaking God's 3rd and only unforgiven commandment are almost everything on the timeline since the trinity. That's why they'll be utterly destroyed (Daniel 7:11, 7:26, Obediah, etc.) Rome's trinity brought The LORD God's Name into their violence. Every forced baptism "in the Name of the Father, and of the Son, and of the Holy Spirit." Every time a priest utters those words making the sign of the cross before raping an altar boy or girl, then forgiving the victim. Yes, you heard that correctly. Crusaders marching on villages with "Shield of the Trinity," etc.

Every crusade, inquisition, conquest, and war waged by the 4th Beast cost money; couldn't have happened without it. Pope Damasus I, Innocent III, and Cardinal Law operated within a budget. We already covered how Pope Innocent III funded crusades, preaching rewards in heaven for contributing to mass-murder committed while misusing God's Name. Of course, that's not how he said it; nor does Pope Francis say he's asking for money to pay lawyers and confidentiality agreements to protect child rapists. Instead, he asks for charity. How does Pope Francis spend it? First how he doesn't:

"Vatican Uses Donations for the Poor to Plug Its Budget
Deficit Only 10% of donations to the Peter's Pence
collection go to charitable works" (Francis X. Rocca, Wall
Street Journal, Dec. 11, 2019) "Only 10 percent of it goes
toward the poor, and yet that's the lead line... every June
when they take this international collection." (Raymond
Arroyo Fox Nation's Deep Dive)"

"Historically, the Peter's Pence – it goes back centuries
– is to support the pope and all his expenses, including
charity, so it's nothing wrong to use it to pay the bills at the
Vatican. On the other hand, it's advertised as a charitable
fund. The Vatican's finances have been a disaster for a
long time...That was part of what got Pope Bergolio
[Francis] elected. He said he was going to reform the
corruption in the Vatican. It hasn't happened..." (Father
Gerald Murray, Holy Family Church NYC) How's money
that's not going to charity's being spent?

"The Catholic Church has spent $10.6 million in the
northeastern United States to fight legislation that would
help victims of clergy sexual abuse seek justice... In New
York, for example, the Catholic Church spent $2,912,772
lobbying against the Child Victims Act... in Pennsylvania...
$5,322,979 lobbying to keep current restrictions in place
on the statute of limitations..." "CHURCH INFLUENCING
STATE: How the Catholic Church Spent Millions Against
Survivors of Clergy Abuse" the Catholic Church has not
only continued to invest in lobbying against the interests of
victims, their investments in this area have actually
increased... as a Catholic born-and-raised person myself...
sadness is a little stronger even than the anger. But maybe
if Catholics themselves get angry about this, then maybe
the institution itself will change... start with members of the
church." (Catholic Church spent 10.6 million to lobby

against legislation that would benefit victims of child sex abuse, CBS, Christina Caatides, 6/6/19)

"“One funding stream alone - to the tune of $70 million dollars - came from one wealthy individual... You can give the order to such and such to give $50,000 in retainers to any big firm in Pittsburgh or Philadelphia and the money just goes out." Not only is that information protected by client privilege, but the church doesn't have to file an annual report with the IRS... Nobody really knows what assets they have... there is no accountability to expose those payments... Neuberger said." (Where does a priest get the money to retain an expensive lawyer, PENNSYLVANIA REAL-TIME NEWS, July 9, 2018)

"It's unimaginable, I think, the damage that's been done to this community through the abuse on the scale that it was... abused at the school in the 1960s, '70s and '80s... Catholic Church Insurance (CCI), an insurance company owned by the church... went into run-off in May, meaning it was not issuing new insurance policies... 7,000 policies in force. Before entering run-off, it had more than 16,000. Most will end by June next year... $381.3 million in liabilities relating to abuse claims... 1,880 alleged perpetrators of child sexual abuse... The board has proposed a legally binding "scheme of agreement." Under the scheme... CCI won't pay abuse claims in full. How much of each claim would be paid would be determined by the scheme's manager, the embattled consulting giant PwC... "They are an enormously wealthy organization the Catholic Church ... so for the Catholic Church to say that they can't afford to meet their liabilities through the Catholic Church Insurance, in my view, is immoral." (Catholic Church-owned insurer says 'high volume' of abuse claims is putting it out of business, by Loretta Lohberger, 10/28/2023) “Diocese of Oakland... 330 sexual abuse lawsuits, filed for bankruptcy... assets valued between $100 million and $500 million... estimated liabilities in the same dollar range..." (Catholic Church in California grapples with more than 3,000 lawsuits, alleging child sex abuse, Alejandra Molina, (5/26/23)

Kenya, India, Austria, Australia, Philippines, Japan, Croatia, Germany, France, China, Italy, France, Indonesia, El Salvador, Mexico, USA, Brazil, Scotland, Ireland, Wales, Tanzania, the list goes on. At schools, orphanages, and churches run by the Roman Church, the same pattern has been found. As the AG of Pennsylvania articulated it: Abuse, deny, cover up, shame the victim, transfer the predator, then cover up the cover up. The Methodist Church and Southern Baptist Convention are following the same pattern.

"The Diocese of Syracuse, New York, has agreed to a $100 million settlement with parishioners who claimed they were preyed on by priests... But, for now, not a dime of that money is coming from the six insurance companies that cover the Diocese of Syracuse... the diocese itself will have to shell out $50 million, the parishes in the diocese will have to contribute $45 million... to settle the 411 abuse claims... when the ushers pass around the collection baskets at Sunday Mass at churches across the Diocese of Syracuse, some of that money could be used to pay the victims, Danielle Cummings, a spokesperson for the diocese, confirmed. "People do give money to the parishes in the general collection," Cummings said. "And unless they specify that this donation is going to a special project, yes, it could wind up going towards the settlement." (Catholic diocese agrees to pay $100 million settlement to hundreds of abuse victims, by Corky Siemaszko, 7/28/2023)

Judge: Christianity and Judaism agree on charity, almost. According to the Jewish Bible: Daniel 4:27, Proverbs 10:2, 11:4, 16:6, 19:17, 21:3, etc., giving charity atones for sins. God always has and always will prefer charity over sacrifices. Likewise, according to the Christian Bible: "Charity shall cover the multitude of sins." (1 Peter 4:8). "You see that a person is justified by works and not by faith alone." James (2:24, 2:13-26). To be fair, the Christian Bible also states that salvation is only through faith and not by works (Ephesians 2:8-9). Regardless, if money's not being spent on charity, then it's not charity. Paying lawyers to defend child rapists isn't charity.

Defense: Most Christians probably don't know that because 1 Peter 4:8 is mistranslated in 29 of the top 32 listed versions on Biblehub.com, with the Greek word for "charity" is replaced by "love." Simply put, the church couldn't continue this evil without money to fund it. Rome's offered the collection basket to the Baal of child sacrifice, and apparently the Methodist Church and Southern Baptist Convention are following suit.

Chapter 20

Turning Over the Supreme Sacred Congregation of the Roman and Universal Inquisition

Defense Counsel: When U.S. State Attorney Generals claim that the Vatican interfered with grand jury investigations and did everything in their power to stop grand jury reports from ever seeing the light of day. They're referring to the same office of "Supreme Sacred Congregation of the Roman and Universal Inquisition" that pulled people apart on the rack until they confessed. The same office that burned people by "slow fire" is currently moving habitual child rapists across state and international borders.

Plaintiff Counsel: Objection! Such a preposterous lie, I don't even...

Judge: Is the Supreme Sacred Congregation of the Roman and Universal Inquisition currently overseeing sexual abuse claims right now, in 2023. Yes, or no? Plaintiff: No. Defense: Yes.

Plaintiff: False! The office of Inquisition hasn't existed for centuries. It hasn't been necessary since deciders stopped abusing the Holy Eucharist and weaponizing the Old Testament against Christians.

Judge: What office of the Vatican is currently overseeing sexual abuse policies and claims?

Plaintiff: The "Dicastery for the Doctrine of the Faith" handles those claims. Slander of Christianity, including the largest charitable organization in the world has gone on long enough. Judge: Noted. What's the discrepancy?

Defense: The timeline had a lot removed. And we'll leave the Medieval, Episcopal, Papal, Spanish, and Portuguese Inquisitions out of this. We'll also leave out Pope Lucius III sending Bishops to Southern France in 1184 and Pope Gregory appointing Inquisitors in 1231. Here's the progression of the specific office that's still in power today:

1089 CE: Pope Urban II set up the Roman Curia which comprises the administrative offices of the Holy See AKA See of Rome, or as Daniel called them the 4th Beast. During Pope Innocent III's reign of terror (1198-1216), the Roman Curia met 3 times a week.

July 21, 1542: Pope Paul IV established the "Supreme Sacred Congregation of the Roman and Universal Inquisition" within the Roman Curia "to maintain and defend the integrity of the faith and to examine and proscribe errors and false doctrines."

1665: Under Pope Alexander VII the "Supreme Sacred Congregation of the Roman and Universal Inquisition" reiterated that priests using the confessional to solicit or provoke sex from penitents are "alien and discordant by the Evangelical truth and clearly so by the sixth and seventh doctrines of the Holy Fathers...and are to be "checked, condemned, and prohibited...The Inquisitors of Heretical Depravity...seek out and proceed against everyone – every priest who has essayed to tempt a penitent."

1908: Pope Pius X renamed the "Supreme Sacred Congregation of the Roman and Universal Inquisition." It became the "Supreme Sacred Congregation of the Holy Office."

December 7, 1965: Under the 2nd Vatican Council "The Supreme Sacred Congregation of the Holy Office" was renamed "Sacred Congregation for the Doctrine of the Faith (SCDF).

1983-1985: All dicasteries of the Roman Curia dropped the word 'sacred.' "The Sacred Congregation for the Doctrine of the Faith" became the "Congregation for the Doctrine of the Faith" (CDF).

1988 and 2001: Pope John Paul II reaffirmed the authority of the CDF.

November 11, 2014: Pope Francis established a special body within the CDF to expedite appeals by priests against dismissal or other penalties imposed on them in cases of sexual abuse.

June 5, 2022: The CDF was renamed "Dicastery for the Doctrine of the Faith" as part of the restructuring of the Roman Curia.

Judge: It's the same office renamed four times. Overruled.

Defense Counsel: The evidence "reiterated" in 1665, combined with the 2023 report in Spain prove Catholic priests have been exploiting the confidential seal of the confessional to commit sex crimes for at least 358 years.

600s Ireland: Individual confessions to priests became common.

600-1200s: The "Penitential Books" were used to assist priests in the private counseling of confessors. The frequency which sodomy of adolescent boys and girls is mentioned in Penitential Books throughout Europe, Africa and the Middle East prove abuse was widely acknowledged during these centuries.

1051 CE: Peter Damian was an Archbishop and Cardinal, later canonized a Saint. He wrote Liber Gomorrhianus" (Book of Gomorrah.) It addressed widespread and generally accepted sexual abuse by clergy. It opens with him calling out his superiors, by name, asking for their removal. In chapter 6, he expressed contempt against priests abusing boys in the confessional. He was particularly disgusted with predator priests administering sacraments to their victims. He addressed damage sexual abuse had already done, asking Pope Leo IX to act. He responded, 972 years ago, the same way Pope Francis responds now.

What did Pope Innocent III do about priests abusing boys in the confessional? He made confession mandatory in 1215 CE. We'll let a former Catholic priest, molested himself by a priest before becoming a priest, explain how the Catholic faith and "Holy Sacrament of Reconciliation" is weaponized today. Simultaneously, it's a good example of the Torah's teaching that idolatry results in violence and injustice.

"It wasn't simply a matter of adult men having sex with children. It was the context of it, that these were men of God and often they used religious symbolism as part of the abuse. So, there was a ritual nature to quite a bit of it. And as a religious person, it seemed almost diabolical to me... I knew him from... 5 years old, and he spent all of those intervening years grooming me for the moment when he knew that I would be the most vulnerable... My mom and dad trusted him, and I trusted him. I went to him for my first confession in second grade... He always seemed to know what I was up to... he also knew what was going on in my family, because... he heard all of our confessions... The bishops are sinners, and we see their sinfulness. Yet the Pope is calling the faithful of the church to engage in penance today. He should be on his knees." (Fr. James Faluszczak)

By this point, it should be come as no surprise that in 2014, Pope Francis appointed a known career criminal to oversee the Vatican's financials. In 1966: George Pell was ordained a priest. He earned his Doctor of Philosophy in 1971. Interestingly, his thesis was titled "The exercise of authority in early Christianity from about 170 to about 270."

"Pell, 76, has been plagued by scandal for decades. In Ballarat, where he served as episcopal vicar for education from 1973 to 1984... children were beaten and sexually assaulted by priests and nuns at the St. Alipius Primary School... "a pedophile's paradise and a child's nightmare." Abuse was rampant throughout the parish... "probably the worst of Australia's 32 dioceses for sexual abuse." ... Australian Royal Commission investigating sex abuse in the church heard testimony in 2015 that all male teachers at the school were molesting children... the abuse was so traumatizing that 12 boys in a fourth-grade class of 33 committed suicide later in life." (Sex abuse scandal has followed Cardinal George Pell for decades, by Derek Hawkins, The Washington Post, June 27, 2017)

That's a 36 percent suicide rate. In 1993, Pell was accused of offering hush money to cover up sexual abuse by a priest. On February 24, 2014, Pell was appointed Prefect of the new Secretariat for the Economy of the Holy See and the Vatican City State by Pope Francis.

2018: Pell was found guilty of child sexual abuse, including penetration; but lawyers won an appeal. A court order supporting the Vatican's policy of secrecy was issued banning Cardinal Pell from being identified. Front-page newspaper headlines included "Nation's biggest story: The story we can't report" In 2019, Pell was sentenced to serve 6 years in jail and register as a sex offender. He served 404 days before lawyers won another appeal.

In 2021 the media was punished, 27 media companies were charged with contempt of court, even though none used Pell's name. Guilty pleas were exchanged for dismissing charges against 15 individual journalists. The Herald Sun, News Corp Australia, Sydney Morning Herald and 8 more media companies were fined between $162,000-$450,000 and ordered to pay $650,000 of the state's legal costs.

Chapter 21

The Children of Israel's Most Ancient Enemy Today

"Gone is the Jewish quarter. Gone are the children. Deported and murdered in World War II. Because they were Jewish. Around 1700 Jewish children from The Hague never returned. Many of them used to play here. Went to school here. Let us not forget and ensure nothing like this ever happens again."(Inscription at the Jewish Memorial at The Hague, Netherlands) More than 12,000 Jews from The Hague were murdered in concentration camps. Also engraved at this same memorial at The Hague is the following:

"Remember what Amalek did to you on the way as you came out of Egypt, how he attacked you on the way when you were faint and weary, and cut off your tail, those who were lagging behind you, and he did not fear God." (Deuteronomy 25:17-18, ESV)

October 28, 2023, Israel: "You must remember what Amalek has done to you, says our Holy Bible. And we do remember. With shared forces, with deep faith in the justice of our cause and in the eternity of Israel, we will realize the prophecy of Isaiah 60:18." (Benjamin Netanyahu)

"Violence shall no more be heard in your land, devastation or destruction within your borders; you shall call your walls Salvation, and your gates Praise." (Isaiah 60:18, ESV) "Violence" is translated from the word "Hamas."

Esau is Jacob's bother and oldest enemy (Genesis 25-32). Amalek is chief of the sons of Esau (Genesis 36:15-16.) Amalek (plural) is the ancient and recurring external enemy of the children of Israel. "He came before all of them to make war with Israel" (Rashi). Esau, the ancestor of Edom (Rome) will be destroyed "Because of the violence done to your brother Jacob, shame shall cover you, and you shall be cut off forever." (Obadiah 1:10).

Amalek is part of the Erev Rav. Basically, Moses was supposed to leave the Erev Rav-Amalek behind during the Exodus. Moses didn't because he had a big heart and thought they could be redeemed. Amalek first made war with Israel in the wilderness during the Exodus. Joshua defeated the Amalek, but not permanently. Amalek went to war with the God of Israel by going to war with the people of Israel. In the end, Amalek will be destroyed. (Exodus 17)

Why and how did Israel's ancient, violent, recurring enemy come to be?

Amalek's mother Timna tried to convert to Judaism, but was rejected by Abraham, Isaac, and Jacob. They didn't believe she wanted to convert for the right reasons. Israel's punishment for Abraham, Issac, and Jacob not welcoming her to convert is her offspring the Amalek (Genesis 32:6-Sanhedrin 99b). Josephus referred to Amalek as a "bastard."

Mount Seir is where Esau settled (Genesis 32:3, 33:14-16, 36:8, Joshua 24:4.) Edom and Mount Seir shall be a possession; and Amalek will be utterly destroyed in the end (Numbers 24:18-20, Judges 4:5, 1 Chronicles 4:42-34, 2 Chronicles 20:22-23, Isaiah 21:11, Ezekiel 25:8, 35:10).

What external enemy gave over the people of Israel to the sword, time and time again since Roman occupation 63 BCE? Esau is the ancestor of Rome. Ezekiel 35 comes right after Ezekiel 34's Prophecy Against the Shepherds.

Plaintiff: Objection! Christianity is the new Israel! Esau represents the Jews.

Judge: If Esau represents Jewish people, then who does Jacob represent?

Plaintiff: Christians. Judge: Based on what?

Plaintiff Counsel: According to the Epistle of Barnabas and Tertullian.

Judge: Even Paul, in his letter to the Romans 9:10-13, concedes that Jacob represents Israel, and his followers should be identified with Jacob. But the reason why your objection's overruled is Genesis 35:10: Jacob is Israel.

Defense Counsel: Paul, in his letter to the Romans 9:10-13 quotes Malachi 1:3 "I have loved Jacob, but I have hated Esau." Why? What has Esau done?

Plaintiff Counsel: Your honor, Defense's painted the Jews as victims of undeserving violence throughout every generation, unfairly blaming Christianity and Islam for most of it. However, the Erev Rav, which preceded Christianity and Islam by over a thousand years caused it. The reality is that Jews have caused, and continue to cause, most of the world problems.

Judge: Like what? Plaintiff: Globalist Jews trying to create a one world government to enslave us. Cashless society. Digital ID/Vaccine Passport; can't buy or sell without it. 15-

minute "smart cities," carbon tax. I can cite examples of what George Soros, Bill Gates, Klaus Schwab...

Judge: Stop. As far as I'm aware, Bill Gates isn't even Jewish. I'm warning both of you, do not attempt to embarrass or incite hatred against an entire group of people by falsely associating them with Bill Gates. Zero tolerance for slander. Even worse, blaming any group for the actions of any one person.

Defense: Jews aren't exempt from the rule that the worst enemies come from within. No surprise the first 2 words out of Plaintiff's mouth were George Soros. Typical Jew-haters cite him as their number 1 example of how evil Jews are. Maybe they don't know that Soros was leading Nazi's to his Jewish neighbors in hiding to be rounded up and sent to death camps.

Plaintiff: Your honor, did you not just warn of a zero-tolerance slander policy? I can cite multiple sources fact-checking that to be false.

Judge: Can you prove those allegations? Defense: Evidence not only proves what George Soros did, and that he has no remorse for doing it. It also proves that Snopes, Reuters, Newsweek, and whatever other fraudulent fact-checks Plaintiff was going to cite are liars too. Much like "let his blood be in our children" written anonymously while under brutal Roman Occupation...

Plaintiff: Objection! In the entire New Testament, there's no mention of any brutal Roman Occupation. Governor Pilate, a fair man, washed his hands of Jesus' blood. He's recognized as a Saint in the Ethiopian Christian Church. Claiming brutal Roman occupation is contrary to the New

Testament which makes clear that the Jews are responsible for killing Jesus.

Defense: Let that sink in. Imagine being a Jew in Nazi Occupied Poland during the Holocaust, writing an account of a rabbi who opposed Nazis. Assuming you were actually Jewish, and not writing anonymously for Nazis: Would you make it a point to mention how fair the Nazi occupiers were, with no mention ceaseless brutality?

Evidence from contemporary sources, not anonymously written, including Josephus, and Philo who described Pontius Pilot as "briberies, insults, robberies, outrages and wanton injuries, executions without trial, constantly repeated, ceaseless and supremely grievous cruelty." Do you think Roman occupied Judea was less brutal than Nazi occupied Poland?

Judge: Do you? Defense: I really don't know if I'd rather be crucified by Romans, freeze and starve to death eating 183 calories a day in Warsaw, or have Nazi doctors perform medical experiments on me at Auschwitz.

According to whoever wrote Matthew 15:26: Jesus was calling non-Jews "dogs." According to John 18:28, non-Jews are so unclean that even being in their presence would make someone else unclean. Peter wouldn't eat with non-Jews (Galatians 2:12). This hatred does not come from the Jewish Bib...

Judge: Before you go any further, provide evidence substantiating your accusations against George Soros, Snopes, Reuters, and Newsweek.

Defense: In a 1998 interview with Steve Kroft of 60 Minutes, George Soros admitted that aiding Nazis during

the Holocaust was easy, and he has no remorse
whatsoever. You can listen to the words come out of Soros
mouth yourself on YouTube or Reddit, in a video
titled ("The '60 Minutes' Interview George Soros Tried to
Ban").

Moreover, Soros' was asked if he believes in God. His is
response was "no." Claiming to be an atheist is every bit as
much breaking the covenant as getting baptized Catholic.
Rudy Giuliani said that he was "more of a Jew than Soros
is." Rabbi Pesach Lerner said Giuliani's statements were
"entirely reasonable."

This article from The New York Post, titled "How George
Soros funds 'fact checkers' to silence dissent" by Matt
Palumbo, published January 25, 2023, explains how
Plaintiff has so much fraudulent information at his
fingertips.

"Because you said, 'These two nations and these two
countries shall be mine, and we will take possession of
them'—although the LORD was there— therefore, as I live,
declares the Lord GOD, I will deal with you according to
the anger and envy that you showed because of your
hatred against them. And I will make myself known among
them, when I judge you. And you shall know that I am
the LORD." (Ezekiel 35:10-12, ESV)

What 2 nations? Israel and Judah.

Plaintiff: Objection. Relevance. That has nothing to do with
the Holy Trinity.

Judge: You've sufficiently explained how the Fourth Beast
of Daniel is relevant to the Trinity and subsequent violence.

How is the Erev Rav relevant to the fourth beast and the Trinity?

Defense: The Erev Rav and Amalek work to oppose and delay the realization of the Oneness of God. Such as banning the creed of the Oneness of God (Deut. 6:4). Or burning people at the stake for witnessing to Oneness of God. The 2 main sins of the Erev Rav are idolatry and sexual immorality. What's a more disgusting combination of idolatry and sexual immorality than Pittsburgh priests having boys pose naked like Jesus on the cross to add to their child porn collection? Judge: Overruled.

Defense: Since the Erev Rav are such an important piece to the puzzle, and the jury deserves to know, we'll start at the beginning.

"The Erev Rav went on to cause havoc and mayhem both to the Exodus generation itself..until the present. the term "Amalek" is reserved for Israel's external nemesis, the Erev Rav is the far more dangerous enemy from within. It is of them that the prophet Isaiah said… those who destroy you and ruin you emerge from within you." (Isaiah 49:17) Now, more than ever, we need to understand: Who is the Erev Rav? How can we identify them today? And, most importantly, how do we stop them?

When the Erev Rav came out of Egypt with the Israelites, they were not "Jewish" in any sense. However, the Israelites themselves were not officially "Jewish" yet either—though they were the descendants of God's chosen one, Abraham, and part of the covenantal tradition first forged with him. It was only when Israel stood at Mt. Sinai and witnessed the Divine Revelation, accepting the Torah upon themselves... The Erev Rav stood alongside them... Though they seemingly became "Jewish", they still retained all of their old idolatrous and immoral ways. Soon after, they instigated the Golden Calf incident… their method was in manipulating people's *da'at*, loosely translated as "knowledge" but referring to the deepest layers of the mind… They knew how to manipulate people psychologically… Erev Rav: they are masters of deception, subliminal messaging, and brainwashing…

like with the Golden Calf, this sin of the Erev Rav was not done privately, but was paraded before everyone, "in the sight of Moses and the whole community of Bnei Israel… the two main sins that the Erev Rav is involved with: idolatry and sexual immorality… Erev Rav is not content to sin privately, but do so publicly, and seek to inspire others to do the same… all the wicked… are the reincarnated souls of the Erev Rav… Worse yet, the Zohar (I, 25a) states that the Erev Rav will be particularly strong in the End of Days, with their final all-in push to corrupt the world…

When their temples and classrooms and organizations and corporations are empty of followers, they will lose their power. When their filthy content is no longer consumed, they will stop producing it… the Erev Rav will soon perish. The Zohar cites the **prophecy of Zechariah 13:2 as referring to the end of the Erev Rav, those "false prophets" of the "unclean spirit", who will be extinguished once and for all: And on that day— declares the God of Hosts—I will erase the very names of the idols from the land; they shall not be uttered any more. And I will also make the false prophets and the unclean spirit vanish from the land…"** (Mayim Achronim, Uncovering the depths of Torah wisdom, Israel's Greatest Enemy: The Erev Rav)

The next summary explains how Amalek is the 4th Beast.
Regarding the following: Moshe is Moses. Edom is Rome.
70 nations are the table of nations (Genesis 10:9).
Hashem is God. In Hebrew, Hashem is "The Name."

"The Talmud identifies "Erev Rav" as people who never do
kindness… Erev Rav is the source of all mixtures…They
can mix us by trying to copy us, just as they copied
Moshe's miracles. The depth of their power to "mix" is as
follows. There are 70 nations, and the Sages state
that Erev Rav is the head of all of them…

Egypt is the root of all exiles, but the four exiles are the
Babylonian exile, the Persian exile, the Greek exile, and
the exile of Edom (Esav). Within the exile of Edom, though,
is the exile of Yishmael. What, indeed, is the connection
between Edom/Esav and Yishmael? We can see it clearly.
We are in the exile of Edom, but within that, we are
surrounded by the Arabs… If we are in the exile of Edom,
how is it that we also in the exile of Yishmael? **The answer
is: they are connected together through Amalek.** The
exile of Yishmael is all due to Amalek. **Amalek exists in
order to fight the revelation of oneness of Hashem.
The force of evil that is Amalek doesn't want the
oneness of Hashem to be revealed…**

Kayin represents ability to "choose" between good and
evil, as he was told by Hashem to choose; on a deeper
level… allows evil to be a possibility in creation. Hevel
represents a higher perspective: he makes everything in
this world into hevel/nothing…. by connecting it to the point
of before creation… Kayin is about what "I acquire", that
acquisitions begin with "me." Kayin/Kinyan is the voice of
evil: "I am the beginning of everything." That is the concept
of Amalek/Erev Rav. Hevel, though, represents the power
to **be aware of what comes before the beginning.** This

is the power of Yisrael…" (bilvavi.net Erev Rav 005 Amalek EXposed)

Justinian banning a verse in his own Bible in 529 CE is a classic example of Amalek's attitude of arrogance, mockery, and contempt. And banning that particular verse, Deuteronomy 6:4, the creed of the Oneness of God, the opposite of Rome's trinity, exemplifies the mission of Amalek.

A deeper understanding, which like the Talmud and Zohar, does not supersede the plain text of the Torah, is Rabbi DovBer's (the Maggid) teaching that our "inner Esau," our evil inclination, attempts to corrupt us in two ways: through the "heat" of desire for material pleasures and "coldness" of apathy towards goodness. We counter these attacks of Esau with positive passion "heat" for holiness and apathy "coldness" towards materialism.

"Why do you spend your money for that which is not bread, and your labor for that which does not satisfy?
Listen diligently to me, and eat what is good, and delight yourselves in rich food." (Isaiah 55:2, ESV)

"For he will not take anything in his death; his glory will not descend after him." (Psalm 49:18, Chabad.org)

Part 3

Turning It Over

Chapter 22

Turning It Over: Trinities and Mediators

Defense Counsel: Moses warned of the 4th Beast long before Daniel's vision. We can go back even further to Abraham defeating the 4 Kings representing the 4 ancient empires. We're warned of the 4th Beast in Numbers 24:18-19, Isaiah 11:14, 15:1-9, 25:10, 34:1-17, 60:18, Jeremiah 9:25-26, 49:7-39, Ezekiel 25:12-14, Joel 3:19, Amos 1:11-15, Zechariah 6,12,13,14, Malachi 1:2. The entire Book of Obadiah is judgment for the timeline of 4th Beast atrocities. Ironically, the Prophet Obadiah was a convert from Edom/Rome to Judaism.

The number 4 is the biblical number for completion. The sages say to look closely at the 4 animals in Leviticus chapter 11, where we're told which animals are clean and unclean.

Clean animals have 2 signs: split hooves, and they chew the cud. The original words for chewing the cud are "ma`aleh gerah" which literally means "it turns it over and brings it up." The Torah continues describing 4 animals that should never be eaten: camel, hyrax, hare, and pig. The first 3 "turn it over" but do not have split hooves. Pigs are the only animals with split hooves that do not "turn it over." According to the sages, in addition to the plain meaning of the text, those 4 animals also represent the 4 Beasts.

The first 3 Beasts turned it over. Babylon turned it over to Persia. Persia turned it over to the Greek Empire, which turned it over to Rome. For example, Baal was deified as the "sky god" in ancient Babylonian cults long before Zeus and Jupiter were deified as sky gods in Greece and Rome.

In the original language, the word "chazar" means both "pig" and "to return to the previous condition." That's the function of a pig, which is basically meant to be a walking garbage disposal, to return that which is unclean back to the earth. The pig represents everything that is unclean. Recall Daniel 7:11, 7:26, the 4th Beast is destroyed before we return to peace, this time called the Messianic Age.

When describing the turning over of pagan-gods and cults, encyclopedias frequently use the words: transformed, discarded, reintroduced, associated with, equivalent, became, combined, mixed, emerged from, was brought to, later appeared, apparently resembled, etc. Recall, the depths of the Erev Rav's power to mix.

More than a dozen pagan trinities preceded Rome's trinity of (Father, son, Holy Spirit). The ancient Mesopotamian Anunnaki deified the trinities of: (Sin, Ishtar, Venus) and (Sin, Shamash, Ishtar) representing the moon, sun, and planet Venus. Sin was represented as an old man with a flowing beard.

In ancient Egypt, trinities included: (Osiris, Isis, Horus) – (Amun, Mut, Knonsu) – (Ptah, Sekhmet, Netertem) – (Khnum, Satet, Anuket) – (Ra, Khepri, Atum.)

Indian trinities include: (Brahma, Vishnu, Shiva.)

Hindu trinities include: (Shakti, Lakshmi, Saraswati.)

1st Beast "holy trinities" include: (Anu, Bel (Baal), and Ea). Baal was the mediator between Ea and man. Ea (Enki) was the father who willingly transferred power to his son,

Baal. In an even earlier Babylonian trinity of (Anu, Enlil, Enki), all 3 "persons" were later and separately replaced by Marduk (Baal). A later Babylon trinity was Sin (moon), Shainash (sun), and Adad (storm). Phoenicians worshipped the trinity (Ulomus, Ulosuros, Eliun).

2nd Beast: Ahura Mazda was likely worshipped alone until the reign of Artaxerxes II (404–358 BCE) when Ahura Mazda was put into a trinity with Mithra and Anahita.

3rd Beast trinities: (Zeus, Poseidon, Adonis)- (Zeus, Hades, Poseidon) – (Zeus, Athena, Apollo)

The 4th Beast had a wide variety of trinities including: (Jupiter, Neptune, Pluto) – (Jupiter, Juno, Minerva). Capitoline Hill in Rome trinities include (Jupiter, Mars, Quirinus).
Capitol Hill in Rome is where the Senate met "on the hill" like in Washington DC now. The Julian trinities of the Roman Principate: (Venus Genetrix, Divus Iulius, Clementia Carsaris) – (Divus Iulius, Divi filius "son of a god," Genius Augusti). And (Dea Roma, Divis Iulius, Genius Augusti) a religious and political trinity. Dea Roma is "Eternal Rome" the personification of Rome, later becoming the personification of Britain, and it didn't stop there. Divis Iulius was the temple. Genius Augusti was the senate.

Germanic Nations worshipped (Wodan, Thor, Fricco.)
Celtic Nations worshipped: (Criosan, Biosena, Seeva,) and the Morrígan aka "Phantom Queen" as a single deity and a trinity of goddesses.

In 381 CE, the 4th Beast's doctrine of the trinity claimed that The LORD God (Who is Holy Spirit), is 2 "separate but equal persons" as the first and third 'persons" of their trinity. According to whoever wrote Matthew, Jesus first made the claim; remember that when we get to Zechariah 13:7.

Rome inserted Jesus of Nazareth as the second person. In addition to being decreed equal to God via Rome's trinity, Jesus is simultaneously worshipped as the mediator between God and man.

In addition to being the mediator in the 1st Beast's trinity, Marduk was also deified as the savior or redeemer. Baal turned over into Marduk after his death and resurrection. According to the "Baal Cycle" of the Ugarit texts dated 1500-1300 BCE: Baal was killed by the pagan-god Mot. Anat killed Mot. Baal resurrected from the dead and built a temple on Mount Sapon.

Marduk is Baal, one of Baal's many names, over 100, including: Mardon, Adad, Hadad, Iskur, Baal-Hamon, Baal-Hazor, Baal-Zephon (Exodus 14:2, Numbers 33:7), Baal-Hadad-Moloch (god of child sacrifice, Jeremiah 32:35) Belos, Zeus-Baal-Hadad. Marduk literally means "bull calf of the sun."

In the Bible: Baals, and baalem are plural. Baal or baalem can be applied to any and every god, except The LORD God of Abraham, Issac, and Jacob alone (Exodus 3:15, 20:1-3, Numbers 23:19, Deut. 6:4, Isaiah 42:8, etc.)

"And the people of Israel did what was evil in the sight of the LORD and served the Baals. And they abandoned the LORD, the God of their fathers, who had brought them out of the land of Egypt. They went after other gods, from among the gods of the peoples who were around them, and bowed down to them. And they provoked the LORD to anger. They abandoned the LORD and served the Baals and the Ashtaroth" (Judges 2:11-13, ESV)

The following have been worshipped as 'dying and rising' or 'resurrection gods' preceding Jesus: Baal/Marduk, Nimrod, Dumuzid/ Tammuz, Osiris, Dionysus "the sin bearer," Bacchus, Iacchus, Helios, Aion, Adonis, Mithra "the mediator." Baldor, Zagreus, Izanami, Quetzalcóatl, Outwitting Death, Bodhidharma.

"... Baal who was worshipped in Ugarit, and Tammuz or Dumuzi as he was known to the Babylonians. In Egypt, he was Osiris, the god of resurrection... transferring the myth of Adonis and Astarte from the Canaanite regions to the Greeks – and from the latter to the Romans..." (World History Encyclopedia, Adonis, From The Canaanite Adon To The Greek Adonis)

There are differing accounts of Baal the mediator's alleged death and alleged resurrection, just like there are for Osiris, Tammuz, Jesus...

Plaintiff: OBJECTION! False! The gospels are not differing accounts of Jesus' resurrection! The four gospel accounts harmonize perfectly.

Defense: We can go through point by point on the following: Number of women at the tomb: 1,2,3, or 5? Were they men according to Mark and Luke, or angels according to Matthew and John? Did Jesus' resurrected body appear to his disciples in Galilee according to Matthew, or in Jerusalem according to the other 3 anonymous gospel authors?

Judge: Going through point-by-point isn't necessary. Overruled.

Defense: Good, because we're making a much deeper point than contradictory gospel accounts added to the Bible by Pontifex Maximus/Pope Damasus I. Recall, since 672 BCE, the Pontifex Maximus' job is to carry on the traditions of Babylonian turned over into Roman ancient cults.

Worship of Baal/Marduk was lambasted by Moses and Samuel prior to the 1st Beast. Jeremiah, Ezekiel, and Hosea follow with the same message into the 1st Beast period (Babylon). Veneration of Baal continued, turning over via Mithraism and Zoroastrianism throughout the 2nd Beast period (Persia).

2nd Beast "Mysteries of the Persians" then mixed with religious practices of the cult of Cybele-Attis, which turned over into the Greco-Roman (3rd and 4th beast) religions known as "Modified Mithraism" and "Roman Mithraism." They spread with the cults of Bacchus and Sol Invictus, becoming popular throughout the Roman Empire, until the late 4th century.

Ironically, the Catholic Encyclopedia does an excellent job explaining the turning over of Mithraism from the end of the 2nd Beast period, through the 3rd, and into the 4th. Even admitting language of their trinity "begat Heaven and Earth, which in turn begat their son and equal" came from Mithraism.

"The origin of the cult of Mithra dates from the time that the Hindus and Persians still formed one people... A pagan religion consisting mainly of the cult of the ancient Indo-Iranian Sun-god Mithra... spread rapidly over the whole Roman Empire... reached its zenith during the third century, and vanished under the repressive regulations of

Theodosius at the end of the fourth century... national worship of Marduk. For a time the two priesthoods of Mithra and Marduk (magi and chaldaei respectively) coexisted in the capital and Mithraism borrowed much from this intercourse. This modified Mithraism traveled farther northwestward... it came into contact with the Phrygian cult of Attis and Cybele from which it adopted a number of ideas and practices... Mithraism was Masonry amongst the Roman soldiery. At the same time Eastern slaves and foreign tradesmen maintained its propaganda. ... But with the triumph of Christianity Mithraism came to a sudden end... The laws of Theodosius I signed its death warrant. The magi walled up their sacred caves; and Mithra has no martyrs to rival the martyrs who died for Christ... the first principle or highest God was according to Mithraism "Infinite Time"... an **ancient Iranian conception**, which survived the sharp dualism of Zoroaster... This first principle **begat Heaven and Earth, which in turn begat their son and equal**... **the sun becomes in a sense Mithra's double, or again his father, but Helios Mithras is one god**... saved by Mithra. Finally, man is well established on earth and Mithra returns to heaven. He celebrates a last supper with Helios and his other companions... now in heaven... **Mithra is the Mediator (Mesites) between God and man**... They believed in the immortality of the soul, sinners after death were dragged off to hell... they stood before God. At the end of the world Mithra will descend to earth on another bull, which he will sacrifice, and mixing its fat with **sacred wine he will make all drink the beverage of immortality**..." (Catholic Encyclopedia: Mithraism-New Advent)

The sacred wine of immortality turned over from the 3rd into the 4th Beast.

"The Jews then disputed among themselves, saying, "How can this man give us his flesh to eat?" So Jesus said to them, "Truly, truly, I say to you, unless you eat the flesh of the Son of Man and drink his blood, you have no life in you. Whoever feeds on my flesh and drinks my blood has eternal life, and I will raise him up on the last day." (John 6:52-54, ESV)

"Then he will say, 'Where are their gods, the rock in which they took refuge, who ate the fat of their sacrifices and drank the wine of their drink offering? Let them rise up and help you; let them be your protection!" (Deuteronomy 32:37-38, ESV)

Continuing from the Catholic Encyclopedia: "... seven degrees of initiation into the Mithraic mysteries. The fathers conducted the worship. The chief of the fathers, a sort of pope, who always lived at Rome... sacred meal was celebrated of bread and haoma juice for which in the West wine was substituted... Sunday was kept holy in honour of Mithra, and the sixteenth of each month was sacred to him as mediator. The 25 December was observed as his birthday, the natalis invicti, the rebirth of the winter-sun... associations to worship Anaitis-Cybele... A similarity between Mithra and Christ struck even early observers, such as Justin, Tertullian, and other Fathers, and in recent times has been urged to prove that Christianity is but an adaptation of Mithraism... Mithra is called a mediator; and so is Christ... Mithra saved the world by sacrificing a bull; Christ by sacrificing Himself... Mithraism was all comprehensive and tolerant of every other cult, the Pater Patrum himself was an adept in a number of other religions; Christianity was essential exclusive, condemning every other religion in the world, alone and unique in its majesty." (Catholic Encyclopedia: Mithraism-New Advent)

"…the Romans adopted the pantheon of Greek gods, although they changed many of their names. However, besides this array of deities, they also acquired several of their cults… Under this Greek influence, the Roman gods became more human… However, unlike in Greece, in Rome an individual's self-expression of belief was not considered as important as adherence to ritual… almost all of these cults disappeared with the arrival of Christianity when Rome became the center of this new religion. The Cult of Cybele lasted until the 4th century CE, at which time Christianity dominated the religious landscape and pagan beliefs and rituals gradually became transformed or discarded to suit the new faith." (World History Encyclopedia, Cybele)

"Under this Greek influence, the Roman gods became more human." Greek Dionysus turned over into Roman Bacchus. 3rd Beast' Dionysus was the first pagan-god not having 2 lower-case-g gods for parents became Bacchus. Jesus of Nazareth would be the next god to have a human mother.

The most famous and widely worshipped resurrection gods through the exiles: Egypt: Osirus
1st Beast Babylon: Marduk, Tammuz
2nd Medo-Persia: Mithra

3rd Greek: Adonis, Attis, Dionysus

4th Rome: Bacchus, Jesus

In 2 Kings 18:5 we're told that King Hezekiah was and always will be the greatest Judaic King of all time. No king, including the future messiah will be greater. Why? Because he "…broke the pillars and cut down the Asherah.

And he broke in pieces the bronze serpent..." (2 Kings
18:4).

"The Egyptians, the Babylonians and the Persians rose,
filled the planet with sound and splendor, then faded to
dream-stuff and passed away; the Greeks and Romans
followed and made a vast noise, and they were gone...The
Jew saw them all, survived them all." (Mark Twain)

Chapter 23

Turning Over: Queens of Heaven

Catholics venerate Mary "Queen of Heaven," "Blessed Mary ever virgin," and "Holy Mary Mother of God," all referring to Jesus' mother. Muslims also venerate Mary as the perpetual virgin mother of Jesus whom they consider to be a prophet. Muslims reverence for Mary AKA Maryam is second only to Catholics. Maryam is the only woman named in the Quran; in which she is "above the women of the worlds." However, Muslims do not tolerate the claim that anyone is God's mother because they know God is not a man and doesn't have a mother, or father. (Numbers. 23:19, Isaiah chapters 40-46).

In preparation for this trial, we listened to videos of Catholic priests lecturing on how holy the Queen of Heaven is. They even point out that the Queen of Heaven is found in the Old Testament. As does the New Advent Catholic Encyclopedia (Blessed Virgin Mary) which has the audacity to reference Jeremiah chapters 3 and 31. Yet, like the priests, do not mention Jeremiah chapters 7 and 44, where Queen of Heaven veneration couldn't be further from the blatant and easily verifiable lies Catholic priests are teaching today.

"Moloch coincided with the introduction of the worship of the "queen of the heaven," ... The worship of the Moloch along with the worship of the "queen of the heaven" are therefore to be seen against the background of the widespread worship in the Assyro-Aramean culture of Adad/Hadad, the king, and Ishtar Ashtarth/Anath, the queen... "abhorrence,"... found in Jeremiah 7:18, and 44:19..." (Jewish Virtual Library, The Cult of Moloch)

Venerating the Queen of Heaven preceded the 1st Beast and turned over through all 4. Isis, Nut, Ashtoreth AKA Astarte AKA Inanna (Ishtar), Anat, Cybele, and Mary. Most Queens of Heaven were the mother, sometimes sister, of dying and rising gods that were often included in a trinity.

Here's a brief progression Queen of Heaven worship/veneration/idolatry, starting before the 1st Beast, and turning over through all 4. Queens of Heaven, "Mother and child," and 'ashtoreths' turned over like the baals.

Isis was venerated as "Queen of Heaven" and as part of a trinity in Egypt preceding the 1st Beast.

"Isis... Her brother Osirus is her husband, and after his death, she conceives the child Horus the Younger with him using magical means... she is the "Queen of Heaven." ... she assimilated the traits and followers of several lesser goddesses..."
(museumofmythology.com/Egypt/Isis)

"Isis... and her husband and son replaced the Theban Triad of Amon, Mut, and Khons, who had been the most popular trinity of gods in Egypt. Osiris, Isis, and Horus are referred to as the Abydos Triad. Her cult began in the Nile Delta... worshiped by the Greeks and the Romans... Her cult in Rome was the greatest rival to the young religion of Christianity, which drew upon the image of Isis and the child-god Horus for the depiction of the Madonna with the Christ child. Her cult would remain one of the most popular in the ancient Mediterranean until Christianity triumphed over the pagan faiths in the 4th-6th centuries CE, and worship of Isis was outlawed along with that of the other pagan gods." (World History Encyclopedia, Isis)

Astarte AKA Ashtoreth was venerated prior to, and during, the 1st Beast period (Babylon) and turned over throughout all 4. Centuries after Samuel, the Prophet Jeremiah continually lambasted idolaters for worshiping the Queen of Heaven. More information can be found in Judges 2:13, 6:30, 2 Kings 16, Isaiah 57:3-10, Hosea 13, Jeremiah 7:16-25 & 44:2-25.

"Hebrew scholars now feel that the goddess Ashtoreth mentioned so often in the Bible is a deliberate conflation of the Greek name Astarte and the Hebrew word boshet, "shame," indicating the Hebrews' contempt for her cult. Ashtaroth, the plural form of the goddess's name in Hebrew, became a general term denoting goddesses and paganism. King Solomon, married to foreign wives, "followed Astarte the goddess of the Sidonians" (1 Kings 11:5). Later the cult places to Ashtoreth were destroyed by Josiah. Astarte/Ashtoreth is the Queen of Heaven to whom the Canaanites burned offerings and poured libations (Jeremiah 44)..." (Encyclopedia Brittanica, Astarte)

Astarte/Ashtoreth turned over and was identified with (became) other pagan goddesses though the 2nd, 3rd and 4th beasts. Astarte is Ashtoreth is Ishtar, the Queen of Heaven that The LORD God through the Prophet Jeremiah lambasted the children of Israel for venerating.

"**Ishtar is the** Akkadian **counterpart of** the West Semitic goddess Astarte. **Inanna**, an important goddess in the Sumerian pantheon, **came to be identified with Ishtar...** her similarity to Ishtar caused the two to be identified. In the figure of Inanna several traditions seem to have been combined... she was known as Queen of the Universe..." (Encyclopedia Brittanica, Ishtar)

"Ishtar, by various names, continued to be an important deity until the advent of Christianity in the Roman empire and Islam in the Arabic world and Persia... In Babylon, she was sometimes portrayed **Madonna-like as the mother of the god Marduk.** In later times, it should be noted, the **priestesses of Ishtar were virgins who were not permitted to marry**..." (New World Encyclopedia, Ishtar)

"Anath, the sister and helpmate of the god Baal... she was often designated "the Virgin" in ancient texts... she was primarily known for her role in the myth of **Baal's death and resurrection**... **Anath and Astarte were blended into one deity**, called Atargatis..." (Encyclopedia Brittanica, Anath)

"II Kings 17... Anammelech who has been correctly related by scholars to Anath who bears the title "Queen of Heaven," the standard term for Ishtar in Akkadian (*šarrat šamê*; cf. Sum. *nin.anna.ak* = Inanna). The pair Adad and Ishtar, or the "king" and the "queen," are the ones to whom children are dedicated... Atargatis (= combination of Ishtar and Anath) who listen to prayer...The worship of the Moloch along with the worship of the "queen of the heaven" are therefore to be seen against the background of the widespread worship... of Adad/Hadad, the king, and Ishtar Ashtarth/Anath, the queen, that began in the ninth-eighth century B.C.E... Amos 5:26 ... "abhorrence," ... of your image[s] the star of your god[s] which you made for yourselves." The *kamānu/kawānu*, found in Jeremiah 7:18 and 44:19, is a cultic cake in the form of a star which is the image of Ishtar, who is called in Akkadian *kakkab šamê*, "the star of the Heaven." The image of Ishtar... "Your king" in this verse is none other than her consort, Adad the king, sometimes identical with the sun-god Shamash." (Jewish Virtual Library, The Cult of Moloch)

Cybele-Attis cult worship turned over through the 3rd and into the 4th Beast. Cybele's the mother of one of the 3rd Beast resurrection gods: Attis. Due to Dionysus, Bacchus, and Jesus having human mothers, Cybele is the last non-human woman to be widely venerated as Queen of Heaven. Let's find out how the Greco-Roman Cybele brings us to Rome's Mary.

"Cybele... worship spread... Cybele's cult in Greece was closely associated with, and apparently resembled, the cult of Dionysus... Cybele was worshiped by the Greek population as "The Mother of the Gods, the Savior who Hears our Prayers" and as "The Mother of the Gods, the Accessible One."... Roman devotion to Cybele ran deep. **Not coincidentally, when a Christian basilica was built over the site of a temple to Cybele to occupy the site, it was syncretistically dedicated as the Basilica di Santa Maria Maggiore**... The popularity of the Cybele cult in the city of Rome and throughout the empire is thought to have inspired the author of Book of Revelation to allude to her in his portrayal of the mother of harlots who rides the Beast... her son, Attis, who was castrated and resurrected. Her most ecstatic followers were males who ritually castrated themselves, and then assumed "female" identities by wearing women's clothing... The evergreen pine and ivy were sacred to Attis..." (New World Encyclopedia, Cybele)

"It is well known that Pope Francis has a great personal devotion to our Blessed Mother, Mary... he always goes to the Basilica of St. Mary Major [Santa Maria Maggiore] in Rome to offer a prayer to Our Lady. He prays before the Blessed Sacrament, which is reserved in a tabernacle with a golden relief of the Coronation of Mary... While, obviously, Mary is not part of the Trinity, nor the Redeemer, she has an essential role in redemption...

Mary's coronation is depicted in a manner that does not make her part of the Trinity but gives a sense of completion to the Trinity's involvement in our lives... Mary truly is Queen of Heaven and Earth in the same manner as Jesus is King... The feast of the Queenship of Mary was established by Pope Pius XII in 1954 just after he had infallibly declared the dogma of the Assumption of Mary into Heaven. In his encyclical letter, Ad Caeli Reginam, proclaiming the Queenship of Mary... Pope Francis has urged us to "knock at the door of Mary."... Mary, Queen of Heaven and Earth, pray for us!" (Living the Truth in Love-The Queenship of Mary by Rev. Gerald M. Barbarito Bishop of Palm Beach)

"Yet I persistently sent to you all my servants the prophets, saying, 'Oh, do not do this abomination that I hate!' But they did not listen or incline their ear, to turn from their evil and make no offerings to other gods." (Jeremiah 44:4-5, ESV)

Chapter 24

Weeping for Tammuz into Weeping for Jesus and Easter

Throughout Ezekiel chapter 8, The LORD God is showing Ezekiel "vile abominations" that get progressively worse. The women weeping for Tammuz' death in Ezekiel 8 brings us to Mary Magdaline weeping for Jesus' death in John 20.

The annual weeping for Tammuz (1st Beast) tuned over into Attis' annual spring Holy Week (3rd Beast). It began with entering of reeds, days later Attis' death was remembered, culminating with the celebration of Attis' rising from the dead on Hilaria. That turned over into Jesus' Holy Week (4th Beast), beginning with Palm Sunday, days later Jesus' death is remembered, culminating with the celebration Jesus rising from the dead on Easter.

From the annual Weeping for Tammuz to Lent and Easter, there's other cult traditions mixed in. The most relevant progression from 1st Beast to 4th of celebrating the annual death of dying and rising gods, before celebrating his resurrection is Baal-Tammuz-Attis-Jesus. To keep this convoluted mixing and turning over as simple as possible we'll stick to those 4. Here's the evidence:

Preceding the Weeping for Tammuz: "... mimicking the mourning of Anat in the period between Baal's death and resurrection." (New World Encyclopedia, Baal)

Weeping For Tammuz: "Among the earliest rites were those observed for the dying and reviving god figure, Tammuz, known by scholars today as rituals of ceremonial mourning in which the god dies and returns to life... These festivals followed the same basic paradigm as those observed earlier by Sumerian kings and served the same purpose: to honor the gods, legitimize the king's rule, and unite the people in religious belief and practice." (World History Encyclopedia, Festivals in Ancient Mesopotamia)

Weeping for Tammuz into the 3rd and 4th Beasts: "Hilaria, in Roman religion, day of merriment and rejoicing in the Cybele-Attis cult and in the Isis-Osiris cult, March 25 and November 3, respectively. It was one of several days in the festival of Cybele that honoured Attis, her son and lover... March 24, fasting and mourning at his death; and March 25, the Hilaria, rejoicing at his resurrection**...** November 3, the Hilaria of the Isis-Osiris cult, marked **the** resurrection of Osiris..." (Encyclopedia Brittanica, Hilaria)

The following cult rituals of Attis' directly preceded the 4th Beasts' fasting during Lent, entering with palms on Palm Sunday, Jesus' death on Good Friday, Jesus' resurrection on Easter:

"...the cult reached Rome around the end of the 3rd century BCE... eventually achieved official recognition during the reign of Emperor Claudius (41 - 44 CE) ... offering immortality to her adherents... Attis as an early dying-and-reviving god... It began on March 15 with a procession of reed-bearers (cannophori) and a ritual sacrifice... On March 22, after a week of fasting and purification, a pine tree (the symbol for Attis) was brought to Palatine Hill temple. Later, there was a banquet — a day of joy or Hilaria. Next came the Day of Blood, March 24, representing the castration and death of Attis. The celebration closed on the March 25 with a ritual bath or lavation of Cybele's image... almost all of these cults disappeared with the arrival of Christianity when Rome became the center of this new religion. The Cult of Cybele lasted until the 4th century CE, at which time Christianity dominated the religious landscape and pagan beliefs and rituals gradually became transformed or discarded to suit the new faith." (World History Encyclopedia, Cybele)

Let's take a step back chronologically from Attis to Tammuz. Then we'll go straight from Babylon to Rome. Women weeping for Tammuz in Ezekiel 8:14 to Mary Magdaline weeping for Jesus in John 20:11-15, where we're told she was the first witness to Jesus' resurrection.

"As shown by his most common epithet, Sipad (Shepherd), Tammuz was essentially a pastoral deity...When the cult of Tammuz spread to Assyria in the 2nd and 1st millennia BCE, the character of the god seems to have changed from that of a pastoral to that of an agricultural deity... The cult of Tammuz centred around two yearly festivals—one celebrating his marriage to the goddess Inanna, the other lamenting his death... The celebrations in March–April that marked the death of the god also seem to have been dramatically performed... date palm..." (Encyclopedia Brittanica, Tammuz)

Dumuzi is Tammuz. Like the dying and rising god preceding him, Baal is Marduk. The names are often used interchangeably. Also note that Ezekiel 18 destroys Cult of Tammuz' dogma of Vicarious Atonement (someone else dying or paying the price for anyone else's sins).

"...in the end, Inanna/Ishtar was resurrected ...the god died...Commenting on this myth, Powell offers the following interpretation: "Inanna's descent to the underworld is her death, and the end of fertility on earth. Her return to the upper world is her resurrection, the return of life on earth. But, in this case her consort Dumuzi. Herein lies the logic of ritual (even human) sacrifice… Tammuz could have been a mortal man apotheosized through the love of Ishtar/Inanna, archaeologists have recently discovered a list of Sumerian kings that includes two monarchs named Dumuzi: Dumuzid of Bad-Tibira, the shepherd... [and] Dumuzid of Kua, the fisherman... parallels between Middle Eastern deities and the resurrected Christ. For instance, it is in this vein that Paul Carus states: "The ancient Tammuz is one of the most important prototypes of Christ. He is a god-man, an incarnation of the deity who is born as a human being, dies in the course of time and eakes to life again." (New World Encyclopedia, Tammuz)

"He said also to me, "You will see still greater abominations that they commit." Then he brought me to the entrance of the north gate of the house of the LORD, and behold, there sat **women weeping for Tammuz**. Then he said to me, "Have you seen this, O son of man? **You will see still greater abominations than these**." (Ezekiel 8:13-15, ESV)

"In cult practice, the dead Tammuz was widely mourned in the Ancient Near East. A Sumerian tablet (Ni 4486 from Nippur reads:

"She can **make the lament for you**, my Dumuzid, **the lament for you**, the lament..she can make it reach the shepherding country, the **sheepfold** of Dumuzid "O Dumuzid of the fair-spoken mouth, of the ever kind eyes," **she sobs tearfully**, "O you of the fair-spoken mouth, of the ever kind eyes," **she sobs tearfully**. "Lad, husband, **lord,** sweet as the date…O Dumuzid!" **she sobs, she**

sobs tearfully...**" These ceremonies were observed
even at the very door of the Temple in Jerusalem, to
the horror of the Jewish prophet Ezekiel**..." (New World
Encyclopedia, Tammuz)

"... Mary stood weeping outside the tomb, and as **she
wept** she stooped to look into the tomb. And she saw two
angels in white... They said to her, **"Woman, why are you
weeping?"**... she turned around and saw Jesus standing,
but she did not know that it was Jesus. Jesus said to her,
"Woman, why are you weeping? Whom are you
seeking?" Supposing him to be the **gardener**..." (John
20:11-15, ESV)

"Then he said to me, "Have you seen this, O son of man?
You will see still greater abominations than these." And
he brought me into the inner court of the house of the
LORD. And behold, at the entrance of the temple of the
LORD, between the porch and the altar, were about
twenty-five men, with their backs to the temple of the
LORD, and their faces **toward the east, worshiping the
sun toward the east.**" (Ezekiel 8:15-16, ESV)

"The word "Easter" comes from Old English, meaning
simply the "East." The sun which rises in the East, bringing
light, warmth, and hope, is a symbol for the Christian of the
rising Christ...The Easter Vigil is the "Mother of All Vigils"...
All faith flows from faith in the resurrection: "If Christ has
not been raised, then empty is our preaching; empty, too,
is your faith." (1 Cor 15:14)...Just as we have borne the
image of the earthly one, we shall also bear the image of
the heavenly one." (1 Cor 15:36-37, 42-49)" (United States
Conference of Catholic Bishops)

"The word Magi refers to a class of ancient Zoroastrian
astrologer-priests who once lived in the Persian Empire.

Today, the word is most commonly used in Christian circles to denote the *Three Wise Men* (Magi), who came "from the East to Jerusalem," following a bright star, to worship the Infant Jesus (Matthew 2:1) ... their gifts were gold, frankincense, and myrrh... Some translations of the Bible, such as the King James Version and the New Revised Standard Version, render *magos* as "Wise Men." Yet, the same Greek word is rendered as "sorcerer" or magician in the account of "Elymas" the sorcerer in Acts of the Apostles 13. The term is also used to identify Simon Magus in Acts 8... Mithraism, a religion derived from Persia, was the largest single religion in Rome... According to the Gospel of Matthew the Magi were the first religious figures to worship Christ... Christian groups, such as the Jehovah's Witnesses, who do not see the arrival of the Magi as something to be celebrated. They stress the biblical condemnation of sorcery and astrology in such texts as Deuteronomy 18:10, Deuteronomy 18:11, Leviticus 19:26, Isaiah 47:13, and Isaiah 47:14..." (New World Encyclopedia, Magi)

"And the LORD said to him, "Pass through the city, through Jerusalem, and put a mark on the foreheads of the men who sigh and groan over all the abominations that are committed in it." (Ezekiel 9:4, ESV)

They turned that into the opposite: A cross marked on foreheads of participants in a 40-day period of fasting in preparation the 4th Beast's dying and rising god. Pope Gregory 1 (590-604) established Ash Wednesday as the first day of Lent. In 1091 Pope Urban II decreed "on Ash Wednesday, everyone—clergy and laity, men and women will receive ashes."

Enter with palms a week before, the pagan-god dies, there's mourning, the pagan-god rises, celebration. **The**

most important point is that no dying and rising god is anyone's savior according to Isaiah 42:8 - 43:11.

Most relevant cult progression into Easter: Baal-Tammuz-Attis-Jesus.

Cult progression into Christmas: Mithra-Sol Invictus-Dionysus-Jesus.

At least a few resurrection god's "birthdays" are on December 25th. Most Christian scholars concede that Jesus of Nazareth was born in the late spring or early summer. However, December 25 is the most logical time to celebrate Jesus' birthday. The winter solstice has always been the standard time for cults to celebrate the "birth" of dying and rising pagan sun-gods along with the "rebirth of the sun." Spring has always been the standard time that man-gods rise from the dead. Recall the timeline December 25, 336.

From the 1st Beast to the 4th, idolators have been making up holidays to pagan gods. The mockery of the 4th Beast is that most Christians know Santa Claus, the Easter Bunny, eating swine, painting eggs, and maxing out credit cards in December have nothing to do with God's holidays. They question this stuff as children. Presents and artificially colored sugar help the lies go down. Evangelicals argue about how pagan Halloween is. Imagine if they knew what cults that Easter and Christmas were turned over from.

The words Easter and Christmas aren't even in Rome's New Greek Testament. Except for one blatantly fraudulent mistranslation of the word 'Passover' to 'Easter' in Acts 12:4 only in the Kings James Version. Every other English Bible version accurately translated the Greek word for

Passover all 29 times the word Passover is mentioned in the New Testament.

What does God think of turned over pagan holidays, celebrated by people who've never made any attempt to celebrate or teach their children any of God's holidays that are for all generations, as instructed in their own Bible?

"I hate, I despise your feasts, and I take no delight in your solemn assemblies." (Amos 5:21, ESV)

"Do not add to the word which I command you, nor diminish from it, to observe the commandments of the Lord your God which I command you." (Deuteronomy 4:2, Chabad.org)

"Beware, lest you be attracted after them, after they are exterminated from before you; and lest you inquire about their gods, saying, "How did these nations serve their gods? And I will do likewise."

You shall not do so to the Lord, your God; for every abomination to the Lord which He hates, they did to their gods, for also their sons and their daughters they would burn in fire to their gods." (Deuteronomy 12:30-31, Chabad.org)

When you come to appear before Me, who requested this of you, to trample My courts?

You shall no longer bring vain meal-offerings, it is smoke of abomination to Me; New Moons and Sabbaths, calling convocations, I cannot [bear] iniquity with assembly.

Your New Moons and your appointed seasons My soul hates, they are a burden to Me; I am weary of bearing [them].

And when you spread out your hands, I will hide My eyes from you, even when you pray at length, I do not hear; your hands are full of blood.

Wash, cleanse yourselves, remove the evil of your deeds from before My eyes, cease to do evil.

Learn to do good, seek justice, strengthen the robbed, perform justice for the orphan, plead the case of the widow. (Isaiah 1:12-17, Chabad.org)

Chapter 25

Turning Over the Pinecone

Defense Counsel: Recall the timeline 753-716 BCE. Did Romulus get his temple to Jupiter in Rome?

Today, we can see several statues of Jupiter, including Claudius as Jupiter, seated Jupiter, etc. As well as plenty of statues of Zeus among more than 70,000 idols that people stand in line to venerate at the Vatican. Not to mention, a large telescope named Lucifer.

Most relevant sky-gods: 1st Beast: Baal – 2nd Beast: Ahura Mazda – 3rd Beast: Zeus – 4th Beast: Jupiter.

I'm going to walk you through these images of ancient engravings:

Baal seated on a throne with his right foot out so people could kiss it.

Jupiter seated on a throne with his left foot out.

And this photo taken at the Vatican: Statue of Peter on the throne. Peter's right foot sticking out just like Baals is worn down from so many people kissing it.

We submit these images of of: Baal, Marduk, Asheroth, Astarte, Nimrod, Cybele, Zeus, Jupiter Sabazios, Tammuz, Nisroch, and Dionysus each holding a pinecone.

I'll walk you through the most relevant images, starting with Egypt:

This is Osiris with his pinecone tipped staff.

1st Beast: Baal AKA Marduk with wings among fruits and pinecones, and Baal's holding out a pinecone.

2nd and 3rd beasts: "Thyrsus Wand", or magic wand tipped with a pinecone associated with the cults of Dionysus.

3rd and 4th beasts: Attis holding a shepherd's crook and pinecone.

4th Beast: These are pictures of various bishops holding what appears to be the same shepherd's crook. In several Christian churches, including the Roman Catholic, it's called a crozier or crosier AKA pastoral staff, or bishop's staff.

Next, this is statue of a giant pinecone called "Fontana della Pigna" which previously stood at the Temple of Isis. It now stands at the "Courtyard of the Pine" at the Vatican. In the Divine Comedy, Dante references Rome's pinecone to describe Nimrod's head: "His face appeared to me as long and large. As is at Rome the pine-cone of Saint Peter's"

"Sacrifices in the garden" with stylized tree branches are tied to the Cult of Tammuz and Ishtar are lambasted by The LORD through the Prophets Isaiah 1:29-30, 17:10, 65:1-4, 66:17, Ezekiel 8,9,33. Jeremiah 17, 44. Prior to that, worship of the baals and Ashtoreth involving the same was excoriated in Leviticus, Judges, and Kings.

"Great Mother of the Gods, ancient Oriental and Greco-Roman deity, known by a variety of local names; the name Cybele... her lover, the fertility god Attis, had emasculated himself under a pine tree, where he bled to death. At

Cybele's annual festival (March 15–27), a pine tree was cut and brought to her shrine, where it was honoured as a god... the altar and the sacred pine with their blood..." (Encyclopedia Britannica, Great Mother of the Gods, Ancient Greek and Roman Deities)

Even the site of the Vatican was turned over from the 3rd to the 4th Beast. From Cybele and Attis to Mary and Jesus. "Even before the arrival of Christianity... The area was also the site of worship to the Phrygian goddess Cybele and her consort Attis during Roman times." (New World Encyclopedia, Vatican City) Cybele was Attis' mother and lover. There is no evidence of incest between Mary and Jesus. Only gospel accounts of Mary becoming pregnant not by the man she was engaged to, apparently without prior knowledge or consent from her or Joseph.

In 1506 Pope Julius II commissioned the Belvedere Courtyard (known as the Courtyard of the Pine) to connect the Vatican Palace with the Sistine Chapel. In 1608 Pope Paul V moved the 4-meter-tall idol of the pinecone from Old Saint Peter's Basilica to the courtyard.

"Founded on the initiative of Pope Gregory XVI in 1839, the Gregorian Egyptian Museum occupies nine rooms, with a broad hemicycle that opens onto the terrace of the of the "Niche of the Pinecone", in which various sculptures are located...intended to invoke the environs of the Nile. The collection is particularly interesting on account of its relationship with the territory, rich in material from Roman Egypt and from Egyptian-influenced Rome. Indeed, many monuments from the most ancient nucleus were brought to Rome at the behest of the emperor to embellish buildings, shrines, and villas, such as the statuary group of the Gardens of Sallust (Horti Sallustiani), now displayed in the hemicycle. There are also many Egyptian works of Roman production…" (MVSEI VATICANI, museivaticani.va)

"At the head of every street you built your lofty place and made your beauty an abomination, offering yourself to any passerby and multiplying your whoring. You also played the whore with the Egyptians, your lustful neighbors, multiplying your whoring, to provoke me to anger." (Ezekiel 16:25-26, ESV)

Part 4

Zechariah 13

Chapter 26

The Great Awakening of Jeremiah 16 and Zechariah 13

Why is prophecy about the entire world finding out the truth, about the false prophet shepherd who is identified by wounds between his hands in-between 2 chapters about the Final War? What happens to those who go to War against The LORD God of Israel by going against the people of Israel?

"And this shall be the plague with which the Lord will strike all the peoples that wage war against Jerusalem: their flesh will rot while they are still standing on their feet, their eyes will rot in their sockets, and their tongues will rot in their mouths." (Zechariah 14:12, ESV) Why?

"Because you cherished perpetual enmity and gave over the people of Israel to the power of the sword at the time of their calamity, at the time of their final punishment, therefore, as I live, declares the Lord GOD, I will prepare you for blood, and blood shall pursue you; because you did not hate bloodshed, therefore blood shall pursue you." (Ezekiel 35:5-6, ESV)

What's the good news? What happens to people who don't do that?

Sukkot, Feast of Booths, Feast of Tabernacles, and Festival of Shelters are all the exact same holiday. The date, instructions on how to celebrate, and why, are given in Leviticus 23:33-42. After the great awakening of Zechariah 13 and Final War eclipse the Exodus as the greatest miracles of all time, who will keep The LORD God's appointed holiday of Sukkot?

"Then everyone who survives of all the nations that have come against Jerusalem shall go up year after year to worship the King, the LORD of hosts, and to keep the Feast of Booths." (Zechariah 14:16, ESV)

In the final generation before the Messianic Age, a progression of events will surpass the Exodus as the greatest miracles in recorded history (Jeremiah 16:14-15, 23:7, Zechariah 13:1-9, Psalm 22:27, Isaiah 52:15, Daniel 12:1-2). Zechariah chapters 8-14 take place "in those days." The message delivered by Jeremiah (ch.16, 17) and Zechariah (8,13,14) is heavily tilted towards non-Jews from the ends of the earth. The Messianic Age is for everyone. The whole world finds out the truth. Many turn back to The LORD God alone.

"O Lord, my strength and my stronghold, my refuge in the day of trouble, to you shall the nations come from the ends of the earth and say:
"Our fathers have inherited nothing but lies, worthless things in which there is no profit. Can man make for himself gods?
Such are not gods!" (Jeremiah 16:19-20, ESV)

After realizing they inherited lies and vanity, fraudulent context altering mistranslations, and pagan holidays: What are the nations going to do in the last days before the Messianic Age?

"Thus saith the LORD of hosts; In those days it shall come to pass, that ten men shall take hold out of all languages of the nations, even shall take hold of the skirt of him that is a

Jew, saying, We will go with you: for we have heard that God is with you." (Zechariah 8:23, KJV)

How humbling might that be for Southern Baptist missionaries telling Jews they're going to hell for not breaking the covenant? Zechariah 12 and 14 are about the Final War. We're going to focus on the chapter in between.

"And it shall come to pass on that day, says the Lord of Hosts: I will cut off the names of the idols from the earth, and they shall no longer be mentioned. And also the prophets and the spirit of contamination I will remove from the earth." (Zechariah 13:2, Chabad.org)

Recall the Zohar's teaching that Zechariah 13:2 is an end to the Erev Rav and Amalek. That alone would make for a most exciting day. Filth out of our children's classrooms, back to the garden, food with seeds, no more war.

Zechariah 13:6-9 is even more epic. The biggest lie ever told, by any metric, exposed to the entire world. Many will return to The LORD God alone. Recall the last verse of Isaiah 52, gentile rulers will be shocked when they find out who the Messiah is. First, they find out who the Messiah is not.

Zechariah 13:2 is about multiple people. One man is identified in Zechariah 13:6-7, and 2 religions that identify him as a prophet are identified in 13:8-9. One of those religions claims that man was fully human and is fully God. The other does not claim he's God; but does regard him as a prophet. Of the utmost importance, both religions recognize Moses and Zechariah as prophets of The LORD God. We're given 4 identifying characteristics:

1. It'll shock nations to the ends of the earth when he's revealed to be a false prophet. He's the only false prophet singled out, to be revealed at the end of the age in the entirety of the Jewish Bible (Zechariah 13:1-9).

2. He's identified by wounds between his hands (Zechariah 13:6).

3. The famous prophet, identified by wounds between his hands, is also identified as a shepherd. Not just any shepherd, The LORD God calls him "My shepherd" and "the man who is associated with Me!" (Zechariah 13:7)

4. When his followers find out the truth, they'll know to turn to The LORD God of Abraham, Issac, and Jacob (Zechariah 1:2-3; 8:23; 13:8-9; 14:9,16).

They already know that The LORD God "the Father" is God.

Only 1 man fulfills all 4 criteria. He doesn't just check the boxes. He's by far the most famous person in world history regarding all 4. Nobody's a close second. Prophesy recorded 2,500 years ago by Zechariah has begun. Rome's trinity comes to an end in Zechariah 13:7. Jesus struck right in the middle...

Plaintiff: OBJECTION! Your honor, besides the fact that accusing Jesus Christ of being a false prophet takes blasphemy to a new low, his claim is illogical. Christians and Jews, priests, rabbis, and at least 90 percent of pastors agree that the Holy Trinity is found nowhere in the Old Testament. Progressive Revelation of the Holy Trinity unfolds in the New Testament.

Judge: Zechariah 13:6 is the only verse in the entire Jewish Bible that most rabbis, priests, and pastors claim is about Jesus. You've offered testimony claiming verses in Zechariah chapters 8, 9, 10, 11, 12, 13, and 14 are prophecy about Jesus. The 1952 Catholic Bible even added the bold subtitle "Sufferings of Christ,' claiming Zechariah 13:6 and 13:7 are about Jesus.

Defense: Point 1 is based on The LORD God's criteria for false prophets as recorded in Deuteronomy 13 and 18. I'll skip the technicalities, such as Jesus said John the Baptist is Elijah (Matt. 11:13-14); John the Baptist said he's not Elijah (John. 1:21-22).

"And Jesus came and said to them, "All authority in heaven and on earth has been given to me. Go therefore and make disciples of all nations, baptizing them in the name of the Father and of the Son and of the Holy Spirit, teaching them to observe all that I have commanded you. And behold, I am with you always, to the end of the age." (Matthew 28:18-20, ESV)

That's exactly what they did "by force if necessary" on 4 continents. Interestingly, Jesus telling us he'll be with us until the end of the age is consistent with Zechariah 13:2.

Plaintiff: OBJECTION! The beautiful message of the gospels is that Jesus willingly paid the price for our sins. Men misusing his words does not make Jesus Christ a false prophet!

Defense: The 4th Beast wrote the playbook, then followed it. Hitler was correct that the Catholic Church did an excellent job of following Jesus' instructions for 1,600 years. Matthew 28:19 brought God into it. Violence done in the name of "the Father, son, and Holy Spirit."

Judge: A bold claim "All authority in heaven and on earth has been given to me." Torah teaches that idolatry results in violence and injustice. And explicitly not to add a word, or any commandment (Deut. 4:2). There's no commandment or instruction in the Torah to baptize all nations in any name.

Plaintiff: Your honor, Deut. 4:2 cannot be used against Jesus! Jesus delivers the same message in Matt. 5:18-19. Defense' claimed that God's against punishing people for the sins of others. Now he claims Jesus Christ will be held accountable for what the Conquistadors did. Is he also suggesting that we're reincarnated, and we'll pay for what our ancestors did to Jews and Indians? For your own sake, please do not allow this blasphemy...

Judge: Interesting, considering your position that Jesus died for everyone else's sins. And that Jesus added to God's commandments in that same dialogue. Nobody will be judged for anyone else's sins (Deuteronomy 24:16, all of Ezekiel 18, and 33:19-20). As to your last point, all I can say is we better hope not; otherwise, there's going to be hell to pay unless we repent.

Defense: "The Jews then disputed among themselves, saying, "How can this man give us his flesh to eat?" So Jesus said to them, "Truly, truly, I say to you, unless you eat the flesh of the Son of Man and drink his blood, you have no life in you. Whoever feeds on my flesh and drinks my blood has eternal life, and I will raise him up on the last day. For my flesh is true food, and my blood is true drink. Whoever feeds on my flesh and drinks my blood abides in me, and I in him." (John 6:52-56, ESV)

What've we learned? Let's take Jesus of Nazareth's instruction full circle. Pope Innocent III makes transubstantiation official in 1215. Host Desecration accusations and trials follow. Entire communities locked in synagogues and burned, except children under 6 who were raised Catholic, unless they couldn't be forced to eat pork, then they were sold into slavery. Currently, their descendants are down on their knees, in cathedrals built on ashes, in Germany, Austria, France, Spain, eating Jesus' body and drinking his blood.

Jesus said it's better to be eunuch, going so far as to say if you are able, then you should castrate yourself for the sake of the kingdom of heaven (Matthew 19:12). The U.S. Council of Catholic Bishops substitutes the word marriage for eunuch. We've seen the results of the Vatican's policy on celibacy. Nowhere in the Jewish Bible is any instruction or recommendation for castration, self-mutilation, nor celibacy given. Per usual, the Torah says the opposite. Also note, Isaiah 55 "Strangers returning home" God has mercy, welcoming back eunuchs, along with everyone who broke the covenant.

Jesus said: "Do not think that I have come to bring peace to the earth. I have not come to bring peace, but a sword. For I have come to set a man against his father, and a daughter against her mother, and a daughter-in-law against her mother-in-law. And a person's enemies will be those of his own household" (Matthew 10:32-36, ESV)

That's the antithesis of what the Messiah's supposed to do (Isa. 2:4, Mic. 4:3, etc.) And nothing ever written has resulted in so much violence and injustice as what Jesus said according to whoever wrote Matthew 27:25, 28:18-19.

Chapter 27

"What Are Those Wounds Between Your Hands?"

"And if anyone asks him, "What are these wounds on your chest?" he shall answer, "With these I was wounded in the house of my dear ones." (Zechariah 13:6, New American Bible, Official Vatican Website: Vatican.va)

Can you think of any historically significant person who's known for having wounds on his chest? Anybody? Me neither. Here's the footnote:

"Wounds on your chest: literally, "wounds between your hands." The false prophets, like the prophet of Baal (⇒ 1 Kings 18:28), apparently inflicted wounds on themselves; to defend himself against the accusation of being a false prophet, a man will deny having inflicted wounds on himself and say instead that he received them at home, "in the house of my dear ones." In the liturgy this test is applied to Christ in an accommodated sense." (New American Bible, Zechariah 13:6, Vatican.va)

Here's the same verse from a different mainstream Catholic website:

"Ask they, What wounds be these in thy clasped hands? [2] Thus wounded was I, he shall answer, in the house of my friends." (Zechariah 13:6, The Knox Bible, New Advent.org)

"[2] Literally, 'between thy hands', a difficult phrase most inadequately interpreted by some moderns as meaning 'on thy back'. If the sacred author had meant 'between thy arms', he would surely have said so, as in IV Kg. 9.24." (Zechariah 13:6, the Knox Bible, New Advent.org)

Couldn't agree more. The attempts to hide Zechariah 13:6 doesn't stop with the Vatican. Recall the PowerPoint presentation: We typed "Zechariah 13:6" on the search bar of Biblehub.com. We found 22 the top 30 translations results were mistranslations. Then we went through every footnote in every one of the 22 to prove that the translators who substituted the words "back," "arms," or "chest" did so knowing the accurate translation is "wounds between your hands." Would you intentionally mistranslate a Bible verse in which The LORD God identifies Himself as the Speaker?

Like Jesus' name isn't mentioned once in the entire Jewish Bible that mentions David by name over a 1,000 and Moses 700; the name of the individual singled out in Zechariah 13:6-7 is not mentioned. The only physical identifier given is wounds between his hands. Why would The LORD God and Prophet Zechariah zero in on the wounds between his hands? How many times has Plaintiff told you that it all comes down to Jesus' resurrection?

"Eight days later, his disciples were inside again, and Thomas was with them. Although the doors were locked, Jesus came and stood among them and said, "Peace be with you." 27 Then he said to Thomas, "Put your finger here, and see my hands; and put out your hand, and place it in my side. Do not disbelieve, but believe." Thomas answered him, "My Lord and my God!" 29 Jesus said to him, "Have you believed because you have seen me? Blessed are those who have not seen and yet have believed."

30 Now Jesus did many other signs in the presence of the disciples, which are not written in this book; 31 but these are written so that you may believe that Jesus is the Christ, the Son of God, and that by believing you may have life in his name." (John 20:26-31, ESV)

"And one will say to him, "What are these wounds between your hands?" And he shall say, "That I was smitten in the house of my friends." (Zechariah 13:6, Chabad.org)

John 20:31: Life in whose name? Why replace "The LORD, the God of your forefathers, the God of Abraham, the God of Isaac, and the God of Jacob" with Jesus or some say Yeshua? Regardless, that's not God's Name forever, throughout all generations, until the end of time (Exodus 3:15).

The subtitle "The Purpose of This Book" is as clear as every homily I've ever heard about "Doubting Thomas." Thomas calling Jesus God, while locked inside a house with friends examining the wounds between Jesus' hands, was used by Plaintiff and bishops as evidence supporting Rome's trinity. "The Decide" was a combination of Matthew 27:25 and Rome's trinity becoming official, the bloodiest combination in the last 2,000 years.

Amazingly, Jesus is also the most prominent person history specifically identified as not having wounds in his hands, by over 2 billion Muslims.

According to the Quran: Jesus was not crucified. After the Jews handed him over to death; Allah raised him up to heaven. Somebody else who appeared to be Jesus was crucified in his place.

Like Judaism, Islams most important fundamental precept is the Oneness of God, which explicitly means no plurality. Here's what the Quran says about Rome's trinity: "Say not, 'Trinity.' Desist! It will be better for you, for God is One God, Glory be to Him! (Far exalted is He) above having a son. To Him belong all things in the heavens and on earth. And enough is God as a Disposer of affairs" (Q4:171).

All Muslims believe: Jesus was a prophet like Moses and Zechariah. No man is God, and saying that any man is God, including Jesus or Mohammed, is the worst form of idolatry. In some places, it's punishable by death. Jesus did not die by crucifixion or by any other mortal means; that God raised him up as a prophet. And they believe Jesus is coming back.

100 percent of Muslims believe that Jesus did not die from being crucified. However, they don't agree on the circumstances of Jesus appearing to be crucified. Ahmadi Muslims believe Jesus survived the crucifixion. I'm going to quote the Q'uran just once more because it's relevant to Zechariah 13:6 and even more relevant to Zechariah 13:7,8,9. "We" is the Jews:

"and said, 'We have killed the Messiah, Jesus, son of Mary, the Messenger of God.' (They did not kill him, nor did they crucify him, though it was made to appear like that to them; those that disagreed about him are full of doubt, with no knowledge to follow, only supposition: they certainly did not kill him- (Surah AN-NISA AYAT 157 (4:157 Quran) Abdul Haleem)

And just 1 abbreviated standard Islamic commentary on that verse, all of which are pretty much the same. "Their" is the Jews:

"Their criminal boldness had reached such proportions that they attempted to put an end to the life of the one they themselves knew to be a Prophet, and subsequently went around boasting of this achievement... they were fully aware that the person whom they were subjected to criminal treatment had been appointed by God as the bearer of His message. It seems strange that a people should recognize a man to be a Prophet in their hearts and still try to assassinate him. The ways of degenerate nations are indeed strange. Such people are absolutely unprepared to tolerate the existence of those who reproach them for their corruption and seek to prevent them from evil... the Jews... after having subjected Jesus – according to their belief – to crucifixion, they might have been overcome by jubilation and in a fit of self-congratulation might have boastfully exclaimed: 'Yes, we have put a Prophet of God to death!'... Jesus was raised on high before he could be crucified, and that the belief of both the Jews and the Christians that Jesus died on the cross is based on a misconception... Pilate sentenced him to death after the Jews showed their deep hostility to Truth and righteousness by openly declaring that, in their view, the life of a thief was of higher value than that of a man with such a pure soul as Jesus. It was then that God raised Jesus up to heaven... The fact that the person who had actually been crucified was someone other than Jesus does not in any way detract from the guilt of those Jews..." (Quran 4 Verse 157 Explanation, Ibn Kathir, MYISLAM.org)

According to Christianity, Roman soldiers killed Jesus and Jews are responsible. Ahmadi Muslims believe Jesus survived the crucifixion and Jews are responsible. Other Muslims believe Jesus wasn't even crucified, but the Jews are still responsible.

The "self imposed blood curse of the Jews" Matthew 27:25 was anonymously written 500 years before the Quran. Same story. Same theme. Same servant/witnesses who God chose to preserve, protect and share the Torah with the world are to blame, in all generations. No story ever written has resulted in so much mass murder all over the world, and terror to this day.

Please, take at least 30 seconds to consider: If the person you hated the most in your entire life were to be crucified; would you be standing there yelling, "his blood be on us and our children"?

Maybe it's just me, but the very last thing I'd be shouting, in public, regardless of who was being crucified, or for what, is a blood curse on my own children and grandchildren. Maybe that's why it was anonymously written. Who knows. We don't know who wrote it. But we know exactly who added it to the Bible, and how his successors used it to massacre millions.

Chapter 28

"O Sword, Awaken Against the Shepherd

Associated with Me"

"O sword, awaken against My shepherd and against the man who is associated with Me! says the Lord of Hosts. Smite the shepherd, and the flock shall scatter, and I will return My hand upon the little ones." (Zechariah 13:7, Chabad.org)

Why is The LORD God calling someone "My shepherd" and "the man who is associated with Me!" if The LORD God is against that man, and going to strike him?

No sentence is more important to this Trial of the Trinity and Zechariah 13:7 than the first sentence of God's 2nd commandment:

"You shall not have the gods of others in My presence." (Exodus 20:3, Chabad.org)

In what name are traditions of ancient cults (turned over) that The LORD God continually sent prophets with a clear message to immediately cease being any part of, continued to this day?
What man, associated with The LORD God via Rome's trinity do over 2 billion people celebrate his birthday and annual resurrection festivals?

What man-god do over a billion people break The LORD God's 2nd Commandment every Sol Invictus Day by getting down on their knees before idols of?

What man is associated with The LORD God in prayers, creeds, images and idols all over the world?

There're dozens of resurrection gods, shepherd gods, sun-gods, mother and child gods, miracle worker gods, etc. But, none of the first 3 beasts dared divide The LORD God, Who is Holy Spirit, into "persons." None dared include the LORD God in any of their trinities. None decreed their dying and rising god equal to the Creator of heaven and earth.

The 4th Beast made Jesus of Nazareth the image of The LORD God who said you saw no image so don't you dare make one, or bow down to one, ever. And don't ever listen to anyone who tells you anything to the contrary. (Deuteronomy 4:2, 4:12, 4:15-19, 5:1-10, 13:1-5, 18, etc.)

In 381 CE, the 4th Beast decreed it official that God Who is ONE Spirit is 2 "separate but equal persons." I don't know how anyone could possibly be more "**in My presence**" or "associated with" than being sandwiched between 2 separate "persons" of The LORD God in Rome's trinity.

Recall how Plaintiff, used the following anonymously written verses added to the Bible under Pope Damasus I:

"Now may the God of peace who brought again from the dead our Lord Jesus, the great shepherd of the sheep, by the blood of the eternal covenant," (Hebrews 13:20, ESV)

Jesus: "I am the good shepherd. The good shepherd lays down his life for the sheep." (John 10:11, ESV)

Jesus: "... Tend my sheep... Feed my sheep... Follow me." (John 21:16,17,18, ESV)

Jesus: "I am the good shepherd. I know my own and my own know me, just as the Father knows me and I know the Father; and I lay down my life for the sheep." (John 10:14-15, ESV)

The LORD God: "Awake, O sword, against my shepherd, against the man who stands next to me," declares the Lord of hosts. "Strike the shepherd, and the sheep will be scattered; I will turn my hand against the little ones. (Zechariah 13:7, ESV)

Prophecy Against the Shepherds of Israel "Thus says the Lord GOD, Behold, I am against the shepherds, and I will require my sheep at their hand and put a stop to their feeding the sheep. No longer shall the shepherds feed themselves. I will rescue my sheep from their mouths, that they may not be food for them." (Ezekiel 34:10, ESV)

Recall the Torah's teaching that idolatry results in violence and injustice. Where'd Pope Innocent III get the power to order crusades? Where'd Pope Nicholas V get the power to reduce people to perpetual slavery in 1452?

We'll let the Vatican and Catholic Encyclopedia explain how they interpret their own anonymously written sources to grant themselves power. Same power abused today, interfering with grand jury investigatins, and moving habitual child rapist employees across state and international boarders.

"Feed my lambs.. Feed my sheep" [John 21:16-17]. Catholics interpret this as Christ making Peter his vicar and pastor with the responsibility to feed his flock (i.e. the Church) in his own place'... Pope Innocent III appealed to the title of Vicar of Christ. Occasionally, Popes like Nicholas III used "Vicar of God" as an equivalent title."

(Herbermann, Charles, ed. (1913) "Vicar of Christ" Catholic Encyclopedia)

"Vicar of Jesus Christ" is the second official title of the Pope (the first being "Bishop of Rome") (Annuario Pontificio, published annually by Libreria Editrice Vaticana, edition of 2012, p. 23) Key word is official, really, it's the third. Recall the first title 716-672 BCE on the timeline.

Recall the song by Troubadour Guilhem Figueira (timeline 1215) that was so popular it was banned in Toulouse 50 years later: "Deceitful Rome, avarice ensnares you, so that you shear the wool of your sheep too much..."

The following "Vicars of Christ" are proven murderers: Pope's Damasus I, Sixtus III, Leo I, Symmachus, Hormisdas, Vigilus, Pelagius, St. Gregory the Great, Saint Gregory II, Stephen III, Saint Pascal I, Eugene II, Boniface VII, Benedict VIII, Adrian IV, Urban II, Alexander III, Lucius III, Clement III, Innocent III, Gregory IX, Innocent IV, Clement IV, Boniface VIII, John XXII, Urban VI, Benedict IX, Martin V, Eugenius IV, Nicholas V, Caliextus III, Paul II, Sixtus IV, Innocent VIII, Alexander VI, Paul III, Julius III, Paul IV, Pius V, Pope Benedict XIII. Most of those popes were undoubtedly the biggest global terrorists of their generation.

Stephen VI had his dead predecessor Pope Formosus dug up and put on trial in the Cadaver Synod of 897. Pope Clement V granted crusaders the right to release 4 souls from purgatory.

Pope Theodorus dipped his pen into consecrated wine, the blood of Jesus, before signing death warrants to sanctify murder. Pope John VIII ordered men's throats slit and cited New Testament texts to justify ordering eyes plucked out.

Pope Gregory V ordered a political opponent blinded, nose cut off, tongue ripped out, then led through the streets backwards on a donkey.

When it would have been bad enough for him to be silent, Pope Pius XI issued a reminder of "The Decide" on March 14, 1937 while the Nazi's were building Concentration Camps during the Holocaust. If the job description of Pope's Paul VI, John Paul II, Benedict XVI, and Francis was to prioritize protecting predator priests at the expense of innocent children and spreading the scourge of child sexual abuse: They'd all get an A+. Actually, according to the duty of Pontifex Maximus laid out by King Numa, Francis is doing his job carrying on ancient cult practice, including the most disgusting.

St. Peter's Basilica in Rome, above the "Chair of Saint Peter" in the golden background which is a tribute to Sol Invictus: "'O Shepherd of the Church, you feed all Christ's lambs and sheep" is inscribed in Latin and Greek. The chair is symbolic of the authority of Bishop of Rome as Vicar of Christ on earth. Pope Innocent III had "Feed your Sheep" and "This is the Door of the Sheep" engraved on the main door leading to the tomb of St. Peter in 1199.

"Pope Francis on Monday recalled a favourite imagery of a pastor... "I wish you to be shepherds with 'the smell of the sheep', the Pope said, repeating once again..." (Vatican News, June 7, 2021)

The LORD God: "I myself will be the shepherd of my sheep, and I myself will make them lie down, declares the Lord GOD. I will seek the lost, and I will bring back the strayed, and I will bind up the injured, and I will strengthen the weak, and the fat and the strong I will destroy. I will feed them in justice." (Ezekiel 34:15, ESV)

"I will rescue my flock; they shall no longer be a prey. And I will judge between sheep and sheep. And I will set up over them one shepherd, my servant David, and he shall feed them: he shall feed them and be their shepherd. And I, the LORD, will be their God, and my servant David shall be prince among them. I am the LORD; I have spoken."
(Ezekiel 34:22-24, ESV)

Notice the future messiah (referred to as David) is not God; he's God's servant. Also note, King David knew exactly who his shepherd is:

"The LORD is my shepherd; I shall not want." (Psalm 23:1, ESV)

Chapter 29

Objection! Jesus Quotes Zechariah 13:7

Plaintiff: Your honor, this is past the point of ridiculous. Jesus himself quoted Zechariah 13:7! Recorded by Saint Matthew and Saint Mark. Why would Jesus quote a verse about him being struck at the end of the age? Makes no sense. The Old Testament Book of Zechariah is quoted over 70 times in the New Testament, 31 in the Book of Revelation.

Even more ridiculous, Defense insinuated that Rome wrote and/or edited the gospels. Even claiming Paul was an agent of Rome. Yet, supposed agents of Rome quoted and referred to Zechariah more than 100 times in the New Testament of the Holy Bible. Defies logic. Much like his degenerate conspiracy theory that Christians and Muslims are descendants of Jews.

Defense: Vitally important messages are delivered to non-Jews to prepare them for the Messianic Age in Zechariah chapters 8-14. Yet many Christians don't even know that because they're taught Revelation instead. It's true that the author of the Book of Revelation, John of Patmos, borrowed quite a bit from Zechariah, Ezekiel, and Daniel; obviously to give credibility...

Plaintiff: Objection! Jesus cannot the shepherd who is to be struck!

Jesus quoted Zechariah 13:7! Jesus is going to strike the shepherd in the final days when he returns.

"Then Jesus said to them, "You will all fall away because of me this night. For it is written, 'I will strike the shepherd, and the sheep of the flock will be scattered.' (Matthew 26:31, ESV)

Defense: Open your eyes! "Jesus said to them, "You will all fall away because of me" while quoting Zechariah 13:7! You're being mocked by the 4th Beast.

Judge: You're arguing that Jesus is not the shepherd. Yet Jesus identifies himself as the shepherd in John 10:11, 14-15, 21:16-17. Additionally, Jesus is identified as the shepherd in Hebrews 13:20 and Revelation 17:17. Moreover, according to Matthew 26:31, Jesus did not say he will strike the shepherd. "For it is written" he's quoting the Prophet Zechariah from the Jewish Bible. Overruled.

Plaintiff: The Father calls Himself the shepherd in Isaiah 34. Jesus and the Father are one (John 10:30)! "For the Lamb in the midst of the throne will be their shepherd, and he will guide them to springs of living water, and God will wipe away every tear from their eyes." (Revelation 17:7, ESV)

After the false shepherd is struck, then Jesus will take his place as our final shepherd. Jesus is our only salvation! Jesus is the New Covenant!

Defense: Your honor, we can discredit the book of Revelation, and Jesus being anyone's savior with 2 sentences:

"and crying out with a loud voice, "Salvation belongs to our God who sits on the throne, and to the Lamb!" (Revelation 17:10, ESV)

"I, I am the LORD, and besides me there is no savior."
(Isaiah 43:11, ESV)

"Besides me there is no savior" leaves no room for the
word "and" in Revelation 17:10, period. Isaiah 43:11
means Jesus did not save anyone. Jesus has no part in
salvation or the forgiveness of sins Deut. 24, Ezek. 18...

Judge: The court rules with Isaiah 43:11. Any further
objections?

Plaintiff: Jesus was crucified and raised from the dead. He
ascended into heaven and is seated at the right hand of
the Father. The shepherd will be struck, on earth, prior to
the arrival of the Messiah. Jesus is the Messiah. We await
his second coming. The shepherd will be stuck before
Jesus returns. Therefore, Jesus cannot possibly be the
shepherd who'll be struck.

Defense: "At that time shall arise Michael, the great prince
who has charge of your people. And there shall be a time
of trouble, such as never has been since there was a
nation till that time. But at that time your people shall be
delivered, everyone whose name shall be found written in
the book. And many of those who sleep in the dust of the
earth shall awake, some to everlasting life, and some to
shame and everlasting contempt." (Daniel 12:1-2, ESV)

Judge: Daniel 12:2 answers the question: Is it possible that
any prophets referred to in Zechariah 13:2 are already
dead? Any final objection?

Plaintiff: Your honor, expert witness testimony will prove
Defense has mislead the jury, taken Zechariah 13 out of
context; and falsely accused our Lord and Savior Jesus
Christ of being a false prophet. Please allow Dr. Micheal L.

Brown PHD, a convert to the New and everlasting Covenant of Christianity from the Old Covenant of Judaism, author of over 40 books, and professor of theology explain how it's impossible that Jesus is the shepherd to be struck?

Judge: This testimony from Dr. Brown is a refute to Rabbi Tovia Singer's teaching of Zechariah 13. I'll allow it. But I want to hear what Dr. Brown's refuting before I hear his rebuttal.

Plaintiff: Your honor, the court and jury deserve to be forewarned that Dr. Brown has proven Rabbi Singer to be an untrustworthy source. Additionally, and quite unfortunately, Singer's already turned thousands of souls away from our Lord and Savior Jesus Christ. He is, in fact, leading people to hell (Mark 16:16). According to the Holy Bible, 2 Peter 3:24-18, both defense counsel and that rabbi are "ignorant and unstable" because they reject the teachings of Saint Paul the Apostle. According to John 8:34-47 neither has any truth in them...

Judge: A Jewish rabbi teaching the Jewish Bible. Explain to me how that's different than what Jesus did regularly according to Luke 4:16, 17, 42?

Plaintiff: Jesus is the only Son of God, eternally begotten by the F...

Judge: Using Greek texts added to the Hebrew Bible by the Roman Catholic Church to discredit a Jewish rabbi teaching the Jewish Bible is disallowed. The jury has a right to be presented with the information. So do I. Play it.

Defense: I'm not sure which of these responses Dr. Brown's objecting to. The first is Rabbi Singer responding to 2 questions: Is Jesus the person being spoken of in Zechariah 13? And are 1.5 billion people (approx. 66.6 percent of Christians) going to die according to Zechariah 13:8?

In the second, he explains: Which 2 nations are going to be utterly destroyed according to Zechariah 13:8 and why. The final war. Precursors to the messiah. That Zechariah 13:8 does not necessarily mean 33.3 and 66.6 percent, and what does it mean, in the language it was written. He even explains how the Anti-Christ fits in. He also touches on the "turning it over" that we already covered. Judge: Play all three videos. The refute last.

(TeNaK Talk episode 1407 – Will the Messiah be DIVINE??) *on YouTube was fast-forwarded to 19:30 and played through 35:30. Next, the entire 20 minute and 2 second video titled* ("Will two thirds of the Jews be killed? Rabbi Tovia Singer: Christians misinterpret a crucial passage.") *played in court.*

Plaintiff: Objection! Contradictory testimony. The rabbi just stated that Rome was finished by AD 410. Daniel's prophecy of the fourth beast being destroyed has already come to pass. That renders Defense' timeline irrelevant to this Trial of the Holy Trinity.

Defense: Want to hear witness testimony of children raped in the past year by priests who forgave them "in the name of the Father, and the son, and the Holy Spirit?" I didn't misspeak; the adult rapist forgave the child victim. Crusaders yielding the "Sheild of the Trinity." Orders given to "baptize in the name of the Father, son, and Holy Spirit by force if necessary." Priests making the sign of cross "in the name of the Father, son, and Holy Spirit" before sexually assaulting descendants of the Christianized at

Indian schools well past 476. Or we can play ("Christianity Converted to Rome, the Fourth Beast" - Rabbi Tovia Singer) if Plaintiff wants further explanation. Or we can go through thousands more mass-murders and conversions by the sword post 476 CE.

Judge: Unnecessary. The most relevant evidence is that the children of Israel are still in the fourth exile of Rome. Therefore we know that the Fourth Beast has not yet been destroyed. Overruled. Now, I want to hear Dr. Browns refute. *Dr. Brown's entire 11 minute and 19 second video titled (Objection 4.37: The only true prophecy about Jesus in the Tenakh is Zechariah 13:1 6) played in court.*

Judge: Defense, so far you've focused on Zechariah 13:1,2,6,7. Rabbi Singer, focused on verses 13:1,2,6,8,9 in the first and offered a broader scope in the second, addressing 13:3,4,5,7 briefly. Conversely, Dr. Brown focused on 13:3,4,5 to argue his three major points of contention. First, he claims Jesus is not a false prophet. Second, Jesus was not killed by his parents. Third, Jesus was not a farmer, gardener, or any tiller of the soil. You've spent enough time addressing his first objection. Respond directly to Dr. Brown's second and third points.

Defense: I'm not sure that focus is the best word. But at least Brown got something right: Jesus' parents didn't kill him. However, that's entirely irrelevant because we're not told anyone's parents already killed them.

Zechariah 13:3 opens with "And if anyone again prophesies." Moreover, we know that the man identified in Zechariah 13:6-7 will not, in the future, be killed by his parents because he's going to be struck by The LORD.

Point 3. According to Mr. Brown, Jesus was a carpenter because his father Joeseph was a carpenter (Matthew 13:55, Mark 6:30). However, according to the 4th gospel, Jesus said: "I am the true vine, and my Father is the gardener." (John 15:1, NIV)

John 15:1 and Zechariah 13:5: the King James Version use the word "husbandman." Neither's a mistranslation. Gardener, farmer, husbandman, and tiller of the soil are all accurate. Jesus was used agricultural metaphors in his parables when decreeing himself the savior (Mark 4:1-20, Matthew 13:1-23, Luke 8:1-15). Additionally, Jesus was mistaken for the gardener in Mary Magadaline's weeping for Jesus, an unmistakable ode to the weeping for Tammuz the shepherd and gardener. Interesting as that may be, it doesn't matter. Browns 3rd point of contention is entirely irrelevant for the same reason as his 2nd. Zechariah 13:5 opens with "but he will say." It hasn't happened yet. "Will" in "he will say" means...

Judge: Dr. Brown's arguments have proven to be entirely without merit. I'm disallowing his testimony as an expert witness and instructing the jury to disregard all of it.

Defense: One of the many ironies of Zechariah 13:7, is that the more Jesus is associated with The LORD God, the worse the case against him becomes. I'm glad the jury heard PHD Brown, the great memorizer of 4,000 out of context Bible verses. His testimony makes it easy to understand why certain people are being mocked throughout Isaiah 40-46.

I have questions for PHD Brown: If Christianity is the truth, why is Zechariah 8:23, 14:16 in your own Bible? Why aren't Jews told that in the final days they'll tell Christians God is with them and grab onto them to learn how to eat the body, drink the blood, decorate Christmas trees, kneel before a wooden idol, and celebrate the dying and rising god festivities on Easter Sol Invictus Day? Why is everyone going to be keeping Jewish holidays in the Messianic Age? How are non-Jews even going to know what day Sukkot starts, or how it's been celebrated for thousands of years? I don't know what explanation PHD Brown might give for Zechariah 14:16. But, it makes no difference. God gives us the answer 6 chapters earlier: Zechariah 8:23.

Making any legitimate comparison whatsoever between The LORD God and any man, pagan god, or anyone else is impossible. Conversely, comparing Jesus to Tammuz, Mithra, Osiris, Attis, etc. is easy. Entire books are filled with legitimate comparisons between Jesus and, other "sun-gods," "dying and rising gods, "virgin mother and child gods," Tammuz, Horus, Mithra...

Plaintiff: OBJECTION! Repetitive! Defense can blaspheme Jesus Christ, making these degenerate comparisons all day long and prove nothing.

Judge: You've covered dying and rising gods. Where're you going with this?

Defense: Plaintiff's acknowledgment that comparisons between Jesus and 18 other dying and rising gods; and Rome's trinity with a dozen preceding trinities can be made all day long is sufficient. Because, and this next sentence in itself slays Rome's trinity, The LORD God said:

"To whom will you liken me and make me equal, and compare me, that we may be alike?" (Isaiah 46:5, ESV)

Chapter 30

Return of the Sons and Daughters of Adam and Noah

Point 4. What happens to people still deceived by the false prophet shepherd with wounds in his hands, the man associated with The LORD God?

"And it shall come to pass, that in all the land, saith the LORD, two parts therein shall be cut off and die; but the third shall be left therein." (Zechariah 13:8, KJV)

What's the good news? What happens to those who repent of idolatry and turn back to The LORD alone?

"And I will bring the third in fire; and I will refine them as one refines silver, and I will test them as one tests gold. He shall call in My name, and I will respond to him. I said, "He is My people"; and he shall say, "The Lord is my God." (Zechariah 13:9, Chabad.org)

As Rabbi Singer explained, "two parts" and "the third" is not 2/3 and 1/3 as in 66.6 and 33.3 percent. It's 1 part emerging from 2 parts in the final days before the Messianic Age. The 1 part emerges from 2 religions. The 2 largest religions in the world both recognize the Prophets of Israel, Moses and Zechariah in paricular as Prophets of God. And both grew via conversion by the sword. The Jewish Bible prophesied the rise and fall of Christianity and Islam, and that of many of them will return to The LORD alone at the end of this age (Deuteronomy 4:27-31, Zechariah 13:6-9).

Recall the sages teaching of Leviticus 11. The pig, the 4th Beast doesn't turn it over; it brings it back. Christianity concedes that right up until Jesus' resurrection, Judaism was the only true religion in the world, and the only monotheistic religion period. When Christians find out that the 4th Beast converted their ancestors then taught them context altering mistranslations, they'll know exactly Who and where to turn to. Muslims will know exactly Who to turn to as well. That's the point of the last verse of Zechariah 13.

Recall Deuteronomy 4:27-28: descendants of the children of Israel will be scattered all over the world and worship gods of wood and stone. According to Christianity, forgiveness comes from Jesus' crucifixion on a tree or cross of wood. How are sins forgiven according to Islam?

"Touching the Stone is one of the things by means of which Allah expiates for sins. Ibn 'Umar said: I heard the Messenger of Allah (peace and blessings of Allah be upon him) say: "Touching them both [the Black Stone and Al-Rukn Al-Yamani] is an expiation for sins." (Narrated by At-Tirmidhi, 959. This Hadith was classed as sound by At-Tirmidhi and as authentic by Al-Hakim (1/664). Adh-Dhahabi agreed with him)" (Islamqa.info, Virtues of the Black Stone)

"Ibn 'Abbas said: The Messenger of Allah (peace and blessings of Allah be upon him) said concerning the Stone: "By Allah, Allah will bring it forth on the Day of Resurrection, and it will have two eyes with which it will see and a tongue with which it will speak, and it will testify in favour of those who touched it in sincerity." (Narrated by At-Tirmidhi, 961 and Ibn Majah, 2944)

Like Abraham, Moses, Ruth, and Obediah, most of the people who come to make up this third part will've been taught lies; but they sought and found The LORD God. That's the third part that God refines like gold (Deut. 4:29-31, Zec. 13:8-9). The 1 part that emerges will not start a new religion. Those who don't convert to Judaism will embrace an even older and far simpler religion. In fact, it's the oldest religion in the world. This is when it started:

"The Lord God took the man and put him in the garden of Eden to work it and keep it. And the Lord God commanded the man, saying, "You may surely eat of every tree of the garden, but of the tree of the knowledge of good and evil you shall not eat, for in the day that you eat of it you shall surely die." (Genesis 2:16-17, ESV)

Adam, the first man, was given the following 6 commandments that every person on earth, in every generation, is expected to keep: 1. Do not worship idols. See God's 2nd commandment Exodus 20:3-6 for further explanation.

2. Do not curse God. 3. Do not murder. 4. Do not commit adultery or sexual immorality. 5. Do not steal. 6. Set up courts of law to enforce the other commandments. Although this 6th commandment was given about 1,656 before the next was given to Noah; typically, it's listed 7th because it's to enforce the other laws. Read Psalm 119 if you want to understand the purpose of all God's commandments, which is the relationship.

"I will multiply your offspring as the stars of heaven and will give to your offspring all these lands. And in your offspring all the nations of the earth shall be blessed, because Abraham obeyed my voice and kept my charge, my commandments, my statutes, and my laws." (Genesis 26:4-5, ESV)

As we can see that's God saying the opposite of what Paul said his letter to the Romans 4:1-3 that Abraham was saved by faith alone. Abraham kept those 6 laws.

The 7th and final law is about food and not being any part of causing unnecessary pain to an animal. Before we get to that instruction given to Noah and all his descendants forever, which is everyone. What were Adam and Abraham's instructions regarding food?

"And God said, "Let the earth sprout vegetation, seed yielding herbs and fruit trees producing fruit according to its kind in which its seed is found, on the earth," and it was so. And the earth gave forth vegetation, seed yielding herbs according to its kind, and trees producing fruit, in which its seed is found, according to its kind, and God saw that it was good. (Genesis 1:11-12, Chabad.org)

Anyone know of a grocery store in the USA that still sells grapes with seeds? When the Messiah comes, is he going to explain that we never needed genetically modified seedless grapes, lemons, and watermelons?

Notice, every attack on us, our children, plants and animals is an attack on the Torah. "Experts" changed the definition of the words natural and organic before elected officials became unable to define the words man and woman.

Genesis 2:16-17 is still happening. What are the fruits of food science knowledge paired with disrespect for God's creation, people, plants, animals, water, soil, and a level of arrogance I can't comprehend? Of course, I don't work in a lab figuring out how to get more Red 2, 3, 40, Yellow 5, 6,

Blue 1, 2, BHT, Trisodium Phosphate, etc. into children's breakfast cereals.

What's the antithesis of what The LORD God entrusted us with: "Genetically modified organisms (GMOs) are plants, animals, or microorganisms whose genetic makeup is artificially modified or altered... Despite biotech industry promises, no evidence shows any GMOs... increased yield, enhanced nutrition, drought tolerance, or any other consumer benefit... vast majority of crops in North America are genetically modified... sugar, corn, soy, and canola are genetically modified. Livestock, agriculture, and aquaculture products are also considered to be high-risk for GMOs. Because over 80% of GMO crops grown around the world have been engineered for herbicide tolerance, resulting in a significant increase in the use of toxic herbicides, increasing its negative impact on the environment and human health. Several countries around the world have banned the use of GMOs." (worldpopulationreview.com, Countries that ban GMO's 2024)

Cheers to 27 countries in Europe, Asia, Africa, and South America that have banned GMOs; and Italy for being the first to ban the abomination of lab grown "meat." Most governments and media, especially in North America, ignore this assault on our food, soil, water, and bees while gas lighting us about SUVs and cow farts.

It should come as no surprise that the company genetically engineering our food to withstand up to 15 times more poisonous herbicides is the same company selling the herbicides. In 2018, the chemical weapons company Monsanto that manufactured Agent Orange in West Virginia and New Jersey that killed soldiers in Vietnam merged with Bayer Pharmaceutical. The same Bayer that manufactured Zyclon B for Nazi gas chambers. That's who's behind the science of most GMO "food" in about half the world's countries. How fascinating is it that after the Messiah arrives, people will be turning weapons into farming tools (Isaiah 2:4)? Back to the garden.

Noah was the first person given permission to eat meat. This came with instructions (Genesis 9:1-17). The 7th Noahide Law is: Do not eat the flesh of any living animal. That's the 7th law every single person is expected to keep.

Long ago, people would cut a limb off an animal, such as a cow, goat or sheep that was still alive. They cauterized it. The animal would live in pain until the meat ran out and they cut off the next limb. Since refrigeration's become common, this practice has stopped. However, not some, but the vast majority of meat that's consumed nowadays, all over the world, is put through tremendous unnecessary pain. If you want to see it, hear it, or listen to former employees talk about it, YouTube has plenty of free videos of cows, pigs, and chickens being abused like you wouldn't believe. Such as "Hormel: USDA-Approved High Speed Slaughter Hell." It's good to know what we're putting into our bodies, after all, it becomes our bodies. More importantly, it's part of God's commandment: The 7th Noahide law.

Every hunter I know, regardless of what religion they are, is not breaking this commandment. They have the utmost respect for the entire process. The deer's killed with 1 shot, the most painless way possible. The deer was living a wonderful life and never saw it coming. The opposite of animals waiting terrified in the death line, listening to screaming animals being processed before them. Hunters also drain the blood into the ground, following instructions in the Torah, probably without even realizing it. Kosher and

Halal butchers also kill the meat in the most humane way possible...

Plaintiff: Objection. False. The Jews treatment of animals is no less grotesque. Defense wants to bring up YouTube videos, here's one titled "Horrific Cruelty Filmed in Kosher Slaughterhouses." The Muslims are no better as we can see in "Meet your Meat, the Barbarity of Halal Slaughter."

Judge: Seen those, and many more. First, that doesn't apply to all Kosher and Halal slaughterhouses. Even the worst Kosher and Halal aren't as bad as other slaughterhouses. But what I've seen is more than disgraceful enough.

Defense: Look, no Jew, Christian, or Muslim that I've ever met is intentionally breaking this commandment. Jews and Muslims pay a premium for meat to be killed painlessly and processed properly. Every Chrisitan, Jew, and Muslim I know treats their animals very well; some even better than they treat people. To what degree ignorance of what you purchase then put into your mouth is an acceptable excuse, I don't know.

Judge: The bottom line, until the end of time, the rainbow is a reminder of the everlasting covenant between God and all of Noah's descendants, which is everyone. It also includes every animal (Genesis 9:8-19). That means God cares about cows and chickens too; not just dogs and cats. Jury, regardless of which side you choose, every time you see a rainbow remember God's covenant because you are a son or daughter of Noah and child of God.

Defense: Notice the Sabbath isn't included in the 7 laws of Noah. I'm going to read from a deposition of a former Christian who repented of idolatry and turned back to The

LORD God alone. She doesn't want to convert to Judaism: "Every Jewish person I meet asks me about my mother... I repented directly to the God of Israel before finding out my mother has Jewish blood on her mother's side... that had nothing to do with... What if my mother never told me... I never doubted that the 10 commandments applied to me... Now a rabbi's telling me I'm not allowed to keep the Sabbath, that it's stealing... God sanctified the Sabbath prior to Moses (Genesis 2:3). If it's only for Jewish people because of Deut. 5:14-15 then why does Rabbi Moses say everyone alive Deut. 5:3... What about Isaiah 56:6-7, am I not included? Is God not speaking to me in Isaiah 56? Isaiah 66:23...

Plaintiff: Objection! You disallowed testimony from Christians saved by our Lord Jesus Christ from drug addiction, alcoholism, cancer, depression...

Judge: I don't dispute the sincerity of their testimonies. However, Deuteronomy 13 and 18 render them inadmissible along with every other claim in the name of any other god besides the Name in Exodus 3:15. And you don't need to say another word about the Sabbath. It's not a Noahide Law to keep it or not keep it. The rabbi's point is don't say your commanded to keep it because you're not. Don't complicate it; and "Stop regarding man in whose nostrils is breath, for of what account is he?" (Isaiah 2:22, ESV)

Defense: One final point on the 7 commandments of Noah, like all 613 of Moses, they are to be followed because God said so. If you think it's morally wrong not to murder and steal; good for you. We're created in the image of God who thought the same thing before we did. Respecting the fact that God gave these commandments, and that's the reason they should be kept strengthens the relationship with our Creator. Awareness of the Oneness of God and the relationship is the source of our power (Psalm 119).

The 4th Beast and Amalek turned it over and mixed it up so much that some people don't even know who they are or why they're here. Recall the story of Abraham raised in idolatry, taught lies as a child. Then he sought the truth, rejected the lies, smashed the idols, and found the One true God waiting for him. What a wonderful opportunity we have to do the same.

Who are you going to believe? The LORD God, Moses, Isaiah, Jeremiah, Ezekiel, Daniel, and Zechariah; or Paul and anonymously written gospel accounts? That's what it comes down to, free will. Deuteronomy 32:38 and the first sentence of Isaiah 43:11 have the same message, nobody else, no other god, no man is going to save any of us. The LORD God is merciful and just. Want mercy? Repent to The LORD God alone. Want justice? Don't.

We haven't even seen the worst of it yet (Dan. 12:1, Zech 13:8-9,14:12, etc.). What could possibly be worse than the timeline we just went over?

"Can you imagine in 10 years when we are sitting here, we have an implant in our brains... because you all will have implants..." (Klaus Schwab, Chairman World Economic Forum) Considering that, what's being done to most of the food, AI, WW3 on the brink, etc., please God let the messiah come soon.

Plaintiff and whoever wrote Matthew 23:39 told you that when enough Jews praise Jesus' name, he'll return. That, like everything else Plaintiff's told you, is the opposite of the eternal message of the Torah. The messiah comes when enough people stop worshiping lower case g gods, men, cults, idols. Stop breaking God's first 2 commandments and turn back to God alone.

If we used our free will to seek God like we're told in Deuteronomy 4,6,13,30, etc., we would've already triggered the messianic age, resulting in the 4th Beast, Amalek, and Erev Rav ceasing to exist. Their hands out of our pockets, slow poision out of our food and water, and filth out of children's classrooms. The source of our power is awareness of the Oneness of God.

Choose Whom You Will Serve "Now therefore fear the Lord and serve him in sincerity and in faithfulness. Put away the gods that your fathers served beyond the River and in Egypt, and serve the Lord. And if it is evil in your eyes to serve the LORD, choose this day whom you will serve, whether the gods your fathers served in the region beyond the River, or the gods of the Amorites in whose land you dwell. But as for me and my house, we will serve the LORD." (Joshua 24:14-15, ESV)

"But as for me and my house, we will serve the Lord." Often quoted by Christians as meaning Jesus or a combination of Jesus and The LORD God. It is 100 percent certain that Joshua's household served The LORD God alone; with no mediators and no separate but equal person of any trinity.

"To you it was shown, that you might know that the LORD is God; there is no other besides him." (Deuteronomy 4:35, ESV)
"know therefore today, and lay it to your heart, that the Lord is God in heaven above and on the earth beneath; there is no other." (Deu. 4:39, ESV)

"In that day mankind will cast away their idols of silver and their idols of gold, which they made for themselves to worship..." (Isaiah 2:20, ESV)

In Isaiah 56, 'foreigners' is often translated to 'strangers', same thing. They're descendants of those who were standing, or not standing there that day, and are currently worshiping gods of wood and stone (Deut. 4:27-28, 29:10-15).

Salvation for Foreigners "And the foreigners who join themselves to the LORD, to minister to him, to love the name of the LORD, and to be his servants, everyone who keeps the Sabbath and does not profane it, and holds fast my covenant—these I will bring to my holy mountain, and make them joyful in my house of prayer; their burnt offerings and their sacrifices will be accepted on my altar; for my house shall be called a house of prayer for all peoples." The Lord GOD, who gathers the outcasts of Israel, declares, "I will gather yet others to him besides those already gathered." (Isaiah 56:6-8, ESV)

Judgment and Salvation "I was ready to be sought by those who did not ask for me; I was ready to be found by those who did not seek me.

"I said, "Here I am, here I am," to a nation that was not called by my name.

I spread out my hands all the day to a rebellious people, who walk in a way that is not good, following their own devices; a people who provoke me

to my face continually, sacrificing in gardens and making offerings on bricks;

who sit in tombs, and spend the night in secret places; who eat pig's flesh,

and broth of tainted meat is in their vessels" (Isaiah 65:1-4, ESV)

A Call to Return to the LORD "The LORD was very angry with your fathers. Therefore say to them, Thus declares the LORD of hosts: Return to me, says the LORD of hosts, and I will return to you, says the LORD of hosts." (Zechariah 1:2-3, ESV)

"For I the LORD do not change; therefore you, O children of Jacob, are not consumed. From the days of your fathers you have turned aside from my statutes and have not kept them. Return to me, and I will return to you, says the LORD of hosts. But you say, 'How shall we return?" (Malachi 3:6-7, ESV)

"if my people who are called by my name humble themselves, and pray and seek my face and turn from their wicked ways, then I will hear from heaven and will forgive their sin and heal their land. Now my eyes will be open and my ears attentive to the prayer that is made in this place. For now I have chosen and consecrated this house that my name may be there forever. My eyes and my heart will be there for all time." (2 Chronicles 7:14-16, ESV)

The defense rests. Judge: You've been presented with both sides. Come to your own conclusions. Thank you for your time and consideration. <u>Glossary</u>

Index

A

Abbas · 248
Abel · 84
Abraham · 2, 5, 15, 22, 25, 27, 38, 49, 135, 166, 171, 190, 193, 223, 229, 249, 250, 255
Abuse · 136, 137, 138, 139, 142, 143, 144, 145, 147, 148, 149, 150, 151, 153, 155, 156, 157, 159, 161, 162, 163, 164, 237

B

Babylon · 190, 192, 195, 198, 202, 203, 208
Baptized · 2, 13, 16, 70, 71, 73, 76, 85, 89, 93, 94, 97, 98, 99, 100, 102, 104, 105, 117, 144, 170
Bergoglio Jorge Mario · 50, 142
Baz maher-shalal-hash · 10

C

Church Catholic · 30, 31, 47, 56, 87, 90, 94, 96, 110, 111, 118, 122, 123, 124, 132, 134, 135, 136, 139, 140, 142, 143, 145, 147, 149, 150, 151, 153, 154, 155, 156, 224, 242
Christmas · 49, 57, 58, 212, 246
Crusades · 47, 80, 84, 87, 96, 154, 235
Creed Nicene · 7, 57, 64, 66, 69

D

Daniel · 1, 23, 43, 44, 45, 46, 49, 50, 60, 154, 158, 160, 170, 190, 191, 221, 239, 241, 243, 255
Deuteronomy · 1, 9, 13, 18, 19, 20, 21, 22, 23, 24, 25, 29, 30, 31, 32, 34, 35, 36, 38, 65, 69, 86, 108, 133, 165, 174, 197, 211, 213, 224, 225, 234, 247, 248, 254, 255, 256

Dicastery · 160, 161
Damasus Pope I · 12, 60, 62, 63, 64, 66, 67, 68, 154, 195, 234

E

Easter · 5, 57, 75, 76, 90, 98, 206, 207, 210, 212, 246
England · 74, 75, 84, 94, 96, 97, 98, 110, 149
Ephraim · 13
Exodus 20 · 20, 21, 29, 30, 31, 35, 73, 153, 233, 249
Exodus 2, 5, 13, 15, 38, 106, 193, 229, 254
Ezekiel 18 · 8, 9, 13, 20, 208, 225

F

France · 70, 72, 75, 76, 78, 82, 83, 85, 86, 90, 91, 93, 94, 96, 97, 98, 99, 100, 116, 124, 131, 132, 150, 157, 160, 226
free will · 34, 35, 36, 45, 255, 256
Francis Pope · 47, 50, 67, 109, 141, 142, 143, 148, 149, 150, 154, 161, 162, 163, 164, 204, 237

G

Genesis · 13, 21, 27, 56, 133, 166, 167, 173, 249, 250, 252, 253, 254
Germany · 70, 75, 79, 85, 86, 89, 97, 98, 99, 104, 111, 116, 117, 121, 122, 123, 124, 125, 126, 128, 129, 132, 151, 157, 226

H

Haleem Abdul · 230
Hitler Adolf · 110, 120, 121, 122, 125, 126, 127, 129
Hosea · 9, 12, 13, 14, 34, 46, 106, 133, 134, 195, 202
Host Desecration · 4, 77, 80, 88, 89, 90, 97, 99, 104, 116, 226

I

Immanuel · 10

Isaiah 42 · 2, 8, 21, 30, 34, 193, 212
Isaiah 43 · 8, 9, 12, 14, 19, 28, 30, 34, 39, 241, 255
Innocent Pope III · 4, 31, 77, 80, 81, 82, 83, 84, 85, 86, 87, 127, 136, 154, 160,
    162, 226, 235, 237
Isaiah 45 · 2, 39, 40
Israel's · 4, 11, 165, 166, 171, 172

J

Jeremiah · 5, 3, 12, 13, 18, 19, 22, 28, 29, 50, 59, 60, 61, 108, 133, 135, 190,
    193, 195, 200, 201, 202, 203, 205, 216, 220, 221, 255
Job · 15, 20
John · 7, 8, 13
John 6 · 197, 225

L

Law Bernard · 139, 140, 141

M

Mazda Ahura · 49, 192, 215
Maximus Pontifex · 49, 52, 54, 55, 57, 66, 67, 68, 80, 195, 237

N

Numbers · 5, 8, 20, 34, 37, 38, 39, 44, 108, 166, 190, 193, 200

O

Oneness of God · 9, 29, 171, 174, 230, 255, 256

P

Pig · 51, 57, 190, 191, 248, 258
Pork · 51, 89, 99, 226
Psalm · 5, 6, 7, 8, 12, 21, 28, 33, 37, 38, 115, 133, 174, 221, 238, 249, 255